LOVE
UNMASKED

Also by Becky Dean

Love & Other Great Expectations

Picture-Perfect Boyfriend

Hearts Overboard

LOVE UNMASKED

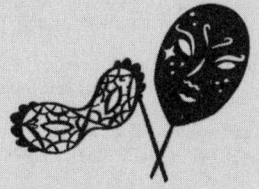

Becky Dean

Delacorte
Romance

Text copyright © 2025 by Becky Dean
Cover art copyright © 2025 by Libby VanderPloeg

All rights reserved. Published in the United States by Delacorte Romance, an imprint of Random House Children's Books, a division of Penguin Random House LLC, New York.

Delacorte Romance and the colophon are trademarks of Penguin Random House LLC.

GetUnderlined.com

Educators and librarians, for a variety of teaching tools,
visit us at RHTeachersLibrarians.com

Library of Congress Cataloging-in-Publication Data is available upon request.
ISBN 978-0-593-64787-5 (trade) — ISBN 978-0-593-64788-2 (ebook)

The text of this book is set in 11.25-point Adobe Caslon Pro.
Interior design by Michelle Canoni

Printed in the United States of America
1st Printing
First Edition

For every fan who has found family through fiction

Chapter One

The mask was going to be my downfall—or possibly land me in airport jail. I should have considered how the pointy wings on the sides, which had looked so elegant in my sketchbook, would appear in real life on an X-ray machine.

A TSA agent was tugging my carry-on suitcase off the conveyor belt and toward the table reserved for suspicious characters. Which now included me. The man's first thought was not likely to be *This girl has impressive artistic abilities and a strong understanding of the aesthetics of the Elven Realms universe.* I suspected it would trend more toward *This girl is packing stabby things clearly intended for wrongdoings.*

Even scarier was what my classmates would think if they saw the contents of this bag.

Most of the group had gone through ahead of me and waited several yards away. A dozen students from my school, plus that many from two other schools in our area. Bryce Carter caught my gaze and smiled. I waved and returned the smile, trying to hide my worry.

He started toward me. While I normally appreciated our shared desire to help everyone, I waved him off and mouthed, *I'm good,* which was a lie, unless *good* could be defined as "desperate and close to hyperventilating."

Next to Bryce was another of my friends, Dai Tanaka, who would have gladly caused a scene to distract the authorities if he knew I needed help. Except he didn't know. Neither of them did, and I had to keep it that way if I wanted to hold on to everything I'd built the last four years.

Word could not get out that Evie Whitmore, vice president of Central High, yearbook art manager, peer mentor, constant winner of the perfect attendance award, shoo-in for the senior-class Most Outstanding Citizen prize, was carrying cosplay outfits.

The TSA agent donned blue gloves, like this was a crime scene or he was preparing for surgery or something equally gruesome that involved blood and my imminent demise.

My art teacher, Mr. Owens; my best friend, Natasha Gutierrez; and two final classmates were the only ones left behind me. Natasha stuffed her laptop back into her leather backpack and grabbed her white Vans. As always, she exuded the air of organized competence befitting the senior class president. She was the sole person who knew about my obsession with fantasy books and my secret plans for the upcoming week.

I loved my friends, who were considered the popular crowd, but we were hardly the crew in *Mask of Souls,* sharing every secret and fighting to the death to protect each other. I had found a place, and sure, it didn't always fit perfectly or feel like home.

But it fit well enough, was nice, and made my life easier. Like that outfit that wasn't exactly what you wanted, but after weeks of searching, you doubted that the idea in your head actually existed, so you settled for something less than perfect, but real and still good.

Natasha would save me, but I didn't want her to suspect I didn't have this situation handled. She must have sensed something was up, though, because she hustled the last two students on in her usual take-charge way.

The agent's hands were now properly gloved, and he was turning my bag so the zipper faced him.

Wait ten more seconds, dude. Life or death, here.

My fingers crossed in hopes of a sudden zipper jam.

Mr. Owens hadn't passed through security yet. Where was he? How close was danger?

The TSA agent was frowning at me.

I gave him a bright *I'm harmless* smile to hide my sudden urge to throw up on the conveyor belt, which seemed like a bad idea since it would keep circling around and around, and then I'd feel bad for whoever had to clean up the mess.

Shuffling in my socks, I joined the agent at the end of the screening area. He unzipped the suitcase and started rummaging through my belongings the way Natasha and I did in the bargain makeup bin at Ulta.

The mask was carefully wrapped in a sweater to protect it, right on top. If the agent removed it, what else would be visible? My sketchbook full of fantastical drawings? The two Elven Realms costumes I had designed and a seamstress I found online had made to my specifications? All would lead to so many questions that I didn't want to answer.

Past comments that had led me to hide my interest in the books looped through my mind—from the self-proclaimed nerds at the bookstore who had told me someone like me couldn't be a true fan, from my oh-so-delightful older brother who said fantasy was childish and I'd never make friends in high school if I admitted I liked that stuff. Of course, he'd waited until after our dad died to say those things, since Dad was the one who'd spurred my interest.

"Excellent craftsmanship," the man said.

I whirled back to my TSA nemesis. Safe from my classmates for now, but airport prison remained a possibility.

His words registered.

I blinked. "What?"

He was holding up the mask and inspecting the silver swoops and golden swirl accents, the winglike shape, and the blue silk ribbons.

My stomach flipped. The clear barrier separating us from the rest of the airport would give anyone who looked our way a view of everything. But my classmates had moved on.

I exhaled hard.

"*Mask of Souls,* right?" the guy asked. "Elven Realms? My daughter loves those books."

Embers stirred inside me. And pride. I'd worked hard to get the design right after carefully reading every description in the books, then spent hours at the 3D printer in the school art studio. I'd longed to show it off to someone, but the one person who would have appreciated it, who should have been on this trip with me, was gone. The man's simple comment, the way he said *daughter,* dropped a boulder in my stomach.

"I do too," I said, my voice thick.

"Did you make this?"

I nodded. "It's plastic, not metal. That's okay for a plane, right?"

He turned it over again. "Yeah, it's fine. This is impressive. What's it for?"

Sneaking out to find an underground fan club, thereby endangering my reputation and my GPA. "I'm on my way to Venice. It's for fun."

"My daughter would love it. I don't suppose I could send her a picture."

Sure, wave it around, pose with everyone in sight, wear it and plaster your picture on the airport's Employee of the Month wall. Don't forget to shout my name while you're at it.

Except I couldn't deny the request of a dad who wanted to make his little girl happy.

"Go ahead," I said.

He snapped a photo, and as he pocketed his phone, his love for his daughter drew me in, transporting me to the days before we lost my dad. He'd been the one to foster my love of reading, the only one who knew how much I loved the Elven Realms. My mom had no clue I was still obsessed, partly because keeping it for myself made life easier, and partly because the first time I'd left a fantasy book lying around after Dad's death, she'd told me to clean up after myself in a businesslike tone but with suspiciously shiny eyes. I didn't want to add to her burden by talking about things that made her sad.

"How old is your daughter?" I asked the man. "Has she read the other Elven Realms books too?"

"She's fourteen. Always has a book. I can't keep up."

"If she likes *Mask of Souls*, make sure she's read the Dreaming Forest series."

Memories bubbled up, causing a burn in my throat and nose, but I shoved them down. I'd only had twelve years, but my dad had tried to keep up with me too. I wanted to tell this man's daughter how lucky she was.

We chatted for another minute. Talking about my favorite books in person was weird after limiting my interactions to strangers on the internet. But soon I could do it more freely than in an airport. I would meet people like me, and the mask would ensure none of them knew who I was.

Excitement was replacing nerves.

Mr. TSA was kind enough to rewrap the mask before returning it to my bag.

"You're all set," he said. "Enjoy your trip."

I wasn't getting hauled in for questioning or locked up in a magical elven prison. No one had seen my costumes. And I hadn't broken down in the security line. Had I really escaped?

"Evie, there you are."

The voice came from someone stepping through the body scanner. My breath froze.

Mr. Owens.

I slammed my suitcase shut. My heart hammered even though I hadn't done anything wrong.

Yet.

Packing cosplay outfits wasn't illegal. My teacher didn't know about my plans to sneak out, go rogue, and violate his trip rules once we reached Venice, while wearing said outfits. He never would have guessed, either, since I was the person who never got in trouble, never did anything remotely wrong.

"Just the person I wanted to see." Mr. Owens didn't seem to notice that I was guarding my luggage like Ana de Rossi making her stand against the armies of the dark elves.

I shifted my bag open a fraction to check the contents without letting my teacher see. Everything was in place. I quickly zipped it closed.

"What's up?" I asked as I grabbed my sneakers.

"I have a favor to ask." Mr. Owens almost toppled over trying to tug on his still-tied tennis shoes without sitting.

I liked Mr. Owens. He was eccentric but encouraging. I'd been taking art classes with him for four years, and he kept trying to convince me to do more—enter contests, explore college art programs. To make him happy, I always told him I'd consider it. Which wasn't a total lie. I wasn't *not* thinking about it, because I was thinking about pretty much everything. Or nothing at all. Depended on the day. He let me experiment with different mediums outside of class, and I cleaned brushes for him, because I liked the smell and feel of the art studio, and because I had a pathological need to be helpful. Also, I felt guilty using supplies without contributing in return.

"Anything you need," I said.

"It may inconvenience you," Mr. Owens said. "We've had a last-minute addition to the group, and our newcomer needs a partner for the week. I was hoping you'd work with him. I know you and Natasha had plans, and I'm sorry to ask, but I trust you to help him."

I trust you. Help him. Words guaranteed to make me agree to basically anything.

Helping was my thing. Beyond the art studio, I also volunteered in the tutoring center, served on committees, and was the go-to welcome guide when a new student transferred to our school—even if the last one hadn't gone so well. Excuse me for wanting to know more than your name, Mr. Brooding Loner, who'd ignored my questions and hadn't spoken in more than single syllables. I'd felt like I was trying to talk to my brother, who had the conversational skills—and general personality—of a cactus. Wrapped in barbed wire.

It would be disappointing not to work with Natasha. She was smart, so our report would have sealed my A in art—assuming I didn't get caught sneaking out and have the entire week blow up in my face. But it was an honor that Mr. Owens trusted me, and Natasha would understand.

"What will Natasha do?" I asked.

"I'll let her join another team, so one group will have three. But I thought our newcomer would be more comfortable one-on-one."

I'd still have plenty of free time with Natasha, Bryce, and Dai this week. I couldn't let someone be alone and uncomfortable. "I'll do it."

Like I ever would have refused once Mr. Owens called it a favor. Mom always said that setting limits was good, that *no* was a complete sentence—except she never said no to anything, and I couldn't either or I risked disappointing someone.

"Who is it?" I asked.

I hadn't seen anyone new with our group when we arrived and met the students from the other schools.

Mr. Owens motioned to the guy stepping through the scanner behind him.

Yeah, I definitely should have asked that question before agreeing.

Of course it was him.

Mr. Zero Words. Mr. Unappreciative. Mr. Broody Loner.

Aka Gabriel Martinez.

His olive skin and stylish black hair, with a sharp line shaved on one side, framed guarded eyes. I could admit he was classically handsome, but his dark brows made a permanent slash across his face, and his jaw was always clenched in a way that said he was prepared for battle, or readying himself to jump into a pit of venomous snakes.

I met him in late January, when he'd transferred to our school with only months remaining of senior year. When I'd asked how he was, he replied, "I'd be better if I weren't here."

Those were the most words I'd gotten out of him for the

next half hour as I showed him around campus. I hadn't realized kindness was so offensive.

Why was I incapable of saying no? If there had ever been a time to disappoint a teacher, this surely would have been it.

"Good news, Gabriel," Mr. Owens said. "Evie has agreed to be your partner."

Gabriel's flat expression told me that he did not, in fact, find the news good.

I was on my way to see a city I'd dreamed of for years. Touring it with a sullen partner incapable of conversation had not been part of the plan.

But I would make it work. He couldn't resist my efforts to be friendly for an entire week. People liked me. Gabriel would just require extra work to figure out what made him tick and how best to get to know him.

"I said I was fine on my own." His voice was a low rumble, his tone as flat as his eyes.

Okay, maybe he could resist my efforts. But I was as determined to make a friend as he was to push me away, and I would win this battle.

Mr. Owens remained unfazed by Gabriel's rudeness. "One of the rules this week is no going off alone. I know most of you are legally adults, but this is a school trip, and it's my responsibility to make sure everyone is safe."

I nodded wisely as if I hadn't spent weeks carefully plotting how to break that rule.

But I did feel bad about it, and I doubted Gabriel could say the same.

"Plus," my teacher went on, "the project would be a lot of work for one person."

The project. Great. My AP Art grade depended on a guy who wouldn't respect me enough to look me in the eyes when he tried to get out of spending time with me.

This trip was officially for Art and Architecture Club seniors and those taking advanced art or architecture classes. I hadn't seen Gabriel in class or in the club. In Natasha's case, the club was an extra on top of a hundred other activities, no matter that she'd received early acceptance to USC and, short of getting arrested in Italy, her fall semester was set.

I . . . could not say the same. But I wasn't dwelling on that now. Or ever.

"I can handle it," Gabriel said. "I work better alone."

I barely contained a snort. But Mr. Owens was counting on me.

"I'm sure it will be fun to work together," I said. "We have two hours until our flight. Why don't we discuss the project while we wait?"

Gabriel finally looked at me, scorn in his eyes. His scowl was a storm cloud, dark and ominous. My smile brightened. Like Mom always said, a positive attitude wins more friends.

"Great idea," Mr. Owens said. "I'm glad you two are figuring it out."

He shouldered his backpack and marched off, leaving Gabriel and me to follow.

"He won't change his mind," I said. "So we might as well do our best to make this work."

Gabriel grunted.

"I'm interpreting that to mean you're sorry and you're willing to work with me."

One eyebrow shifted up a fraction, the only change to his face. "Why would I be sorry?"

I gritted my teeth to keep my smile. "Think of it as having someone to help, so you don't have to do all the work."

"I can manage."

"I'm sure you could, but Mr. Owens didn't leave that as an option, which means you don't have to. That's what partners are for."

"Mr. Owens is gone. You don't have to pretend to be nice to me."

My nostrils flared. "Believe it or not, some people are nice when no one is watching."

His forehead creased in skepticism.

Time to try another tactic. "How did you end up on the trip?" I asked. "Mr. Owens said it was last minute."

"It was."

"Why?"

"I decided to run away."

I dodged a lady with a service dog and hurried to his side again. "But you have to have a passport."

"Maybe running away is a regular thing."

"Arizona would be cheaper."

"No canals there. I only run to places with canals."

It sounded like a joke, except his expression and tone remained the same.

"Where else have you run to? Amsterdam? Las Vegas? Venice Beach?" I stopped, having officially exhausted my canal knowledge.

"I wish I were in any of those places right now so I could jump in a canal to escape this conversation."

Even though he sounded entirely serious about going for a swim to get away from me, I kept my face pleasant. "If you don't like conversation, this will be a long week for you. Do you plan to jump in lots of canals?"

"If you keep talking this much." He moved on, and I scrambled after him, towing my suitcase and its incriminating contents, which I'd nearly forgotten about thanks to Gabriel's rudeness.

What was his problem?

I just needed a new strategy. I would keep trying. Everything would be fine. Spending the days with Gabriel might not be fun, but it wouldn't ruin my main plans for the trip, the secret, nighttime ones. I could write our report. All Gabriel had to do was not screw it up. And if I could get him to be nice . . .

Who was I kidding? That would take magic greater than that of the fictional elves.

Chapter Two

Gabriel had apparently not liked my plan to discuss the project. He veered into the bathroom and didn't emerge after several minutes of me awkwardly hanging out by the door. There was no way the line in the men's room was that long.

He was either having digestive problems or he was avoiding me.

Okay, let's be honest. He was avoiding me.

I certainly wasn't insulted that an airport bathroom was preferable to talking to me. I would not take it personally.

I was totally taking it personally.

This shouldn't have surprised me. After that tour, I'd continued making an effort—greeting him in the halls, asking his opinions for student government surveys, ensuring he received invitations to senior events. He'd ignored me then too. But this week, we had to talk.

Just not outside a bathroom, because people were starting to give me weird looks. I abandoned my post and trudged to our gate.

I plopped down with my friends, keeping my suitcase tucked behind my legs.

"What are you thinking right now?" Bryce asked.

I froze. I had an answer I'd planned to use but hesitated a second while I recalled it. "How the dowager countess was the best character on *Downton Abbey*."

"Slow on the reply, but I'll allow it." He grinned. "Mainly because I never watched that show."

"Blasphemy," I said. "I know what we're doing on the plane."

Bryce grabbed Natasha's arm. "Save me from the British people."

"Gladly," she said. "That show is worse than my sister's telenovelas."

"Traitor," I told her.

"I love telenovelas," said Dai. "That's how I learned Spanish when we lived in Argentina. Although my teachers didn't appreciate the more colorful words I picked up. . . ."

"What are you thinking?" I asked Bryce.

"How three countries have placed Bigfoot on the endangered species list."

Natasha groaned. "How do you come up with these things?"

Bryce laid a hand over his heart. "I only speak truth, Natasha."

It was our larger friend group's ongoing game. Anyone could ask what you were thinking anytime, and you had to have an answer more interesting than *nothing* or *school*. If you were too slow or the other person deemed your reply boring, you got a strike, and when someone reached ten, they owed everyone coffee. I found it stressful, always having to keep a fun, lighthearted, and random-but-not-too-random reply ready. As opposed to Bryce, who presented conspiracies with such a straight face that none of us knew if he believed them or just liked annoying Natasha.

"We need to talk," I said. "Not about Bigfoot," I added when Bryce opened his mouth.

He smirked at me, and I grinned and shook my head. Bryce was cute, but he didn't make my stomach swoop. We'd flirted with the idea of going to end-of-senior-year events together, semi-dates, but we'd never dated for real. I didn't necessarily see a romantic future with him, but I enjoyed his company. Time for that later, though.

"There's been a change in plans," I said.

Natasha straightened. "What kind of change?"

She sounded determined, not nervous. She loved making plans, the grander the better. Often with spreadsheets and lots of ordering others around. This wouldn't faze her.

"Mr. Owens wants me to work with someone else. I'm sorry. He says you can pick any other group to join."

"Who does he want you to work with?"

"Apparently Gabriel Martinez has joined the trip."

They looked around, frowning. If I hadn't seen Gabriel with my own eyes, I would've doubted the truth of that statement too. His absence wasn't helping sell my story. He was more elusive than Bigfoot.

I debated telling them he was having stomach problems, but I did want him to like me.

"He came with Mr. Owens," I said instead. "And he needs a partner."

"I heard he got kicked out of his last school," Natasha said.

Bryce leaned forward. "I heard he was arrested for stealing hamsters from pet stores and releasing them on city buses."

"That's oddly specific," I said.

"He's in my English class, and he never talks," Dai added.

"Okay, enough," I said. My brother, Jonathan, had been the subject of lots of false gossip, and I hated it. "Those are just rumors. Maybe he's shy."

"Wasn't he rude when you gave him a tour?" Natasha asked.

"He wasn't the friendliest, but it's fine. I am sorry, though." I aimed the apology at her. "About this week."

"You can work with us," Dai said.

Natasha scanned the rest of our group. "I suppose that would be easiest."

Though we were friendly with everyone, and we'd been on several art or architecture field trips over the years, none of the others were close friends.

Natasha whipped out her phone. "Evie and I had planned to study political and religious symbolism as displayed in the city's art and architecture. What are you guys doing?"

She aimed the question at Bryce, who blinked. His eyes darted to Dai. "Tanaka's taking care of that, since it's his thing."

Dai was the only one of us who planned to pursue architecture. Bryce had joined the club junior year when his parents said that playing three sports wasn't enough for colleges and he needed to look more well-rounded. Natasha's, Dai's, and my involvement had sold Bryce—along with the number of local, one-day field trips that would get him out of classes.

"We were going to focus on Moorish influences," Dai said. "I've been intrigued by it since my mom took me to Spain last year."

Dai was in the popular crowd because of his past. He had lived in five countries and traveled extensively, but he never bragged, never acted like it made him special. And he loved to make people laugh, usually by doing wild stunts, so most of the time it was hard to see him as worldly or sophisticated.

"What if we studied multiple influences?" Natasha asked.

Dai shrugged. "I'll write the Moorish parts."

"Great." Natasha turned to me. "You can keep our idea. I'll send you the outline."

Her outline was as long as a normal person's full report. It would be daunting without her help, but she was nice to offer, so I couldn't refuse. "Are you sure? You put so much work into it. I can come up with something new."

"No, it's fine. This is for a grade for you."

"Thanks. Hopefully Gabriel agrees to it."

Not that I fully cared if he agreed, since I had no idea whether he even liked art and I suspected I'd be doing all the work. Especially if he never left the bathroom.

"Why did you pick the symbolism topic?" Dai asked.

Natasha stashed her phone. "It sounded impressive, and I like politics."

And I'd agreed because my only idea had been comparing Venice's architecture to descriptions of Venezari in the Elven Realms books, which would have required admitting I knew enough to complete a project like that in the first place. Not to mention the presentation I'd have to make to my art class after the trip.

The guys pulled out their phones to play games, and Natasha asked me to help review plans for the upcoming career fair. Over the last few months, I had enjoyed talking to people from a variety of fields, calling potential attendees, organizing booths—but the project had driven home how aimless my future was. Even now, staring at Natasha's list of participants, nothing screamed at me, *You should do this for the rest of your life.*

I ignored the familiar panic and listened to Natasha, agreeing when she asked what I thought, occasionally taking breaks to distribute the snacks I'd brought to share.

When they called our flight for boarding, Gabriel emerged from whatever secret realm he'd been hiding in, just in time to join the line.

"Are you feeling okay?" I asked him.

"Why wouldn't I be?"

"You were in the bathroom for a long time."

"Partnership extends to stalking my bathroom habits?"

"Sorry for being concerned. Maybe you hate flying. Maybe you ate a bad sandwich for lunch. Maybe you picked up an amoeba at the beach that—"

"Maybe I didn't want to listen to you pretend to be friendly."

"Just because *you* don't know how to be friendly doesn't mean it's pretending when everyone else does it."

"I didn't say everyone."

Only me. Lovely.

Before I could ask how I'd managed to offend him when I

viewed our primary interactions as *him* trying to offend *me*, he walked away, leaving me frowning at his back.

Two long flights should have offered ample opportunity to talk with Gabriel, but the times I got up and lingered by his row, he was wearing headphones and pretending to sleep. Yes, pretending. As in, made eye contact as I approached but closed his eyes by the time I reached him and refused to open them when I said his name.

Seriously, who did that?

But Gabriel's rudeness and my intense curiosity about what made him that way didn't matter. Not now.

Because after the flights, including an overnight one, and Bryce dodging my attempts to make him appreciate the Grantham family, we were here, in the city I'd been dreaming of.

We retrieved our bags, went through customs, and loaded into a large private bus at the airport. A short drive took us over a wide bridge. The sun glinted off water stretching on either side. My friends were chatting, and I half listened, half fought the urge to press my face against the window for the first possible glimpse of the city.

The town was car-free, so we parked on the outskirts and split into smaller groups to board water taxis.

Several students climbed into a low boat with gleaming wood panels. It looked glamorous and old-fashioned, like something from a bygone era where rich people went jet-setting to exotic locales. Even though the sun was shining, the breeze was cool as we cruised down the turquoise Grand Canal. Our speed was slow, and water swished gently against the hull.

Magic simmered inside me, a bubbly feeling that this couldn't be real and yet also a sense that this was the realest thing I'd ever experienced. The only thing missing was my dad, who had promised we'd see the city together one day, eat pizza, and dream of the Elven Realms. I felt him beside me, watching over me, and let the wind dry any threat of tears.

Buildings of cream and peach, orange and scarlet, pink and tangerine swept past on both sides. Old brick and stone, some crumbling or stained, and the overall terra-cotta tone, felt historic and elegant rather than run-down.

The boat rocked in the wake of other vessels, everything from small personal watercrafts to water-buses with ads on the side. The tang of seawater filled my nose, familiar from the beach near home yet also new and exciting. Glimpses down narrow side canals promised secret finds. My imagination raced with ideas for drawings, and my fingers itched for pencils to sketch with.

People sat along the water eating at tables under umbrellas, and windows glinted in the afternoon sun. We passed under bridges, where moss and barnacles clung to the bottoms. The canal kept winding through the city, longer than I'd expected, and I would have been perfectly happy to cruise for hours.

It was happening. I was really here.

I was Ana and Clio and Izak and the others, and I could imagine their version of Venezari overlaid with my modern

Venice, and the gleaming elven city of Moravion layered on top of that.

I was trying not to bounce up and down and squeal.

I was cool. I was worldly. I did stuff like cruise through the canals of Venice, with the breeze in my hair and sunglasses perched on my head.

Okay, fine, I was a huge secret nerd, and inside I was screaming like a fangirl at Comic-Con when the movie adaptation of her favorite book was announced.

I wanted to reread the scene in the series' second book, *Bridge of Echoes*, where Andriana de Rossi first glimpsed the elven city. The latest in her family to lead a secret society charged with protecting the human realm and keeping the elven realms secret, Ana had a magical mask gifted from the elves to her ancestors centuries before. The mask allowed her to see hazy glimpses of the normal elven realm and the shadow realm of the dark elves.

In the first book, the elven side remained a dream, snatches of vision or sound that Ana longed to see for real. She didn't fully grasp its grandeur until she entered it and discovered everything was brighter, more vivid, more tangible than she'd ever imagined.

That's how this felt. I had seen Venice through a mask—in pictures, in my imagination. But now it was real, unfurling before me, better than I had hoped. The colors were richer, the air thicker, waking me up, reminding me that magic did exist, and leaving me bursting with thankfulness that I got to experience it.

Bryce had his phone out, filming the views and us. Everyone expected me to be normal, so I waved when he aimed the camera at me and tried to keep my grin to a nonfanatical level.

Natasha peered over the edge of the boat, looking pale. "I knew this was a bad idea."

"Seasick?" I reached for my backpack. "Do you need medicine? I brought lots."

"I'm fine. Not a big fan of boats."

"Then this might not have been the best city to visit," Bryce said. "I'll hold your hair if you need to puke."

"Such a gentleman," Natasha drawled.

"I'll do the same for you," I told him.

He laughed and ran a hand through his short dark hair, ruffled by the wind.

In contrast to Bryce's easy charm, Gabriel's stiff shoulders and head determinedly pointed away clearly said he was apart, separate, alone, even though he sat close to us. Sunglasses blocked his eyes and those eyebrows.

"Happy to see the canals?" I asked him.

His angled head was the only indication he heard me.

"I'd wait for a slower speed to jump in, if I were you."

"Thanks for the advice," he said.

"Just watching out for my partner."

We left the Grand Canal and entered a narrower, calmer waterway. Golden stone buildings lined the canal, with colorful plants exploding from flower boxes and tiny balconies hemmed in by wrought iron railings. Bright pops of color came from the red, white, and green Italian flag and the blue EU one that fluttered against a stone facade.

Our boat stopped by red-and-white-striped poles, coming to rest against what wasn't a true dock, just a small stone sidewalk a few feet from the hotel entry, where an awning offered a sliver of shade. The buildings behind us were in shadow, and not too far down the canal, a small stone bridge offered a way across.

I already loved everything about this place. Boats to get around. The maze the city would be, away from the center of town, with bridges the only way to cross the watery streets. I imagined that Izak, the Krijekan sailor turned gondolier, might offer me a ride as he patrolled for elven incursions. In my mind, I saw Ana perched on that bridge and the silvery shadow of Bastian in the elven realm, stalking behind her from another world.

I filed off the boat with my classmates as Mr. Owens led us into the hotel. Bryce lingered to help with bags, and I made sure no one needed seasickness medicine.

The lobby had a seating area with heavy floral couches and floor-to-ceiling drapes, and a side room with small tables and a buffet. A gray cat slept in an animal bed in the corner. A thick rug covered the marble floor in front of a dark wooden desk, and an intricate glass chandelier hung overhead.

The atmosphere was historic and authentic, appropriate for an art and architecture group. I was glad we were staying somewhere with character, rather than in a cookie-cutter modern hotel that could have been anywhere.

The woman behind the desk came around to air-kiss Mr. Owens's cheeks, and his face turned redder than I'd ever seen.

He cleared his throat. "Valentina. You look lovely. Lovely to see you again, I mean."

"Welcome back, signore." She was around his age, with gleaming black hair, olive skin, and lips in a shade of red I wished I could pull off except my skin was too pale.

"I'm—we're—glad to be back."

Oh. My. Word. He liked her. Adorable.

Bryce was hiding a smile and probably plotting ways to get them together.

The teachers checked us in and called out names, distributing key cards. I was rooming with Natasha, who knew about my nighttime plans and had devised safety measures to make sure I didn't end up abducted.

"Remember," Mr. Owens said, "no going off alone. Be in the lobby at seven for dinner. Breakfast is from eight to ten a.m. Tomorrow morning we have a tour before you'll start your projects, so don't be late. And don't skip dinner tonight. I know you're tired, but it will help you adjust to the time difference if you go to bed at a normal hour."

Projects. I scanned the group for Gabriel. He couldn't dodge me forever.

Apparently he could dodge me for now, though, because I didn't see him.

Natasha and I went upstairs to our room, which had two narrow beds and a partial canal view that I could have stared at for hours. Cream and gold wallpaper covered the walls, and the marble bathroom had a bidet. Against one wall stood an old-fashioned wooden wardrobe, complete with a brass key in the lock. It was perfect.

I hung my costumes in the wardrobe alongside Natasha's

clothes, which she'd organized by day. My first outfit, which matched the one Ana wore when she went out at night to patrol the city, was black, with a short tunic, trousers, and a scarf that could be pulled up like a hood. The other was from the second book, when Ana was in the elven realms, a longer tunic of dark green with patterns of silver thread and soft, loose leggings.

I ran a hand over the fabric, and my throat burned. I wished my dad was here. He'd died before the club started, never learned of its existence, but he would've happily joined me in a matching costume.

Natasha studied my clothing with the same slightly baffled expression she'd worn when I first told her about my plan, but what she said was, "They turned out great."

I was grateful for her support, even if she didn't understand.

I swallowed hard, resolve strengthening. My dad wasn't here, but I was, and I would enjoy the city for both of us.

"Are you going out tonight?" she asked, yawning.

"I don't want to waste any time. I might take a nap now."

"Nope, you'll never wake up."

"That's what I have you for."

But I was too excited to sleep. One step I could take was scoping out potential escape routes. I went to the lobby, scanning for exits. I felt like I was preparing to commit a crime. In a way, I was. A crime against the teacher currently standing right in front of me.

My heart took flight like a flock of Venetian pigeons.

Mr. Owens was leaning against the front desk, talking to Valentina.

"Evie," he said. "Do you need something?"

"What? Nothing. I mean, hi. I mean, I wanted to see if everyone was settled okay."

No one was down here except a group of older Germans chatting in the breakfast area. Our group was clearly settled just fine.

The front door was right by the desk. Was someone on duty all night? Natasha could distract them once or twice, but that wouldn't work repeatedly.

"This is a nice place. The group stays here every year?" I roamed, pretending to admire the furniture while my eyes searched for other doors. A hall led to rooms. Maybe there was an emergency exit at the end?

"We do. Valentina takes care of us."

She beamed at Mr. Owens, and my attention skipped past her to the breakfast room, which had a door with glass panes. Based on the light, it might lead outside. That had potential.

"That's great," I said.

I had questions about their relationship, but I felt guilty for being nice while plotting against them as if they were jailers and I was planning a prison break, so I returned to my room to change for dinner.

The three schools split up for the meal, and our group ended up sitting under umbrellas at a restaurant on the canal. The sun was inching behind the buildings, the light dancing on silvery water, and boats paraded past.

I was still having trouble believing this was real.

Smaller groups formed at the square tables, but Gabriel sat alone.

"Want to join us?" I asked.

Bryce jumped up and dragged a chair next to me, and I shifted to give Gabriel room.

Gabriel looked like he'd prefer to throw the chair into the canal and sit on it there.

"We don't bite," I said.

"Tanaka does sometimes," Bryce said.

Dai narrowed his eyes.

"What are you thinking?" Natasha asked him.

"Cannibalism in the Donner Party," Dai said swiftly.

"See?" Bryce said. "Is it too late to switch roommates?"

I patted his arm. "We'll get you a panic button in case he tries to bite you in your sleep."

Gabriel was staring at us like jumping into the canal was an increasingly better option.

I scooted over more and nudged the empty chair toward him.

He sat with a grunt, his knee bumping mine as he settled in, his posture tense. "If anyone bites me, I'm gone," he muttered.

I blinked. Was that . . . a joke? Did he know how to make those?

We ordered pasta, and after the waiter left, Bryce said to Gabriel, "I didn't know you were coming on this trip." His tone was friendly.

Gabriel blinked at him like, *Well, obviously I'm here.*

"Do you get to stay by yourself?" Bryce asked.

Gabriel nodded.

"Hey," said Dai. "No switching rooms. I'll contain the biting." He took an enormous chunk out of his fresh bread while holding creepy, wide-open eye contact with Bryce, and Natasha and I laughed.

Gabriel was glancing between us, eyes wary, shoulders near his ears, as if he were preparing for an attack.

"Are you interested in art?" Natasha asked him.

"Look," he said. "I might have to work with Whitmore, but you don't have to pretend that makes us friends."

Natasha shrugged.

Bryce frowned like he didn't understand. "You don't want to be friends?"

Dai shoved Bryce's arm. "He's obviously smart enough to know that being friends with you means listening to outrageous theories and being force-fed a disgusting amount of protein shakes."

"You love those protein shakes."

"Keep telling yourself that."

"Protein shakes do seem a more effective social deterrent than biting," Gabriel murmured. Another joke? What was happening?

The waiter deposited a large bottle of water and five small glasses, so I took the bottle and poured for everyone. The pasta followed soon after and the others shifted their attention away from Gabriel, who ate in silence, slowly and methodically. He didn't seem to be listening as we chatted about prom, the planning committee, graduation parties, and the school base-ball team, where Bryce played outfield.

"Did you go to the game last week?" Bryce aimed that question at Gabriel.

"What game?"

"The baseball one. District playoffs."

"Why would I do that?"

"Um. It's fun? And we're good?"

"So if the team wasn't good, it wouldn't be fun and you wouldn't go?"

"I would," Bryce said.

"Because you're on the team," I told him, and he grinned and pointed at me. I shifted to Gabriel. "It *is* fun. Nice weather, music, ballpark snacks."

"Oh, well, if I'd known there were peanuts and Cracker Jacks, I would've gone weeks ago," he said quietly.

I snorted, but no one else heard him. Wait. Laughing was a bad idea. I was encouraging his antisocial tendencies.

"What other snacks tempt you to be social?" I asked. "Hot dogs? Nachos?"

"There's not enough fake cheese in California for that."

"What about basketball games? Football?" Bryce asked, like he couldn't understand why someone wouldn't want to live in a sports arena. "Did you go to those?"

"Sadly, I missed football season."

"Oh, right, you're new."

"It must have been hard to transfer," Dai said. "Coming in sophomore year was bad enough. Senior year would be rough."

"Did you move?" Bryce asked Gabriel. It was a diplomatic question considering the rumors about him getting kicked out of his last school or arrested. Or hamster-related thievery, which I was fairly certain Bryce had made up.

"No," was all Gabriel said.

My friends exchanged glances and sent pitying ones my way. *Poor Evie, who had to spend the week with this guy, good luck with that.*

Conversation shifted, and they left Gabriel out of it, which he didn't seem to mind one bit.

Chapter Three

Sadly, dressing like a ninja did not automatically grant ninja skills.

I wore my first costume, the black one, which was Ana's standard attire when she left her privileged, wealthy life to prowl the streets as leader of the Sentinelle. The secret society of watchmen protected the city and kept an eye out for elven incursions or anything that might reveal the existence of other realms.

The outfit was more incredible than I'd imagined. The soft fabric moved silently, comfortable and empowering at the same time.

Unfortunately, the clothes weren't enough to lessen the giant mess of nerves in my stomach.

I'd made a pros and cons list about whether I should do this. The pro list had included how awesome it would be and the fact that I might never get another chance. How I'd loved the Elven Realms books since my dad and I first read them together, discussing every character and plot twist over iced lattes that had made me feel so grown up. Then I'd learned about the club, and even though he'd been gone for a few years, I'd imagined the elements it might include and what my dad would have wanted to see most. He would've loved the idea, possibly wouldn't even have minded my bending rules for such a great opportunity. Missing it would feel like disappointing him.

The con list had been three times as long and included everything from endangering my chance at the citizenship award to endangering my reputation to endangering my health, because I was physically allergic to breaking rules and already feared I was going to be sick.

"Are you sure you don't want to wait a day? Aren't you tired?" Natasha yawned, which I was choosing to interpret as a result of jet lag and not a commentary on my attire.

My eyes were dry, my mind blurry. Other than napping on the plane, I'd been awake for too long. But . . . "I don't want to waste any time. The club is supposed to be hard to find."

And if I didn't dive in tonight, I might chicken out the rest of the week.

"They can't send you GPS coordinates?" she asked.

"Then everyone would show up and it wouldn't be a secret. The search is part of the experience."

"If you say so."

Fans had done a remarkably good job of keeping details scarce. Clues to the club's location were hidden around the city, but I was hoping I might get lucky tonight without them.

I picked up the mask that had almost ruined me and tied it on. Silver wings swept out from my eyes, covering my forehead, nose, and cheekbones, leaving a hint of my mouth and chin visible. After designing, printing, and painting it, I'd lined the inside with silk for comfort. The swoops that framed my eyes sparkled. It could have come from the elven realm, crafted with magic by the Ellurai themselves.

I examined my reflection, then took the mask off and added thicker winged eyeliner, another coat of mascara, and dark-plum lipstick that I'd never wear in real life. Better. Tonight I wasn't Evie Whitmore. I was a Sentinel, ready to take on the streets of Venezari.

Usually I wore my hair straight and down, brushing my collarbones. Tonight, I braided it into a crown, then put the mask back on. My phone went into the thigh pocket I'd de-signed for that purpose, and I buckled the belt. Its compart-ments were filled with many of the items Ana carried to feed the magic that kept the breaches sealed between the human and elven realms. Not all the items, because blood would be gross, and fingernail clippings creepy, and bullets definitely would have gotten me busted by TSA. But I had vials of tears (aka tap water from the hotel bathroom) and salt and pouches of coins and breadcrumbs. Finally, I strapped the fake knife to my thigh. Even though it was plastic, I'd known to check it and not risk it in the carry-on bag.

I was ready. Tonight, I was the art project, every detail care-fully crafted. Now to find other people who would appreciate it.

"Okay," Natasha said. "You look impressive. Are you sure you know what you're risking?"

I knew exactly what I was risking. But I also knew I would regret not trying.

"Remember," she said, "if you don't come back, I'm calling the cops and tracking your phone. Good luck."

Right. It was time.

Next step, hallway.

My heart raced. And now doubt was hitting.

What if the other fans discovered I hid my fandom and decided I was a fraud? The day in seventh grade when I'd attended the final Elven Realms book release party at a local bookstore with my dad, not knowing he'd be gone in a few weeks, flashed through my head. We'd worn matching Elven Realms shirts, and some kids from school in full costume asked me if I was lost looking for the shoe store and if I even knew the difference between an elf and a dragon. As if a popular girl couldn't possibly enjoy fashionable footwear *and* fantasy books. I hadn't told my dad, even when he sensed something was wrong; I was too embarrassed to admit how much their words hurt. I'd mostly lingered at the back of the store the rest of the night, though it hadn't stopped my dad and me from staying up way too late reading that last book together. I would be forever grateful we'd gotten to finish the series, because I might never have read the last one without him.

Any hope I'd had of making friends in high school who shared my love of the books and accepted all the sides of me had died that night. Would the club be a repeat of that?

Or, worse, what if I never made it that far? What if I got

caught, ruined my perfect reputation, and disappointed my favorite teacher?

I cracked the door. Peered out. Sconces lit the otherwise empty hall.

I had to try. No one at the club would know the fashionable, outgoing side of me to contrast with the nerdy side. Surely jet lag had knocked out the teachers. This was the one thing that was mine, and I was doing it not only for myself but also for my dad.

The carpet cushioned my footsteps as I descended the stairs, but I worried my heart was louder than a tap-dancing giant.

I paused at the foot of the staircase. Would a night clerk be manning the front desk? The hotel had other guests, so they'd have no way of knowing I was a student, but our group filled most of the rooms. Would they report to Mr. Owens that someone had been sneaking out?

Half our group were girls. If someone described the offender as medium height, average build, dressed in black, surely no one would narrow it down to me.

Actually, I would likely crack under pressure and immediately admit the wrongdoing so no one else got in trouble, because I was a huge dork like that.

This was going to give me a panic attack.

Think about the club. It would be worth it. I hoped.

One step at a time. I darted to a pillar and kept it between me and the desk. The breakfast room was nearby, but I would be easily spotted if I made a break for it.

I was really doing this, preparing to step alone into a strange city with no plan, no backup, breaking half a dozen rules. I hesitated behind the pillar, in a no-man's-land of wanting to find that club and wanting not to get sick in the vase of fake flowers on the nearby table.

A creak came from behind me. I whirled around.

At the foot of the stairwell, a figure in black emerged.

My breath lodged in my throat.

Was that . . . an Elven Realms costume?

The guy wore an old-fashioned black coat with a royal-blue sash, a red insignia, and gold tassels like the Venezarian guards wore in the books. Black pants. A plastic sword. A black mask covered his entire face, revealing nothing about his identity.

Our eyes met. Or, rather, our heads faced each other. I couldn't see his eyes. We froze.

That was definitely an Elven Realms costume.

He lifted slightly on his toes like he might bolt up the stairs.

I gulped. My heart hammered in my ears. Another fan. Did he know about the club?

Could he tell who I was? I fought the urge to adjust my mask and edged farther behind the pillar.

What happened now? Were we supposed to pretend we hadn't seen each other, since clearly neither of us wanted to be seen? As if that was possible. The sight of him hovering there in that costume would be branded in my memory for the rest of my days.

His head jerked and his posture stiffened.

Voices. Coming down from the stairs. I flinched.

He strode toward me. Before I could reach for my panic whistle or consider whether I should grab the vase and smash it over his head, he was lightly grasping my arm and tugging me toward the nearby curtains.

Oh. Good call.

Waiting for a shout from the desk that never came, I pressed against him as he wrapped the heavy fabric around us. Dust tickled my nose beneath the mask, and a musty smell threatened to make me sneeze. One of my shoulders was jammed against the window frame, and the Elven Realms guy huddled against me on the other side. His chest rose and fell quickly, same as mine.

A tremor went through me. I was not cut out for crime. I should have mentally prepared myself for this by practicing minor cat burglary or mild trespassing or something.

Also, I was in costume, hiding behind a curtain in a hotel lobby.

No one could learn about this, ever.

The voices were close now, too close, and speaking Italian. The people exchanged words with the man at the desk; then the voices faded, and I heard the front door open and close.

My partner in crime inched the curtain aside and peered out. If he was spotted, I was staying here forever and letting him get caught alone. I would live behind the curtain and haunt the lobby until the entire building was abandoned and crumbling into a canal and I could slink away without a single person seeing me.

"You go first," he whispered, his voice barely audible through his mask. "Duck behind the couch. Wait. Now."

He tugged the curtain back and, trusting him for no reason beyond his costume—which was a terrible reason to entrust someone with your deepest secrets and your entire future—I located the giant sofa and scrambled toward it, ducking to keep out of sight.

I wasn't as graceful as Ana. I tripped over the tassels on the edge of an ornate rug, stumbled, and almost face-planted into the fancy couch. My partner joined me, crouching more gracefully, without the threat of rearranging the furniture with his face.

No one yelled or arrived to drag us out. I sucked in a breath, held it, released it slowly.

The guy pointed to the breakfast room, the same thought I'd had, but it was so close to the desk.

"Wait," he whispered.

He crawled to a nearby table, where a bowl of green apples sat. Real? Fake? I couldn't tell. He grabbed one and sent it rolling to the opposite side of the lobby from the breakfast room, then let out a convincing cat meow.

I barely swallowed my snort.

He waved me on. I didn't have any better ideas, other than aborting this entire mission, so I ran for the breakfast room. I glimpsed the clerk, bent over to pick up the apple, his back turned.

The mystery guy followed right behind me. We edged around the small tables, past the long buffet, now empty. A hand closed around mine, and I let him lead me toward the door.

Hopefully it was unlocked and we could leave before the clerk came searching for a troublemaking cat.

It was, and it led to a courtyard with small metal tables. Two tentlike gazebos with flowy curtains held outdoor couches, and metal heater stands topped with a spot for fire were situated throughout. Planters ringed the space, giving it a garden feel. Two waist-high metal gates, one on each end of the courtyard, led out. In the daytime this space would be pretty.

My friend released my hand and raced toward the nearest gate, swung it open, then skidded to a near stop. He grabbed the wall for support, gripping the vines that covered it. A soft swear escaped him.

Beyond the gate was nothing but water. The hotel backed up to a second canal.

The guy clung to the vines, dangling precariously, trying to haul himself back into the courtyard. One foot was on the ground, but the other hung over the water. The vines were separating from the wall, lowering him inch by inch to his watery doom.

I hurried over and stopped at the edge.

How committed was I to this incredibly new partnership? Committed enough to risk both of us falling in?

Fine, yes, he needed help, which meant obviously I couldn't leave him.

I tested the vines. If I pulled from my end, they might break and he would fall. I huffed a sigh, planted my feet, and stretched out one arm.

My fingers snagged on his waistband. If I weren't worried about remaining quiet, I would have apologized for the wild inappropriateness of nearly sticking my hands down a stranger's pants. I tugged, drawing him close enough that I could wrap my arms around his torso. I braced my foot against the wall and yanked him toward me.

Momentum carried us backward. We landed in a heap on the stone, my spine pressed into the ground, the guy on top of me. I grunted, and he groaned and rolled off so we lay side by side, breathing hard.

"Hello?" came a voice. "Is someone out there?"

Was that Mr. Owens?

My new friend tensed. I couldn't tell if he also recognized the voice or just knew it meant trouble.

Light flicked on in a window overlooking the courtyard.

We scrambled on our hands and knees toward the nearest gazebo. The gauzy white curtain offered far less cover than the indoor drapes. The fabric snagged on my belt, and the movement made the tent pole screech across the stones. I froze.

The light brightened, like a curtain had been opened so someone could look out.

The fabric was stuck on my belt. Staying as low as I could without toppling the entire tent, I grabbed the end and made the curtain flutter.

"Wooo," I moaned like a ghost.

Really, Evie? Because that was going to convince my teacher not to be suspicious?

My face burned beneath my mask. I stopped the ghost charade. We waited.

The light went out, and it was quiet. My new friend detached the curtain from my belt, then helped me stand, and we made a break for the other gate.

We burst into the narrow street, clutching hands, and speed-walked away from the hotel until we were out of sight. Without speaking, we slowed and stopped. It was silent and dark, the stone sidewalk and stone buildings solid and heavy-feeling.

A wild laugh escaped me, short and strangled. My companion joined in with a low chuckle.

I released his hand so I could bend over and suck in air. The only sounds were our heavy breathing and my bursts of nervous laughter.

I was shaking, and my heart refused to slow. That had been far more adventure than I anticipated, and now the cool night air was hitting me, making me shiver.

But I was here, outside, and there was no going back.

Once my breathing steadied, I straightened and edged away to study my new friend. The dim light from distantly spaced hanging fixtures was just enough to see his costume, which might not have been custom like mine, but he'd found pieces that worked. His mask was shiny black, with eye-shaped holes, a carved nose and mouth, and no embellishments. Simple but striking. It covered everything from his forehead to his jaw. His eyes were too shaded for me to determine their color. The rest of his face was a complete mystery. I very much hoped mine was as well.

"Thanks for the help," I said. "I think it was your cat that saved us."

"It was definitely your ghost. Thanks for not letting me fall into the canal." His voice was muffled by the mask.

"Thanks for not taking me into it with you."

Who was he? He was obviously staying at our hotel. From what I'd seen, that meant my classmates and the other students from our area and a group of elderly Germans. I might know him in real life.

"Great costume." His voice was low and rough, like he wanted to hide how he really sounded. Should I do the same? It helped that his mask muffled his words. "Does your belt have . . . ?"

I opened it and let him see the vials, bottles, and pouches. "Nice."

"You too. Luca, right? I like the tassels."

His head bobbed once. I couldn't see anything about him, other than his dark hair. His collar reached the bottom of his mask, and black gloves covered his hands.

"Do you have the hidden weapons?" I asked.

Luca embodied a trope I loved, where a character has to disarm and it takes several minutes because he has so many weapons concealed all over his body, often in places that shouldn't be able to hide a knife or blade.

"If I tell you, that defeats the purpose," he said, quoting Luca, and I smiled.

We assessed each other. Adrenaline was fading to a low buzz, and I recalled my mission, why I'd gone through that stress in the first place.

"Are you going to the club?" I asked.

He remained close to the nearest building, hugging the shadows, like he was worried about stepping too far away from the secrecy they offered. "Do you know where it is?"

"No, do you?"

"No. I was planning to look."

I bit my lip. Tried and failed to make out his eyes in the shadow of his mask. If he hadn't been in Venice long enough to find the place, he could have arrived today, like I had. "Want to look together?"

He hesitated.

"We don't have to," I added.

"I don't know how safe it is at night. I would feel bad leaving you alone. Wait." His voice sharpened. "You don't know where it is, and you were planning to wander a strange city by yourself after dark? There might be dangerous people out here."

"Like you?" I asked.

He placed a hand over his heart. "I promise not to lay a hand on you."

"That's what a serial killer would say."

"It's also what a non–serial killer would say. I would be happy to look for the club with you," he said. "I would be a terrible person if I left you alone and anything happened."

"I'm not totally defenseless. And I researched the city. It's supposed to be safe. Just don't make any sudden moves."

He held up his hands. "I will only move un-suddenly."

"So . . . together?"

"Together."

I should have been insulted that he thought I needed a chaperone, but I did feel safer with someone in costume who'd also been worried about getting caught than I would have by myself.

Was it possible we knew each other? Odds were good that

he was part of my group, but that included eight guys from my school and several from the others.

I sure didn't want to tell him who I was. I didn't know if this guy had the same reservations or was an open nerd who had no problem wearing a fantasy mask in broad daylight, but he had hidden too.

"What can I call you?" I asked.

"How about Angelo?"

I laughed. "Clio's cat. I like it."

Ana's best friend had a stray she named Angelo—angel—although the other characters called it Diavolo—devil. Nice to know my new friend could laugh at himself.

"I'll be Fantasma," I said. It was the name the characters used for the faint glimpses they sometimes had of the parallel realm. The main characters knew they were elves, but the rest thought they were ghosts.

His chuckle was a low rumble. "Nice to meet you, Fantasma."

More tension eased from me as it hit home that I was doing this. "Any idea where to start?"

"I'd planned to wander and watch for anyone else in costume."

"Great plan." I motioned to myself. "It's working already."

He sniffed what might have been a laugh. "Except you don't know where you're going, so you don't count."

"Fair point. My costume is amazing, though."

"Indeed it is." He swept out an arm. "Shall we?"

Chapter Four

It was nearing midnight, and the shops and restaurants were closed, though some had low lights in the windows illuminating goods like shoes, clothes, and purses. In a few areas, motion sensor lights popped on as we approached, making me jump. We passed hardly any people. The water in the canals was so still that the buildings and bridges were reflected perfectly, and glowing lamps made double the light thanks to their twins in the water. The air was cool and damp, and the whole city felt drowsy.

It was perfect and otherworldly, and my heart swelled.

When we crossed a small bridge, I paused in the middle to watch the dark water and dancing reflections.

"Do you need to feed the magic?" Angelo asked.

"I think this one requires a coin."

"Not blood or a secret?"

"Those are reserved for high-risk areas. I'm not sensing any elven incursions here."

"Right. My mistake." He gave me a half bow. "You are the expert, after all. I'm just a lowly city guard."

"Don't worry, I'll protect you from the monsters and invading elves."

"And I'll stand here looking good while you do it."

"Sounds like a fair trade, if not very chivalrous."

"You're the one who offered to handle the monsters," he said.

Our conversation mimicked the one in the scene that revealed the history of how Ana first met Luca the guard, before she befriended him and recruited him for her team. I was grinning, but I didn't know if Angelo could tell since my mask shaded my mouth. Was he smiling too? I wished I could see his face. Except I also didn't, because I didn't want him seeing mine.

Yes, it was supremely nerdy to pretend to be Ana. But my new friend was pretending too, and warmth fizzed through me.

I opened my belt and took out a penny. I was in Venice, and I was in costume, and I was pretending to be my favorite character with a total stranger who wasn't mocking me. I laughed as I tossed the coin into the canal.

"Safe for another night," he said.

I was practically skipping as we moved on. Angelo didn't know who I was, which meant I could be as nerdy as I wanted. The feeling was so foreign that I wasn't sure how to handle the freedom, like a bird who'd lived in a cage its whole life and didn't know what to make of an open door leading to blue sky and real trees.

A mask let you choose to be anyone you wanted, and go figure, I had apparently decided to be one hundred percent me.

My partner had the best strategy for the first night of searching. So, we wandered.

The empty city was creepy but also beautiful. I was glad I wasn't alone.

I wished I could have been here with my dad. I missed his laugh, the passionate way he discussed books. How, when I was a kid, we'd acted out stories where I pretended to be Lucy Pevensie to his Tumnus, or I was Bilbo and he was Gollum, and he'd improvise costumes and do accents. Before life changed and I had to tuck that part of me away.

I forced my thoughts to the present. I'd learned early on after losing Dad how easily the memories could suck me in, so now I was careful when to take them out and dwell on them.

Angelo seemed content with silence, which was smart since I kept forgetting to disguise my voice. But I couldn't be with someone and not talk to them. It was physically impossible, the way if you tried to hold your breath too long, like Bryce had on a dare, your body took over and forced you back to your natural state of breathing—or in my case, talking.

"Are you a fan of all the Elven Realms books?" I asked. "Or just the Mask of Souls trilogy?"

"I've read lots. Some are better than others. I like the Exiled King series and the ones set in Krijeka. But Mask of Souls is my favorite subseries."

"Mine too. I love the setting"—I waved a hand at Venice—"but also the characters are the best."

"I'm guessing Ana is your favorite?" He gestured to my outfit.

"Is that clichéd?"

"There's a reason people love the books. She's a great character."

She really was. Not because she was a rich heiress leading a secret life. But because of her longing for more in the world, her belief in magic, and her desire to leave a mark. Plus her heroism, take-charge attitude, and the fact that she always had a plan, while I did not. A romance with a hot elf didn't hurt.

"Luca for you?" I asked.

"I actually like Pietro, but it felt wrong to impersonate a priest."

Interesting. Most readers preferred Bastian, the mysterious and dangerous elf, or Luca and the way he let his fellow guards tease him so he could hide his secret work with Ana. Pietro was a quieter character, an intellectual who loved knowledge and his faith.

"Does that mean you like breaking into things?" I asked.

Pietro might have been a priest in training, but he had a penchant for picking locks and accessing forbidden areas.

"Sadly, I couldn't bring my lockpicks on the plane."

I sighed dramatically. "TSA rules are the worst."

"Where'd you get your costume?" he asked. "It's great."

"I designed it. Sketched out what I wanted, then hired someone to make it."

"Nice. I cobbled this together myself, which is why it's nowhere near as detailed."

"It looks good. Accurate." Not that he looked good, because I had no idea what he actually looked like.

Was this a terrible idea? I was exploring the alleys of a

foreign city with a stranger in a mask. If he tried anything, I wouldn't even have a description for the Italian police.

But Angelo was walking a respectable distance from me and letting me choose our path, rather than intentionally steering me down the darkest, narrowest streets like he planned to abduct me or dispose of my body in a canal.

Still, it was good that my mom and Mr. Owens didn't know about this.

Not that they would have believed it was me, anyway, role-playing a fictional character.

We took turns pointing out features of the city that reminded us of settings from the books: an old church that could have held secret tunnels where Pietro liked to sneak, a closed market like the kind where Clio hunted for rare or illegal deals.

"Do you have a favorite scene?" he asked.

"How long have you got?"

He spread his arms. "All night."

I grinned. That sense of freedom swept through me again. I should have been tired, and I might regret this tomorrow, but for now, I'd enjoy every minute.

"I love when characters discover the full extent of their powers and use them in epic ways, so the sea monster fight, obviously. Plus Clio mastering the weapon she shouldn't have. I also like quieter scenes, like the first time Ana and Bastian get to talk for real, in person, and he touches her hand. Or Izak reuniting with his brother. What about you?"

"Those are great. I like Luca joking about how monsters

don't exist while saving his fellow guards who don't realize how close they are to getting eaten."

I laughed. "Yeah, that's good."

"Or Pietro standing up to the priests and leaving them speechless."

"Then jumping off the roof to make a dramatic exit," I finished.

"Epic." He repeated my word.

"How old were you when you first read the books?" I asked. Did that question reveal too much? Answering might reveal our ages, which verged on getting personal.

"I found the first in the Dreaming Forest series when I was thirteen. After I finished that trilogy, I picked up the Mask of Souls books." He paused. "It was a hard time in my life, and they offered what I needed. Hope that people could be loyal and heroic and good."

The longing in his words gripped my chest. That was what my dad loved about the series too. "Yeah." My reply was a soft sigh.

"Eventually I worked my way through some others," he said, "but nothing compared."

The feeling of longing continued to squeeze my lungs. "That's what's amazing about books, isn't it? The way they can sweep you away. Let you live another life when you need to not be in yours."

It was something I never would have admitted without the mask.

"Exactly," he said. "Or let you dream of a better life."

I debated telling him about my dad, but years of not talking about him won out.

"I've read every single Elven Realms book in order from the beginning," I said instead.

"I haven't read the newer series," he said. "I guess I'd found what I needed in Mask of Souls and didn't want to ruin it."

"Makes sense." We rounded another corner, and I stopped to stare. "Wow."

The street corner brimmed with golden light, and the bridge ahead reflected in the canal below.

Even though my mask wasn't magical like in the books, even though magic wasn't real, at this moment I felt like it was.

Angelo paused beside me, silent.

"You can almost believe there's another realm just out of sight, can't you?" I asked.

"It would be nice, wouldn't it?"

"The magic, yes. The evil elves and dark creatures, not so much."

His laugh was soft. "The bad makes you appreciate the good, though. If you've known darkness, it's easier to appreciate the brilliance of light. Darkness gives the light more meaning."

Did the dark days since losing my dad make me better appreciate the time I'd had with him? "Experiencing the light makes it hard when you lose it, though."

"True," he said. "That's why characters, why people, keep fighting. To protect the light."

"I hope I would be brave enough to be like them," I said.

"Me too."

The books had been right about masks. They both concealed who you were and made you more yourself at the same time. As if by hiding something as superficial as your facial features, the depths of your soul could shine more brightly.

This person beside me didn't know my name, but after a few hours, he knew truths about me that no one else did. There was safety in knowing those truths were protected.

We didn't see many people, even in the city's central area. None wore costumes, and when we asked if they'd seen anyone else dressed up, they said no.

After two hours of walking, I was tripping over uneven cobblestones. And even ones. And nonexistent ones. My eyes burned, my throat felt scratchy, and I had to be sharp tomorrow. The time difference would only go so far in explaining my exhaustion.

We used our phones to work our way toward the hotel but still hit two dead ends when the map failed by leading us to canals with no bridges, forcing us to backtrack and find a new route. This city would be seriously easy to get lost in.

Too bad I wouldn't be here long enough to learn its secrets, like Ana in Venezari. It had taken years to master high school, learn the intricacies and become the expert who knew what to do in every situation in order to protect myself so I had nothing to fear.

Except, like Ana, I had plenty to fear.

Secrets were a broad bridge leading straight toward fear. Inviting it. After living with them for so long, you tended to forget, until something brought the reminder crashing back—that you weren't in control at all, and everything you'd built could collapse in an instant if the truth got out.

Nighttime was making me philosophical. And pessimistic.

We hesitated around the corner from the hotel, where we'd stopped to talk at the beginning of our adventure.

"Do they lock the door at night?" I asked.

"The one we came out of had a keypad," he said. "Scan your card and you should be able to make it from the breakfast room to the stairs. Move quickly and don't stop."

I nodded.

"Same time, same place, tomorrow?" he asked.

"By same place, do you mean the haunted courtyard, the cat-infested lobby, or behind the dusty curtains?"

"Curtains, for sure. It can be our spot."

"Or," I said, "we can meet here, around the corner."

"That's safer, but far less creative," he said. "I'll go in first. If I come running right back out, you'll know it's not safe."

"You don't have to do that."

"It's fine. Then we won't know where the other is going."

Good point. "If you're sure."

"I'll meet you in this realm," he said.

"Or the next," I finished the quote, and he slipped inside with a salute, leaving my heart to melt at his adorable nerdiness.

Which didn't matter, because we were nighttime companions in crime, nothing more.

Chapter Five

I had made a grave miscalculation. I had failed to account for the fact that Natasha was one of those mystical and possibly evil creatures known as a morning person.

When I'd returned, I'd woken her up enough for her to mumble that she was glad I hadn't been kidnapped, and then she'd gone right back to sleep. I wished I could've said the same, but the thrill of the evening, and meeting Angelo, meant sleep was slow in coming.

Then I woke to the sound of intentional breathing as Natasha did her morning stretches at an unholy hour. Was it even light outside?

"Ughhh."

She didn't hear me—earbuds in, probably playing cheerful chirping birds or crowing roosters or the sounds of sleep being murdered, or whatever else morning people listened to at a time when they should be unconscious.

I burrowed deeper under the covers. Sleep and I were not going to be well acquainted this week. Should I attempt another hour despite Natasha's yoga breathing, or give up and get ready for the day?

I was in Venice. Sleep could wait.

I tossed the covers aside and stumbled to the bathroom. Today would require an excellent makeup job and lots of caffeine.

When I emerged, Natasha removed her earbuds. "How was it?"

"Interesting."

"The club?"

"I didn't find it."

"I told you GPS coordinates would be easier. What was interesting?" She stood and grabbed clothes from the wardrobe.

"I kind of met someone. . . ."

"What? How? Where? Who?"

I snorted. "You left out *when* and *why*. In the lobby, sneaking out, also in costume."

I summarized our escape, leaving out the details like nearly falling into a canal, my impersonating a ghost, and my friend pretending to be a cat.

She sat cross-legged in the middle of her bed, clothes forgotten. "Do you think you know him?"

"I don't know. He sounded young, but his mask covered his whole face."

"Are you going to try to figure it out?"

I shrugged.

"Did you like him?"

He was in costume, searching for the fan club, and we

talked about the books for hours. Obviously, yes. "We didn't give real names. Maybe he doesn't want me to know who he is."

"Aren't you curious?" Natasha asked.

"Of course. But I want to respect his privacy."

She looked unconvinced. "If you say so. I'd want to know."

"You want to know everything."

"Knowledge is power."

"Only if you use that knowledge correctly," I said.

Angelo would have appreciated my quoting Pietro, but Natasha didn't catch the reference. When I'd first confessed my interest in the books our sophomore year, I'd tried to convince her to read them. She'd finished a few chapters, said it wasn't her thing. It wasn't the bonding moment I'd hoped for, but she kept my secret. Mostly, I didn't talk about the books so I didn't bore her. It was easier to focus on what we did have in common.

We finished getting ready, me with lighter lip gloss and eye makeup, my hair down. The opposite of Fantasma. Then we headed downstairs for breakfast. At this hour, the lobby was bright and crowded.

My attention jumped to the curtain that had been my hiding place, then the bowl of apples, before I forced myself to focus on the buffet. If my partner in crime was here, I couldn't reveal any hints that Evie Whitmore had been the one running around the city playing dress-up.

I said good morning to our classmates, smiled at people from the other schools, and helped Dai carry three plates and two cups of coffee to a table. A buzz of excitement filled the air as people discussed the city, the projects, the food.

Natasha's question stuck with me. Was Angelo here? Did I know him? I found myself debating which guys in the buffet line were the right height and build before I made myself stop. If I tried to figure out who he was, it felt like giving him permission to discover Fantasma's identity. Which was ridiculous, because he'd have no way of knowing if I was snooping or not.

The buffet offered an assortment of pastries, sliced meats and cheeses, fruit, eggs, and mini boxes of cereal, plus large silver coffee dispensers, which I took great advantage of.

Valentina was overseeing everything, and I stopped beside her. "Valentina, right? Do you run this place?"

"Yes, I have been the manager for ten years."

"How long has Mr. Owens been coming?"

"This is the fifth year he has stayed with us."

"He must know he'll get great service," I said as my teacher joined us. His face reddened as he smiled at her.

So. Cute.

There were more teachers, from our school and the others, but Mr. Owens was the coordinator, and it was obvious why he kept coming back.

Natasha and I took seats by the door I had sneaked out. She leaned across the table toward me, but her eyes trailed guys getting food.

"Do you think it's him?" She pointed. "Or him? How tall was he?"

I grabbed her hand and shoved it down. "Shh."

Was he here, studying the girls? How hard would it be for

him to figure out who Fantasma was? My dark-auburn hair might be a giveaway, depending on how it had appeared at night. If I said that aloud, though, Natasha would buy hair dye or a wig for me.

And . . . did I want to know? He'd been fun to talk to. Funny. Nice. We had common interests. Liking him would be far too easy—and far too complicated.

Food and coffee helped erase my remaining tiredness. I was ready for my first full day here and the chance to see the city in the morning light.

Until Gabriel Martinez slunk in, and I remembered that I had to spend the day with him.

Armed with strong Italian coffee, I could convince him to work with me. Or at least to stay out of my way. But not too far out, since Mr. Owens expected me to keep an eye on my partner.

Gabriel grabbed a plate of pastries and eggs and walked toward the main lobby.

I darted to my feet and blocked his path. "I'm going to save you from getting charged with stealing dishes. We need to talk."

"Beginning a conversation with *we need to talk* is a great way to make guys run away, FYI. Is that why you're single?"

"How do you know that?"

"I didn't, because I don't care. But you confirmed it." His lips quirked on one side.

"FYI," I said, forcing a smile, since my relationship status mattered little to me, "we're partners, and we need to start our project, which means we need to agree on a topic."

"You mean you want me to agree with what you want to do."

"That would be easiest, since I already have a plan."

"That doesn't sound like partners. Your word, not mine."

I clenched my teeth to keep my smile in place. "Why don't we discuss it while you eat?"

"Is that another word you're using loosely?"

"What, eat?"

"Discuss. Are you planning to listen to my opinions or just tell me all the reasons you're right?" He gazed down at me.

I clutched my coffee cup so tightly it was a miracle it didn't break, but the alternative was launching its contents at his face, and I was too nice for that. Plus, it was too delicious to waste.

"I'm all ears," I said. "But only if you sit."

His jaw twitched. His brows were set in their permanent dark slash, making his brown eyes look black. "Fine."

He took a chair at an empty table in the corner. After peeking at Natasha, who was watching us with concern like me sharing a table with Gabriel might cause my descent into hamster-related villainy, I followed him.

Then detoured to top off my coffee before sitting across from him.

The soft light from the window made his hair gleam and his golden skin glow. Based on his sharp haircut and surprisingly stylish black Vans, frayed jeans, and unzipped-hoodie-plus-denim-jacket combo over a tight T-shirt, he would have made a decent model. I could admit to noticing someone who dressed well, even if his personality left something to be desired.

"If you let me explain my idea," I said, "I'm sure you'll see why it's a good one. Natasha and I were going to study churches, public buildings, and monuments, and analyze how the political symbolism of the art—"

He gave a giant fake yawn. "Bored already, Whitmore."

"Excuse me?"

"You're excused."

"It's just—"

"Where'd you find that idea, a college syllabus?" He took a long swallow of orange juice, and I tried not to watch the way his throat moved and he licked his lip when he was done.

"Okay, so it's ambitious. But it will impress Mr. Owens." And Natasha had put a lot of work into planning it, then let me have the topic. It would be rude to waste her efforts.

Gabriel met my gaze directly. "The parameters of the assignment were to write about any aspect of art or architecture, right? This project is literally designed to let us choose anything that interests us. Mr. Owens isn't expecting a graduate dissertation. He just wants us to prove we're doing something educational this week, other than eating gelato and feeding pigeons."

It was the most words I'd ever heard from him, which somehow made mine vanish.

"Are you honestly saying that out of everything in Venice," he went on, "political symbolism is what you find most exciting? For your *art* grade?"

What I found most exciting was not to be revealed during the light of day with my real face showing. Which made me miss Angelo. I could have told him.

"Why are you here?" I asked. "You've never been to a club meeting. Are you taking art or architecture?"

The classes were small, he wasn't in mine, and I didn't think he'd have been allowed into architecture partway through the final semester of senior year.

"Are we comparing schedules or picking a project?" He bit into a croissant.

I crossed my arms and leaned back. "Since you don't like my idea, let's hear yours."

He took his time chewing and swallowing before answering. "Building and art preservation techniques in a city that floods. Public monuments. The haunted places of Venice. How people are buried in a city like this. The various art mediums employed in the buildings."

I blinked. Not only were those ideas insightful, they sounded way more fun than Natasha's. Instant guilt hit at that thought.

Some of Gabriel's ideas weren't exactly academic, though—hard veto on haunted places.

Besides, this wasn't about fun. It was about an impressive report that secured my grade.

"Or I could try one more time to convince Mr. Owens to let me do my own project." Gabriel's steady gaze held a challenge.

That was what he wanted—to be rid of me. I couldn't say the feeling wasn't mutual. But our teacher had asked me to work with Gabriel as a favor, and I didn't want to let Mr. Owens down. Was Gabriel really okay alone for an entire week?

Okay, so probably, yes. I'd never seen him willingly talk to anyone. Solitude was his natural habitat.

But what if he got kidnapped by the Mafia or carried off by pigeons or eaten by a sea monster lurking in the canals? Not that I trusted my skills to prevent kidnapping. Or murderous pigeons. Or sea monsters. But still.

Plus, I was determined to figure out why he didn't like me and win him over, unable to back down from this challenge.

"He'll never go for it," I said.

"I'm not writing a history report. It won't kill you to pick something fun, something that interests you."

I hadn't even suggested my Elven Realms idea to Natasha. I certainly wasn't telling Gabriel. His ideas rolled through my head. Various art styles had the most promise. Once we started, I could find a way to make it bigger, more impressive.

"I suppose artistic mediums isn't a terrible idea. Like, sculptures and paintings, mosaics, things like that?" I pulled out my phone and searched. "We could visit museums, churches, famous buildings and study the techniques used to complement the architecture."

He grunted.

"What?"

"Nothing."

"You clearly have an opinion."

"Not one you want to hear."

"That doesn't stop you most of the time."

He made another noise, but this one might have been a laugh.

It froze me in place, and I stared at the way his eyebrows softened the tiniest bit. I felt oddly gratified that I had amused him.

And I was tempted to smile in return.

Chapter Six

"It's your job not to lose your partner today," Mr. Owens announced from the center of the room after he left Valentina's side. "After the group tour, you'll have the afternoon to work on your projects independently."

"I don't think he means alone," I muttered.

"I'm flattered that you already know me so well," Gabriel murmured back.

"Not as well as I will by the time the week is over. We're going to be great friends. I can tell."

"Your optimism is astounding." One of his dark brows lifted a fraction, a change from his usual scowl, and the expression was both a challenge and possibly a show of humor.

It imprinted itself in my brain, begging for me to recall each feature's exact position for later comparison. My mind was cataloging his looks, whether I wanted it to or not.

He wasn't what I'd expected. Sure, he'd been rude at dinner last night. But he was also funny. Not in a loud way like Dai, but his comments amused me. I wanted to dig deeper, learn more about him. Like, why the attitude and why he was here and why—

Better if I shut down that train of thought right now. He didn't like people, and, for some reason that sent a twist of pain through my chest, he especially didn't like me. Wanting to understand him was setting myself up for trouble. And trouble was something I avoided at all costs.

I was better off thinking about Angelo and how open and nice he'd been, the interests we had in common, and how much I was looking forward to spending time with him again.

Our large group flooded out the door. The morning was cool, and the light made the golden stone glow. The canal nearby was in the shade, the water a deep green. I wanted to capture it on paper, but that was not part of the project.

It could be, though. Not drawings where I turned regular Venice into Venezari or the elven city of Moravion the way I did for online forums, where my fan art was well known. This project would be for art class. It wasn't a secret that I was decent at art. As a hobby that I wasn't overly enthusiastic about, of course. Because if I had been enthusiastic, that would have meant contests and competitions and galleries, and my mom would have sucked the fun out of it.

But I could do this to add to our report.

Gabriel had stopped and was staring at me.

Oh. Right. I gave him a smile. "Ready, partner?"

"Are you trying to sound like a cowgirl?"

"Yep. Yeehaw."

Seriously? I sounded like an idiot.

But Gabriel's quirked eyebrow, freed from its permanent frown, almost made me willing to say more dumb stuff. Almost. If it made his face do that.

People jostled around us as Mr. Owens led the way, over bridges familiar from the night before. Everything looked different in the daylight. Less otherworldly, but still beautiful. The whole city had a charming, old-world feel, like it had remained untouched by time.

It was early enough that not all the shops were open. Men pushed handcarts full of goods, and the scent of Windex hit me when we passed people cleaning windows.

Natasha ended up by my side near the front of the group as we followed signs that read Per San Marco.

"This cannot possibly be the most direct route," she said. "Are we taking a scenic path?"

Mr. Owens laughed. "That's Venice."

"It's very inefficient." To me, she muttered, "It's a miracle you aren't still wandering the alleys."

"Shh," I said. "It's not that bad." I thought the indirectness added to the city's charm.

"Hmph," she said.

We emerged in Saint Mark's Square, the main public plaza. My steps slowed as the huge open space spread before us, a shocking contrast after the narrow streets and walkways of the rest of the city. Long stretches of off-white buildings with elegant arches lined three sides of the square, and the cathedral's ornate domes graced the other end. An orange brick bell tower pierced the sky, and a flock of pigeons strutted through the square like we were invading their territory.

This was the city's most well-known location, and I paused to let the cool air and historic atmosphere seep in, imagining my dad at my side, marveling at the iconic view.

"I heard you can get them to land on you," said Dai, yanking me from my daze.

Natasha shuddered. "Gross."

Dai withdrew chunks of bread from his pockets.

"Where'd you get that?" Natasha asked.

"Brought it from breakfast." Dai held a chunk in each hand and moved into the square toward the birds.

"Dai, what are you doing? That's not allowed." Mr. Owens took a step toward him, but pigeons were descending, and our teacher seemed to decide that getting closer was unwise.

Birds fluttered around Dai. Three landed on his outstretched arms and pecked at the bread in his upturned palms.

"Do you know how many diseases those have?" Natasha called.

We could barely see Dai's face through the cloud of birds, but he replied, "Then why do people use them to carry messages?"

"Because of a tragic lack of cell phones throughout history," Natasha said.

"Did you know they were the first domesticated birds? They're quite smart."

"How do you know that? Did you make that up?"

"My nana is a bird-watcher."

"Pigeons are the best she can do?" One pecked near Natasha, and she kicked at it to scare it off.

A tornado of feathers and squawking now surrounded Dai.

"You alive in there, Tanaka?" Bryce yelled.

"I am the great pigeon tamer," came his voice from among the storm. "My pigeon army and I shall conquer the world."

Nearby, another tourist had also brought food. A second flock was forming.

"Is that a rival pigeon lord I see?" Dai asked. "This will not do. We shall go to war."

"We shall go to our tour," Mr. Owens said. "Mr. Tanaka, leave the pigeons alone."

Dai tossed the remains of his bread to the ground, emerged from the feathery horde, and glared at the child who was stealing his birds away.

"My army betrayed me," he said. "And they pooped on my shirt."

Natasha sniffed. "That's what you get for playing with wild animals."

"That, and the bubonic plague," came Gabriel's voice from right beside me, and I jumped.

"I need a shower now," Dai said.

Natasha wrinkled her nose. "You should have thought of that before you got friendly with the flying rats."

"Do not speak ill of my soldiers."

"I have to smell you all day. Ugh."

Everyone was laughing. It struck me, as it often did, how

easily Dai goofed around without worrying about what people thought. It made them like him more. But it was easier for a guy, a smart and cool one, to be goofy. Mom always said that women had to be careful not to lose respect because it was hard to gain and harder to gain back.

"If Mr. Tanaka has abandoned his plans for world domination through pigeons, it's time to begin," Mr. Owens said. "We'll be touring the basilica and the palace this morning. Many of you may want to return to these locations, depending on the focus of your project, but I wanted everyone to have an official overview of the most famous sites to start the week."

Saint Mark's Basilica was an impressive building of domes, spires, and arches. The church had obviously provided inspiration for the duomo in *Mask of Souls,* where Ana and the others completed their first heist. Sadly, Angelo wasn't here for me to point that out.

A long line had already formed to enter, but we met a tour guide holding an orange umbrella who guided us past the people. He gave us audio devices and earbuds so we could hear him if we were separated. When we passed through the massive front doors, I gaped, then hurried on as my classmates flooded around me.

The interior was as grand as the outside. Gold-leaf mosaics covered domed ceilings high above and made the cavernous space glow. Marble pillars gleamed. Even the floors were covered in intricate mosaics. As we shuffled from area to area, the guide described the history and architecture, the elements of the church, the Byzantine treasures held here.

I half listened while mostly soaking in the grandeur and trying not to trip as I stared.

The patience required to make the mosaics, with so many tiny pieces, was impressive. This place had a feel of permanence. The building, and the art, had endured, to be marveled at centuries later. It was a little intimidating. What would I ever do with my life that lived up to this? The weight of history, along with my family's accomplishments, pressed down, telling me I had to make something of myself, right now, except I had no idea where to start.

Natasha was dictating notes on her phone. Dai was listening and occasionally commenting to her, I assumed for their project, while Bryce took pictures. I needed to find things we could use in our report, but Gabriel was lost in the crowds. Keeping track of your partner was a challenge when your partner's life mission seemed to be to escape the group.

I hoped he wasn't getting into trouble. Surely Mr. Owens wouldn't have let him come if he thought Gabriel might plunder historical artifacts to sell on the black market.

No. I refused to listen to rumors. I would get to know him, give him a chance.

Two of my fellow AP Art students were next to me as we continued the tour.

"What do you think?" I asked.

It was easy to slip into Art Class Mode and discuss techniques. They were planning to pursue animation and graphic design. My fan art hobby made me feel like a fraud, someone who dabbled in the same world but hadn't fully committed. But we chatted, and I gave Matt a spare pencil and Lina a Band-Aid for the blister on her heel.

The tour led upstairs, then outside, onto the balcony, which gave us a bird's-eye view of the square and the crowds below, another angle to see just how big the space was. Wind whispered in my hair, a gentle voice reminding me how incredible it was that I was here.

In the distance, boats cruised the turquoise canal. Giant horse statues loomed above us. I posed with my friends as Bryce filmed us before he zoomed in on the pigeons below.

"Tanaka's army is waiting for him," he said.

"Don't worry, troops. I shall return for you," Dai called.

"Where's your partner?" Natasha asked me.

I sighed. I couldn't fathom ignoring rules so blatantly. Did Gabriel's parents not give him the mega-intense lectures, guilt trips, and disappointed glares that my mom was so fond of? Or maybe, like my brother, Jonathan, Gabriel ignored them.

Then again, ignoring rules was exactly what I'd done the night before. Gabriel might have a good reason too.

Our next stop was the Doge's Palace, adjacent to the basilica. The interior was as impressive as the church's, with ornate ceilings, gleaming floors, and broad staircases. The building housed a museum with rooms decorated in past styles, rich wallpaper and furniture, friezes and carved doors and sculptures. Signs detailed the history of the Republic of Venice, and displays contained old armor and weapons.

I imagined Luca and the others wielding similar items and

surreptitiously took photos of helmets and fancy hilts, shields and axes to use in drawings later.

The guide discussed medieval history, tales of politics and crime. Again, I saw the inspiration for the Elven Realms books, in the scheming politicians. I hoped this building had hidden rooms and passages like the palace in the books, even if I didn't get to see them.

I wished I had someone to point out details to, what I liked and what scenes they reminded me of. I could bring up this place with Angelo tonight. Everyone who came to Venice toured these sites, so it wouldn't reveal my identity to say I'd been here. The idea of having someone to talk to, even if the method was unusual, boosted my mood.

In the dungeons, Dai pretended to be a prisoner moaning for food, then we crossed the enclosed Bridge of Sighs. A romantic name for a place with a sad history, where prisoners had their last glimpse of the world before facing their fates.

Small cutouts in the stone offered a view of the lagoon and the sky. It had beautiful craftsmanship, not that the prisoners cared. They only knew their lives were ending.

Being trapped inside something beautiful was still being trapped.

The guide's words started to blend together. Being out half the night was catching up with me. My eyes were dry, and my brain felt sluggish. Hopefully everyone else was struggling too and would blame jet lag.

After the tour, our group reconvened outside, and Mr. Owens waved us close.

"Okay, everyone, you should have the money I gave each of you. Get some lunch, then get to work. Be back at the hotel at seven tonight for dinner. Don't be late."

I sidled up to Gabriel, who lurked at the edge of the group. "You *are* here."

"Where else would I be?"

"Halfway to Rome? Jumping in that canal you mentioned? You kept disappearing."

"Stalking me again?"

"Keeping track of my partner, as Mr. Owens asked. Can we discuss our project now?" I trailed Natasha as she and Bryce and Dai crossed the square. She'd probably researched a good place to eat, so I'd tag along.

"My expectations are low," Gabriel said.

"Can we *try* to discuss our project?"

"That sounds more doable."

I swallowed a groan. "Did you take notes on the tour? There was a lot we could use for our report."

He tapped his temple. "Mental notes."

"We can visit again later this week. Take our time, enjoy it more."

He looked at me steadily.

"What?"

"Nothing," he said.

"No, you have thoughts."

His gaze didn't waver. "For partners, you don't trust me very much."

I started to say he hadn't given me a reason to. But I was

being unfair. Other than being a bit rude, he hadn't given me a reason *not* to. Scowls and sarcasm weren't automatic indicators of someone's trustworthiness.

I crossed my arms. "Okay, impress me, then."

He rattled off nearly as many facts as the tour guide had, about the mosaics, paintings, marble, the altarpiece and use of jewels in the cathedral, the styles of architecture, and, with a smirk, the religious symbolism of the lions of Saint Mark.

I blinked. Surprise had silenced me.

"How do you remember all that?" I asked, genuinely curious.

"I take good mental notes." His smirk deepened a fraction. "Are you impressed yet?"

The annoying thing was, yes. Yes, I was.

Chapter Seven

Others from our school knew that Natasha was a safe person to follow, so a group of us ended up at a casual café a few streets off the square.

While we waited for our pizza, I asked everyone's opinions about the tour and what their projects were, and Olive asked for a Band-Aid since she'd heard I gave Lina one. I fished one out of my bag, then responded to Sanjay's request for aspirin, before settling in with my friends.

Natasha was already writing.

I poked her. "Look up and enjoy Venice."

"If I do that, I'll see the pigeons. I'm trying to pretend they don't exist."

"I would have thought you were devising a way to eliminate them," I said.

Dai gasped. "You wouldn't dare."

I rolled my eyes at him. "What are you thinking?" I asked Bryce.

"Birds are robots."

"What?"

"All birds are robots," he repeated, "used by the government to spy on people."

"That makes no sense."

"What about birds we eat?" Dai asked, as if this were a serious theory.

"The government is using them to introduce robot parts into our systems so they can convert us."

"How long has this been a thing?" I played along.

"It's recent," Bryce said. "The government has slowly been replacing the real birds, and now they're gone. They're all spies. When they land on wires? That's how they recharge."

"I should warn my nana," Dai said.

Bryce nodded sagely. "They're really watching her."

"Wait, does that mean my army was a robot army? Wicked."

"Seagulls stealing food at the beach?" I asked.

"Harvesting our DNA."

"Pigeons pooping everywhere?" Dai asked.

"How they leave messages."

"This is the dumbest thing I've ever heard," Natasha said without looking up. "Strike for Bryce. And strikes for both of you for encouraging him."

"Hey," he said. "You don't get to hand out strikes just because you disagree with my philosophies."

"That's not a philosophy, that's a delusion."

"Fine, what are you thinking about?" Bryce asked.

"My tia's tamales."

I was impressed that she had a quick answer since she'd

been writing her report, but that was Natasha. Her brain held more topics at a time than a computer with twelve windows open.

"While you're eating freshly made pizza in Italy?" Dai sounded outraged.

"They're good tamales," she said.

I was laughing, and I caught Gabriel watching us with an expression I hadn't seen yet, like he was confused. It went into my mental file. Not that I was keeping one.

"Well, this has been fun, but we have a project to work on." Natasha took one last swig of her drink, closed her notebook, and stood.

Bryce and Dai rose more slowly, and all three of them looked at me.

"See you at dinner?" Natasha asked.

"I'm not going to drown her in a canal, Gutierrez," Gabriel said from his table.

She turned to him. "You'd better not."

"I'm sure he'd find a more creative way to dispose of me," I added.

His lips lifted a fraction, and my heart fluttered. I felt like I'd won a small battle, somehow.

My friends moved on, and I stood too. "Are you ready?"

"No." But Gabriel rose. "What if we wander and see what we find?"

He was testing me, to see if I'd go along without a plan. Hiding the twitch in my jaw, I said, "Okay."

He moved confidently, down side streets, across bridges, his pace steady. He didn't stop to gawk like I wanted to, but he wasn't rushing the way Natasha would have, her destination always more important than distractions along the way. I tried to study him without being obvious, the angle of his head, the way his eyes took in everything, the slope of his shoulders under his denim jacket.

"Have you been here before?" I asked.

"No."

"You seem to know where you're going."

"Yeah, wandering."

"No, but it's like you have a destination in mind and you know how to get there. I love this city so far, but it's confusing, with the canals and bridges and everything."

"Maybe some of us are better with directions than you."

"Yeah, you strike me as a guy who's great at following directions."

"It's my favorite pastime. Sometimes I buy IKEA furniture because I love reading the booklets so much."

I snorted. "Aren't those just pictures, without words?"

"Adds to the fun."

We fell silent, and I studied the buildings, the boats, the people. We passed a variety of shops, some selling leather and emitting a rich, earthy scent, ones with shoes, elaborate masks, glass art. Everything from expensive name brands to tourist stuff to local artists' work. The scent of fresh bread baking mingled with that of handmade herbal soaps and the sweet sugar of gelato shops. Too bad Gabriel probably wasn't a shopper, because I would have loved to explore the stores.

The streets were crowded, and I had to dodge people to

keep up with Gabriel. I heard many accents and languages, which was fun.

My mind scrambled for another topic. Something to get to know Gabriel for real, to break the ice, to make the week less awkward. We couldn't spend multiple days in this weird limbo.

"So do you like art?" I asked. "What did you think of the tour?"

"Do you always talk this much?"

"It's called being friendly."

"Is it for others or for you?"

"What do you mean?"

"Is it to help others or because you aren't comfortable with silence?"

I was perfectly comfortable with it. Sometimes. If I was drawing or watching a movie. Okay, fine, occasionally I talked during movies. I got enthusiastic and wanted to point out the details I liked to make sure no one missed them. My sister had refused to watch movies with me for years now, and my brother, before he left home, had teased me about my habit.

"Most people appreciate the effort," I said.

"No they don't."

"Just because you don't, doesn't mean no one does. One person isn't a valid sample size."

"A third of the world's population are introverts. Most of them dislike small talk and prefer silence."

"Even introverts like to talk about things they enjoy. What do you enjoy?"

"Silence."

Fine. If he wanted quiet, I would give him so much quiet he'd forget I was here. Rude. But whatever.

Was he right? I thought I was friendly because I wanted to make other people comfortable. To get to know them. To find something in common to bond over. But was it more for me? Was it my way of trying to make them like me, without considering what they wanted? My way of fitting in?

No. People genuinely liked to talk about themselves. I was not letting Gabriel get in my head.

Besides, I needed to focus on my other mission for the day, the secret one. Mission: Find the Fan Club. Which would hopefully be more successful than Mission: Earn Gabriel's Friendship.

Internet rumors said that shops and restaurants around Venice had clues about the location of the Elven Realms club. They were supposed to have a symbol in the window or near the door—three circles in a row intersected by a line, to represent the three realms—small and inconspicuous so it wouldn't be noticed except by those who knew to look for it. In between admiring the bridges, water, houses, and flowers, I scanned the places we passed.

We came to another plaza with a stone church, not as grand as Saint Mark's, but with a tower. We studied it, and I took pictures from multiple angles, before entering.

The inside of this one was more like a church and less like a museum or treasure hoard, with wooden pews, an altar, and organ pipes. Several dark paintings adorned the walls, which were bright white instead of gold.

"Renaissance style," Gabriel said. "The outside and these paintings. More traditional than Saint Mark's. Probably because it's not attached to the political center of the city."

I made notes on my phone and tried to hide my shock so I didn't insult him.

I wanted to ask how he knew so much, maybe bond over an interest in art. But as we were leaving, we passed several temporary vendor carts in the square. One had the circles symbol at the bottom of its sign.

I couldn't ask the vendor about the Elven Realms with Gabriel listening.

"Mind if I make a stop?" I nodded to the cart.

"Shopping on the first day?" Why was he so hard to read? Was he mocking? Judging?

"I promised my sister I'd bring her something."

Technically, she wanted multiple things. Whatever looked authentic but was fairly cheap, so she could resell them. Masks, scarves, lace, leather, food. I'd need another suitcase, which she had tried to convince me to bring, claiming she'd pay the extra baggage fee from her profits, assuming I brought her good items. Which meant she would later claim the items weren't good enough and refuse to reimburse me. At fifteen, she was well on her way to outdoing our mom's business empire and mastering the dirtier sides of capitalism. Mom was very proud.

I circled the cart, which contained an assortment of notebooks with marbled covers, leather goods, and wooden toys, in addition to the standard magnets, scarves, and hats.

The woman manning the cart had streaks of gray in her long black hair and kind eyes.

How did I approach this? I felt like a spy. One with no training who would immediately get captured, fold under the enemy's torture tactics, and quickly spill national secrets, setting off an international incident.

Oh well, might as well give it a shot. If this woman had no idea what I was talking about and thought I was a delusional American, I'd never see her again, so it didn't matter. My warm face didn't get the memo. I tried to channel childhood Evie, playing pretend with my dad.

"Are you a sentinel of the realms?" I asked, fighting the urge to duck my head or run away in embarrassment, which would make this even more awkward.

Her lips curved. "I am a friend to those who seek," she said, her words accented.

My heart beat faster. "Does that mean you can help me?"

She handed me a business card with a single sentence written in multiple languages.

I beamed at her. "Thank you! Grazie."

She smiled back. "May you find what you seek."

Relief and excitement were a jumbled ball inside me.

Figuring I should help her in return, I selected a few journals, paying from the envelope of cash my sister had given me and keeping the receipt. If my hunt for the club required visits to multiple stores, this would get expensive. Maddie would be happy.

As the woman bagged my purchase, I read the card. The English line said, *The place you seek seems but a shell.* I didn't know how that helped, but it was my first clue. If I found more, surely I could fit them together. Maybe Angelo would find some too. I imagined him somewhere in the city today, searching for the symbol, same as I was.

My steps were light as I rounded the cart.

Except, when I faced the plaza, Gabriel was nowhere to be seen.

It wasn't overly crowded, just vendors in the middle and awnings and tables at restaurants along the edges. A man in a black suit was setting up a cello.

But no Gabriel.

Seriously? Had he taken the first opportunity to run off? This was going to be a long week.

Gabriel appeared clutching a pastry and a paper bag.

I stared at him.

"What?" he asked.

"I thought—"

"That I ditched you? I debated it." He wore a slight smirk that made his eyebrows rise in the middle. It was a new expression, not quite the same as his mocking one. Close, but different. Surely it wasn't flirting, right? He didn't like me. Or anyone.

"Where's mine?" I asked.

He extended the bag toward me.

"I was kidding."

He held my gaze. "Too cool for baked goods?"

I snatched the bag and reached in to find a croissant. "Were you truly planning to share, or were you hoping to finish them before I came back?"

"I love sharing. I'm so glad you returned for us to enjoy croissants together, Whitmore."

I knew he was being sarcastic, but I smiled anyway. "I am too. I enjoy it very much, thanks."

There was the slightest movement as one corner of his mouth tucked in, and it sent brightness skimming through me. I could get addicted to trying to surprise him and get a reaction like that. What would it take to earn a real smile?

We paused to eat—wow, cream-filled croissants, well done, Venice—and listened as the cellist began to play. Rich, deep tones of Beethoven filled the air. The square suited the large instrument, the strings reaching every part of it.

I was rooted to the ground as the melody and the weight of the city's history hummed inside and swirled around me.

When the cellist finished, we clapped along with the crowd that had gathered.

"Do you play any instruments?" I asked Gabriel, licking cream off my fingers.

"Always with the personal questions."

"Does that qualify as personal? It's not like I asked your deepest hopes and dreams or your most embarrassing moment."

He sighed like I was exhausting him. "No, I don't play an instrument. Are you happy?"

"I don't know, are you happy? Do you wish you played an instrument?"

His lips pressed together in a near smile, which I took as another victory for me.

"Do you at least like music?" I asked.

His gaze held mine, and I wasn't sure if he would answer. "I like anyone willing to put themselves out there like that." He nodded to the musician.

It felt like the realest thing he'd told me.

As we moved on, he dropped coins in the guy's upturned top hat.

Sparks flared in my chest. The gesture was another tiny glimpse of the real Gabriel he tried so hard to hide. A nice person was in there. If I kept trying, eventually I'd draw him out.

"Since you asked," I said, "I don't play an instrument either."

"Having that knowledge makes my life complete."

"I took piano lessons for two years as a kid," I continued, determined not to let him get to me, "but I wasn't very good, so my mom decided I should do something else."

I sensed his attention on me.

"What? And don't say *nothing*."

"Did you like piano?" he asked.

"I guess? It was kind of fun."

"Then who cares if you weren't good?"

Squirming filled my stomach. "Things don't work that way in my family. My mom is big on being the best at everything you do."

"Sounds impossible. Let's check this out."

We'd come to another small church, and Gabriel aimed for it, but his words lingered.

My brother had frequently said the same thing, loudly, arguing with our mom, refusing to play by her rules, saying how unrealistic they were. Their fights stressed me out, and I'd refused to dwell on whether Jonathan had a point, because I didn't want to have his tense relationship with our mom. Agreeing with her beliefs made life easier and happier.

Besides, our mom was great. Supportive. Full of useful life lessons. After Dad died, she'd kept us going. She helped us be the best, celebrated our accomplishments, didn't let us settle. With her encouragement, I'd won class elections, received perfect attendance awards, and racked up college acceptance letters. Accomplishments that were no less impressive because I didn't know what to do with them.

I refused to let Gabriel disrupt the careful balance I'd achieved in my mind.

I studied a painting of the Virgin Mary. This church was a lot like the last one.

"We can't just keep writing about places we randomly stumble across," I said. "I'll find a variety of art and types of locations for us to visit."

Gabriel inclined his head, and his eyebrows didn't move, which I took as agreement.

See, I could read him so well already. We were definitely almost friends.

"Then we have the actual report," I went on. "We should write up something each day, while things are fresh in our minds. I can write it and let you read it over."

"Control issues?"

"I thought you'd appreciate not having to do the work."

"You don't know anything about me."

"Because you don't want me to," I said.

"You're saying you want to get to know me?" His brows lifted in doubt.

"I asked you a bunch of questions when I gave you a tour, and I've been asking all day today. You're the one who keeps shutting me down."

He studied me.

"What?" I asked. "I wasn't the rude one."

"You were prying. On the tour."

Had I been? When I met him that day, I'd already heard rumors, but I thought I'd been careful not to let that affect how I treated him and didn't ask anything that I wouldn't ask anyone else.

"I didn't realize wanting to know where you'd gone to school and what classes you liked and if you had siblings constituted an interrogation." I took a breath, considered what he'd just said, softened my voice. "I give welcome tours because I like meeting new people and helping them adjust to a new place. I'm truly sorry if you didn't feel welcome."

My genuine tone converted his scowl from *100 percent annoyed* to *Oh fine, I'll tolerate you.* "It's . . . possible I overreacted. That day. I was having a bad week."

I did a double take. Was that . . . Gabriel admitting he'd been wrong?

"I'm choosing to take that as an apology," I said. "You're forgiven."

He rolled his eyes. "I have three siblings. That's all you're getting from me."

"You have siblings, and you don't play an instrument." I clasped my hands in front of me and beamed at him, intentionally cheesy. "I feel us becoming friends already."

His mouth did that thing again where I suspected he was trying to smile but either he'd never learned to do it properly or his lips were as stubborn as the rest of him and refused to give in to the temptation.

I wanted to press a finger to the corner of his mouth and see if I could bring out a full smile.

"So," I said, gripping the strap of my bag instead, "the project. What if we add drawings of the things we write about? I'll handle that. Since you want to do all the writing."

His eyes glinted, sharp but amused. "You any good? Don't want you bringing my grade down."

"I'm good enough. Wait. Your grade. Are you taking art?"

"There you go, prying again."

I groaned. "You're so annoying."

"I really am." He stretched before shoving his hands into his pockets.

"Oh no." I grabbed his arm and twisted it to see his watch, one with a thick, worn leather band that was different and therefore intriguing. "Is this on Italy time?"

"No, it's on Cleveland time."

"We're going to be late."

"So?"

"So, Mr. Owens specifically said not to be."

He grunted. "Worrying so much must be exhausting."

"It's called being responsible and polite."

"Being polite is exhausting too."

"Then you should have lots of energy saved, since you don't spend any of it on politeness. Can you please walk faster?"

He sighed loudly and lengthened his stride.

Chapter Eight

Mission: Earn Gabriel's Friendship had suffered a setback. Our group went to dinner near the hotel, and he ditched me immediately to sit alone. So much for the progress I'd thought we'd been making.

He bent over his phone, brow furrowed, the light from the screen illuminating his features. Why did I care? Other than being used to being able to make friends with anyone? It was a mark on my record. A failure. Nothing to do with Gabriel specifically.

But . . . why was he so private? And why did he hesitate at the simplest questions? Did he have friends? Maybe he'd been popular at his last school and transferring during senior year was hard.

I didn't need to know any of that. Because I definitely wasn't thinking about him.

We were partners for the project, nothing more. We didn't have to be friends. But . . . friendly partners would've been nice. Especially when I recalled the times his mouth had contemplated smiling and his eyebrows relaxed from their constant pinched position. The way he'd listened intently to the music and tipped the cellist. The way he knew so much about art.

"How'd it go with Mr. Broody?" Natasha asked.

Her question jolted me out of thoughts I shouldn't have been dwelling on. "It will be fine. How was your day?"

"We made good progress on the list of sites to see, so we'll easily have time to expand our report. But this city has no logical pattern, and the stupid pigeons are everywhere."

I pictured her dragging the guys from place to place, kicking at birds that dared to cross her path. I would have been with her, if not for Mr. Owens's request.

Even though I loved Natasha, maybe I didn't hate Gabriel's general mood of not being in a hurry for anything, ever. It was a more relaxing way to see a new place. Not that I'd tell her that.

After dinner near the Rialto Bridge, we aimed for a gelato shop. The chilly weather didn't matter—in Italy, gelato was required.

When I reached the counter, I saw the Elven Realms symbol in one corner of the display case full of containers of colorful gelato. I let everyone else go first and made sure they'd moved on before I ordered, then leaned over the counter like this was one of Clio's shady deals.

Recalling the first woman's phrasing, I whispered, "Are you a friend of the sentinels of the realm?"

The man winked, and when he handed me a cup of strawberry and chocolate gelato, he also slipped me a card.

My pulse skipped. Having code words was seriously too much fun.

"Thanks!" I started to turn, and saw two classmates were behind me.

I stuffed the card into my mouth.

Genius, Evie.

They smiled at me, and I returned the expression while keeping my lips shut, hoping they would assume I had dessert in there and not paper covered in ink. Wait. Was the ink toxic?

Hopefully my spit wasn't wearing off the clue. *Excuse me, sir, may I have another card? I accidentally ate the first one along with your delicious gelato.*

Trying not to choke, I spun away from my classmates, fished the card out of my mouth, and fought a gag.

The soggy but legible card was in Italian; no translations this time. A street or a business? I'd have to do a search later. I stuffed the card into my pocket and trailed the group toward the Rialto Bridge. The walkway leading to the bridge was packed with people strolling and browsing at booths selling paintings and masks, crafted leather and clothing, anything a tourist might want. Most of it wasn't what my sister had in mind, so I just enjoyed looking.

Were we still supposed to be keeping an eye on our partners? Because somewhere between eating my clue and here, I'd lost Gabriel.

Hopefully Mr. Owens would understand. If he knew Gabriel at all, he'd know that asking me not to lose him was like asking a helium balloon not to drift away if you let go. It would land eventually, but its path and destination were a mystery.

Bryce and Natasha were inspecting items while Dai trailed behind them, hands in his pockets, surprisingly not making a show. This probably wasn't a big deal to him, after all the places he'd traveled.

I half imagined that among the stalls, I'd find Clio's booth of legal goods—and her less-than-legal supply of elven artifacts that she wasn't supposed to keep.

If my sister read fiction, she would have related to Clio, the Hallan merchant who could find anything for a price, as long as you didn't ask where she got it. But I hadn't seen Maddie crack anything but a textbook in years, except maybe a book about how to make more money. The only thing my sister would like about the Elven Realms was my art—because she would have found ways to sell it.

I wanted to shop, but I also wanted to paint. A digital painting for this scene, as opposed to one with colored pencils. The angles of the Rialto Bridge, the reflections on the water, the glow of lights.

At a booth selling colorful scarves, a hand-drawn sign had the symbol. I pretended to examine the scarves, while waiting until no one else was within several feet before using the same line as last time.

With a wink, the woman behind the table handed me a card.

I grinned.

"Hey, Evie, want to help me pick one?" someone said from behind me.

I hurried to drape a scarf around my neck, using the motion to hide my shoving the card into my bra, and then turned around.

Olive stood there, holding three options.

Bad idea. The corner of the card was digging into my armpit, and the position felt precarious, like the card might dislodge. I kept one arm pressed to my side to hold it and wiggled slightly until it wasn't poking me, while I took off the scarf one-handed.

"Of course." I gave Olive the interested, knowledgeable face that made people frequently ask me for style advice. "Let me see."

While she slowly, so slowly, held up the three different scarves, I shifted my arm more.

The card stabbed me. Why had they used such inflexible cardstock? And why couldn't Olive move faster? Then I felt bad, because I did enjoy helping people find the perfect items and get good deals.

When she finally settled on a green scarf and went to pay, I fished out the card. An old woman watched me. Sure, sure. Sticking my hand down my shirt probably looked weird. I smiled at her like this was normal behavior and shoved the card into my pocket.

Hopefully the clues, and any that Angelo might have found today, would be enough to point us in the right direction tonight. I wanted to examine my clues, but Olive was waiting. I stashed those thoughts for now as she linked her arm through mine.

What would she say if she discovered the interests I was

hiding? Would it make her see me differently? We were both in the honor society, and I tried to project Natasha's air of confidence around those friends, focusing on the more prestigious colleges I'd applied to, not that I necessarily wanted to attend any of them.

I'd kept my secrets for four years. No reason to change now.

Later tonight, I would be Ana again, and it would be enough.

The green and silver elven outfit felt like good luck. Ana had worn something similar when crossing the elven realms. She was searching for a way home, but along the way she'd also learned about magic, fallen for Bastian, experienced the wonder of a new place.

Those sounded appropriate for my nightly excursions. Except the fall-in-love part. Though I was excited to see Angelo again . . .

I ignored my weariness and desire for a nap. Tonight was the night. I was slightly less terrified than the previous evening. Sure, the consequences if I were caught paraded through my head. But venturing out once successfully, and having the clues, had lessened my worry.

Angelo and I would solve the clues and find the club, and I wouldn't have to think about unsociable daytime partners or how everyone thought they knew me but really only knew the shiny masks I chose to show them.

I hadn't shared the clues with Natasha, even though she

might have been helpful. They felt like something to be saved for true fans. Plus, she already had a project for the evening—helping me sneak out without having to impersonate a ghost.

Heart pounding once more, I went downstairs and lingered in the stairwell, waiting.

The lobby phone rang.

I listened to the clerk's end of the conversation, knowing what was happening on the other—Natasha claiming she'd left something in the laundry room and couldn't go herself because she'd applied a charcoal mask and couldn't possibly be seen. The clerk was resisting her efforts to convince him to search. Natasha had offered to distract him in person, but I didn't want Angelo to see her, suspect she was helping Fantasma, and connect her to me. Finally the clerk grumpily agreed. I waited, then peeked out. The man disappeared down the opposite hall.

I darted for the breakfast room and out the door.

Tonight, the gauzy white curtains rippled in the breeze, ghosts fluttering without my help.

Movement caught my eye. I whirled. My elbow bumped a heater stand.

A cat darted off. I exhaled hard.

The heater wobbled, tilted. I lunged for it, but I was too slow. It crashed to the ground with a metallic clang.

I froze. My gaze jumped to the window that I suspected was Mr. Owens's.

I hurried to right the stand and then dashed for the gate before the sound alerted anyone to my presence.

Eyes gleamed from the shadows. The gray cat was watching.

"Thanks for nothing," I said.

It yowled and scampered off.

Jerk.

I slipped out onto the street. My heart might never slow down.

The darkness reminded me again how good it was that I had company for this quest. Faint sounds came from apartments nearby—television, music, voices—but the streets and canals were empty of people and boats. Now that I'd seen the city during the day, nighttime offered a greater contrast. Water lapped the canal banks. The air was very still, so silent after the crowds.

When I rounded the corner, a figure waited. I tensed before recognizing the same outfit as the night before.

A thrill went through me, edging out the nerves. Secret nighttime meetings on street corners transported me into the books. We were Sentinels, and the city was ours.

"Hi," I said.

"Hey. You came."

"So did you."

"Great. We've established that we're both experts at stating the obvious." Though his voice remained muffled by the full mask, I heard a smile in his words.

"Is our next step figuring out where to go? Because I found clues today." I couldn't keep the eagerness out of my voice.

"I did too. Want to sit somewhere and compare?"

We found a quiet bridge and perched on the steps. The

water was dark, and so was the sky, no stars visible. It reminded me of when Ana sneaked out to meet Clio, who brought paper cones of fried squid, and they would chat.

"What did you find?" I asked.

"Ladies first."

"Why, because you didn't actually find clues and you want to steal mine?"

"Because you sounded excited to share and I don't want you to explode."

Oh. That was sweet. "I found three. The first told me to look for a place that seems like a shell. So maybe a building that looks abandoned from the outside?"

"Makes sense, since the club is secret. If it had lights and music, everyone would find it. Venice has lots of empty buildings. Tourists driving up prices, rising water levels, flooding."

"That's sad."

"This used to be such a thriving city," he said. "It would be incredible to restore the old places, make it like it used to be."

That sounded like an interest in architecture. Was he from our school's program or one of the others? No. I was not considering Natasha's idea to learn his identity. We were temporary allies and fellow secret nerds, nothing more.

"Okay, here's the second." I showed him the card with the Italian writing but didn't hand it over. Though it was dry now, it had been covered in my spit.

"A street name?" he asked.

"That was my first thought, but it could also be a canal or a bridge. I found a few options."

"We can search more later. What's next?"

"My last clue was *You can approach me by land or by sea,* so I'm guessing it's right on a canal. I saw those garages, basically, where you can drive a boat right up to a building. And we know that lots of buildings like our hotel have street and canal access."

"Great," he said. "There aren't many canals to check."

I laughed. "What did you learn?"

"My first one says *A powerful family once called me home.* Lots of the abandoned buildings are old palaces, so combined with your clue, I think we want one of those."

"That narrows it down to, what, a hundred?"

"I'm not done yet." His voice was playful, and he nudged my arm.

"Sorry, my apologies, do continue."

"The other clue was another name." He showed me the card.

"Okay, so an abandoned palace that you can enter from the street or with a boat, with these names as cross streets or cross canals or whatever."

He pulled out his phone and typed in the names. The screen's glow lit his mask.

I snorted.

"What?"

"You're dressed like Luca, but you're scrolling your phone. I was imagining the trouble the crew would get into if they'd had cell phones." Wow, that sounded dorky.

"Izak could be the Uber of gondoliers."

"Clio would love eBay."

"Or the dark web."

I laughed. "Pietro would appreciate the research potential of the internet."

"And Bastian would think it was foreign sorcery."

"It kind of is."

"True. This one's not too far. Let's start there." He stood and offered a gloved hand, which I accepted and let him tug me to my feet. His grip was strong but gentle, and that coat did indecent things to his shoulders. He hovered above me before quickly turning away.

My heart was beating too fast.

He could be old. He could be married.

Worse, he could be someone I knew.

We checked a nearby corner where a bridge and a canal had names that matched our clues but found it dark and empty. No signs of people, no buildings for a hidden club, unless it was a very small one.

The streets felt apocalyptic, like we were the only two people left in the city.

We meandered to another possible location, chatting about the palace and the duomo. Conversation flowed much more easily than with Gabriel, but the destination was another bust.

"Time for one more?" he asked.

I smothered a yawn. "Yes."

"Are you sure?"

"I'm sure. I don't want to waste any time."

I was also sure I would be drinking lots of coffee again to-morrow. Could too much caffeine make your heart explode, or was that a myth? I should check on that.

We approached the third possible area and crossed a bridge. Something moved in the shadows beneath it. I clutched Angelo's arm and pointed.

It was a man in a small gondola. The man's outfit was what drew me. Despite the darkness and the fact that he was tucked beneath the bridge, I recognized the outline of his hat. He was dressed like Izak, in a black short-sleeved shirt and a wide-brimmed hat.

We hurried across the bridge and stopped at the base, not far from where the boat rested. Up close, I could see the rest of his perfect costume—the buttons undone at his throat, a scarf around his neck, and an orange sash around his waist.

"How goes the night?" I called.

The boat maneuvered to the bank next to us.

"At peace, may the Vilnik keep it so." The man quoted Izak in Italian-accented English.

Up close, I noted his fox mask—the fox was the sacred animal of Izak's people—and the boat, painted with stylized fish in primary colors, to match the native art of Krijeka.

I couldn't stop a grin as another scene formed in my mind that I wanted to capture on paper. It was perfect.

"Can you take us to the club?" I asked. "Do you need a password?"

"I can take you."

Angelo lingered. "Are we doing this?" His voice was low.

"Surely this guy didn't dress up in costume to drown people, right?"

Angelo hummed.

"We're doing it. I'll keep my panic whistle ready."

We moved to the bank, and Not Izak helped us into the boat.

Silently, we glided through the water, away from the bridge, down the canal, and along a building that towered above the water. It looked abandoned, from the crumbling bricks to the barred windows that must have been covered from the inside so no light leaked out. The boat stopped next to a worn wooden door submerged in the water.

Was this yet another bad idea? Maybe this guy dressed up as a book character to take people to his secret torture dungeon. He might keep sharks in there or giant eels, and we were dinner for some deranged aquatic pet that would hopefully drown us before it spent thirty years gnawing on our bones.

He hauled the door up and eased the boat inside. The water continued in a cutout like the shallow end of a pool, just large enough for the gondola. Two lanterns lit the water, but shadows swallowed the rest of the space.

Angelo paused, like he was leaving it up to me whether we entered the creepy, possibly haunted building or leaped into the canal and swam to safety, bone-eating eels or not.

If I strained, I could hear music.

"We're already a true crime documentary in the making. Might as well finish the mission," I murmured, and Angelo huffed a laugh.

I stood carefully in the wobbling boat. We climbed out.

The gondola left immediately, and the door closed behind it. I hoped we were right about that other exit. The space smelled of seawater and felt like a damp garage, cavernous and shadowy.

A person approached, wearing a guard outfit similar to Angelo's. My heart pounded. I was torn between thinking this was extremely cool and fearing this entire endeavor had been a terrible idea.

"Benvenuto. Welcome."

"Hello," I said.

"Which Mask of Souls character always carries candied pecans?"

"Trick question," I answered. "Clio, Ana, and Izak do in various scenes."

"Correct." The man shifted to my mystery friend. "What gift does Pietro give the elven lords in *Bridge of Echoes*?"

"A poem," Angelo said. "Do you need me to recite it?"

Okay, that was hot, a guy in an Elven Realms costume knowing as much about the books as I did. Not that I was thinking about Angelo that way.

"That won't be necessary," said the guard, to my disappointment. "We're open until three. Doors are unlocked at eleven. We ask that you try not to draw too much attention when coming and going. No posting details online. You can take pictures, but don't share them. We all work together to protect this place."

It felt like there would be some jerks who ruined it for everyone, but considering I hadn't found directions or pictures on the fan boards I frequented, their rules seemed to be working.

"I agree to your terms, good sir," I said.

"I agree too," Angelo said.

"You may enter." The guard gestured farther in.

Now that my eyes had adjusted to the low lighting, more details came into focus—archways and columns and a broad stone staircase.

I definitely heard music, instrumental, jaunty like in an old-time pub.

We crept on, past cavernous arches, up the stairs, to a doorway blocked by curtains.

I held my breath. This was it. The moment I'd been dreaming of. My heart skipped. Would it be everything I'd hoped for? Worth the effort and the stress?

Angelo's hand ghosted across my back as he ushered me inside.

And we were transported.

Chapter Nine

It took all my self-control not to freak out.

The room was an exact replica of the tavern where Ana and her crew gathered for secret meetings. A man behind the bar in a red vest. Stoneware mugs. Worn wooden tables. Faded tapestries on the walls, floor covered in straw. A sign hung over the bar with the words THE MASKED OTTER and the image of an otter in a mask. Wooden casks lined one wall, and the scent of roasting meat filled the air. A musician playing a stringed instrument sang in Italian.

Two dozen masked people, almost all in costume, sat throughout the room. Many ate or drank, which meant I could likely order something.

I clasped my hands at my chest to keep from grabbing Angelo's arm and swinging him around. My mind submerged, sinking into the atmosphere, the details. I imagined Ana and Luca and Clio waiting for me in a back room or the city guard storming in at any moment for the confrontation scene with Izak.

It was my imagination come to life. I didn't know where to look first.

Longing for my dad hit me so strong, I flinched. He should have been here, seeing this with me.

I wanted to examine every inch of the room. See every prop and every costume. Some were straight from the books, while some guests had gone for a more generic fantasy aesthetic. But all wore masks, elaborate like mine, or simple like Angelo's, or classic Venetian ones.

The masks plus the dim lighting gave the place a secretive atmosphere. These people could be anyone: famous or not, young or old, Italian or American or anything else. But we were bonded by love for books that had reached every part of the globe.

My heart might burst from the magic of that, the way a story could connect people. No matter how different our lives were, we weren't that different in the end. These people were instant friends, instant family.

I hoped. So far no one had asked me to leave, so it was an improvement over my last attempt to fit in in a place like this.

"It's perfect," I finally said.

My grin probably wasn't visible beneath the mask and in the shadows. Was Angelo staring in awe or smiling? Surely he wasn't disappointed.

We edged farther into the room. They'd done an amazing job with the details. Light emanated from sconces on the walls that flickered with real flames. The dishes were stoneware or old pewter and appeared historically accurate. Tapestries showed scenes of ships and sea monsters.

It could have been a movie set, other than the people with phones. I wanted to sketch a scene of the crew huddled around a table with mugs of sweet wine, planning their heist.

An archway led to a second area where people were playing cards—Primo, I assumed, a popular game that the characters played. Through a side door, past an enormous stone fireplace with intricate scrollwork, people were entering, which meant there was more to see.

I pressed closer to Angelo. "Want to look around and see what else there is? Or, I mean, we don't have to stay together."

"No," he said. "I mean, yes. Let's look around."

Something warm and bright bloomed inside me. We didn't hold hands, but our arms brushed occasionally as we moved through the room. The scents of hay, freshly baked bread, and spices joined roasting meat, and conversation hummed.

We pointed out details to each other, leaning in, like I did during movies or at art museums, except this time, Angelo oohed and aahed appropriately every time I showed him something, and he made observations too. It was interesting to see what he focused on. He also liked the art and the craftsmanship, including small details like decorations or embellishments.

The warmth inside me spread. Maybe I'd found someone I could watch movies with, who would be okay with me talking. Someone with whom I wouldn't have to hide my enthusiasm, who wanted me to share so he could enjoy things too.

Except I didn't know Angelo, not really. Not in real life,

where activities like watching movies were possible. A voice in my head that sounded suspiciously like Natasha's whispered that if I learned who he was, those activities might be an option.

We aimed for a door people had come through, which led to a hall of ornate pillars, with molding on the walls and marble sculptures in alcoves.

"Elven Realms or just old Venice?" I asked.

"Hard to tell. They might have left the palace's original features in place and restored them."

Beyond the pillars, in another long hall, was the marketplace from the books, selling leather, jewelry, weapons, clothes, all with a historical—or a magical elven—feel.

"Is this for sale?" I asked a woman at one of the tables.

"Si, everything. Many artists and craftsmen make the items and sell them here."

"There goes all my cash."

Even if they took credit cards, there was no way I was letting *Secret Elven Realms Marketplace* show up on the bill my mom paid. I wanted to linger and study the corsets, the knives, the belts, the lockets, but there was more to see, and I had more nights.

We climbed the stairs and found a large, shadowy room where people were sparring with swords. One whole wall was covered in weapons. My dad would have loved those.

The second large room on this floor had a fresco ceiling and a glittering chandelier, again possibly left over from the building's glory days. The gleaming floor revealed the room's purpose—it was the dance hall from Ana's daytime life, opulent and grand, where the nobility of Venezari gathered. A small group of people were dancing to elegant music. Some were dressed as human characters, some as elves. Silvery lighting kept the room dim but romantic.

Another hallway served as an art gallery, with an assortment of drawings and masks on the walls. The walkway was dark, but small museum-style lights illuminated the art.

I lingered. Could I add art to this? Did I want to?

A few images and styles were familiar from the online community where I shared my work. Had those artists been here in person? How great would it be to meet them?

"These are good," Angelo said.

"Do you draw?" I asked, then immediately said, "Sorry. That was too personal."

We hadn't discussed keeping details to ourselves, but we had both been careful not to reveal anything of our lives beyond our fandom.

"Not as well as these people." It was a cop-out, but that was fair, since I shouldn't have asked.

The third floor contained smaller rooms, crafted to match various places from the books—Pietro's library, Ana's bedroom, Izak's workshop.

The attention to detail was amazing, down to old-fashioned tools and hairbrushes and leather-bound books.

The windows were covered so no one outside could see in and no light seeped out, but on the inside, each was painted with a view of what the characters would have seen from within a location in the books—the monastery courtyard, the tree along the Central Canal that Ana used to escape each night, the workers' sector of the main harbor.

Even here, the lights were low, like whoever had designed this place respected the guests' desire for anonymity.

Angelo lingered in the doorway of the library, where shelves of books lined three walls and a small wooden desk, complete with scrolls, sat under the window. He drew a book from the nearest shelf and opened it reverently.

"I always wanted to see this." He replaced the book, and we continued down the hall. "What about you? Is there anything you were hoping for but haven't found?"

"The elven realms," I said. "But I hardly expected them to turn a city building into . . ."

I trailed off as we entered the final room.

It was the Dreaming Forest. A silver pavilion, a gray wood table, the gentle green of what I assumed were fake plants given the lack of sunlight, pale yellow and blue twinkling lights. A small pool and fountain, complete with carved animals and floating pink flowers. Trees painted on the walls gave the illusion that the forest extended beyond the confines of the room.

I could have stayed here all night, drawing and absorbing the peaceful atmosphere, the otherworldly air.

It was entirely ridiculous, but my eyes burned with the threat of tears. This was all so amazing and real. The attention to detail, the artistry, and I was here, like I'd dreamed of for years. I could easily forget it was a club and believe I had been dropped inside the books.

I was happy but also relieved. I'd worried, after building this up in my head for so long, that it couldn't possibly live up to expectations, and it did. Exceeded them, even. It had everything I could have wished to see and more.

Angelo and I were silent, taking it in, the trickling water and the soft glow of fairy lights surrounding us.

I might be missing my dad, but I was glad not to be seeing this alone.

I intended to experience every single bit of this place. I would proudly let my nerd flag fly, because here, with my mask, among my people, I was safe.

We slowly made our way to the ground floor and the tavern.

A new round of Primo was starting, and we accepted spots at the table. The books contained no actual rules for the game, other than implying it was like poker, so someone had obviously made up how to play. Thankfully, they were using chips to bet, and it was free to enter. Like they wanted anyone to be able to join.

That bursting feeling swelled inside me again.

A man with an English accent explained the rules and dealt the cards. The people around the table had a variety of accents, which was so cool.

Once I got over the initial panic of being awful at the game, it was freeing not to have any idea what I was doing. No one knew me. It was okay to be bad at something, like Gabriel had said about playing the piano. I felt like I was proving something to him even though he'd never know it.

Angelo folded a great hand and immediately put his masked face in his hands, and we both laughed. What did his face look like when he did that? His smile, his eyes?

I briefly let myself imagine what it would be like to spend the day with him, with my real face. Would I have had the courage to say these things, do these things? Maybe it would depend on who Angelo was, whether he was someone from school I'd see every day, or from another school and it wouldn't affect the daily life I'd built.

No, the risk was too great, the past rejections and warnings too loud. It was safer to keep this here, no matter how much I liked him.

I lost another round. "This might be a good time to leave before I embarrass myself further," I said.

The dealer chuckled. "We're all terrible at first."

"Except this one." A woman jerked a thumb toward the guy on her right, who had the biggest stack of chips. "He made up the rules, but we suspect he changes them nightly to ensure he wins."

I laughed. I had so many questions. Did the guy live in Venice? Had he helped found the club? But I sensed I wasn't supposed to ask.

When I couldn't stop my head from drooping, Angelo touched my arm. I nodded, reluctantly. Magic was all around us, but I had to return to the ordinary world and leave it behind. For now. I would be back. I had six more nights to see everything.

I sighed. "I suppose we should go, shouldn't we?"

"Depends on how you feel about arriving at the hotel as they're setting up breakfast and the other guests are rising."

"Yeah. I'd rather not walk through the coffee line dressed like this."

I tried to take everything in as we located the other door. I bumped into Angelo, a table, the wall, since I wasn't watching where I was going, and he steadied me with a hand on my arm.

A guard stopped us at a set of large, ornate doors. The person in front of us left, and we waited. A couple of minutes later, the guard checked outside, I assumed to make sure the street was empty.

"Go in peace and beware the night," the man said as he opened the door.

We exited onto a quiet, unassuming street, and I turned around to look up at the palace. The stone facade and dark windows gave no indication of what hid inside.

Most days, I remembered my dad with more fondness than pain, the way time wears the edges off grief, leaving a rock behind but one that no longer constantly jabs you with sharp edges. But sadness struck at the thought that he would never know about this place, that we couldn't explore every inch of this new world together.

"Well," Angelo said.

"Well," I agreed, like the word held multitudes and both of us knew we didn't need to say anything more because the other already knew. It felt like the club might vanish if I spoke of it.

He used his phone to navigate to the hotel, which was good, since I had no idea where we were. Angelo stayed quiet, so I did too, letting images from the night play through my head.

His steps slowed as we neared our meeting spot. "Fantasma . . ."

"Yeah?"

"Do you—" He stopped himself.

"What is it?"

"Should we consider taking off the masks? Meeting for real?"

A flare gun went off in my brain, flashing at me to hide or run away or otherwise evade the impending danger. I'd been afraid he wouldn't want to stick together now that we knew where to go. Instead, he'd gone the opposite direction—the direction I had been trying to steer my thoughts away from because it led to a potentially massive cliff.

"Not if you don't want to, obviously," he added quickly. "But I think we've connected and maybe we owe it to ourselves to find out if we could be friends in real life, after this."

The panic shifted to a twisting sensation, like someone was wringing out my heart and lungs. After two nights, I was already getting used to having someone to talk to. I saw what I'd been missing by burying this part of me, and I didn't know if I wanted to return to my life of hiding and interacting solely online.

Maybe it would be worth the risk?

I'd been silent too long. "I have thought about it. . . ."

"Sounds like a *but* there."

"I don't know," I said. "I like what we have here. But I don't know."

He stood very still, head tilted down toward me, and I wished I could see his face. "You don't have to answer now," he said. "I just wanted to suggest the idea. Or . . ."

"Or?"

"What if we agreed to wait until our last night? Or, um, until Saturday night?"

Had he meant to imply that he assumed I was with his group and shared the same schedule?

Waiting sounded less scary. It gave me time to get used to the idea, and I could always change my mind before then. Unsure if I was excited or terrified, I bit my lip and tried to keep my voice from shaking. "Deal."

His head bobbed. "Same time tomorrow?"

"Same time tomorrow," I said, and my heart soared.

Chapter Ten

Why did mornings have to happen so early?

My head felt fuzzy, and there was no way I'd make it through the day without caffeine.

Natasha and I sat in a corner of the breakfast room, and she asked about the night before—not about the club, but if I'd spent the evening with Angelo. I had to force myself to concentrate.

"We shared our clues and found the place together. It was amazing."

"We could figure out who he is," she said. "Aren't you curious?"

I was. But I'd been the one to hesitate, and we'd agreed to wait, so investigating now felt like an invasion of privacy. On the other hand, if I had a hint of who he could be and it would prevent me from being totally surprised on our last night, I might be more likely to go through with the decision.

"We could narrow down the possibilities," I said. "Nothing more."

"Yes!" Her eyes brightened.

"Just basics," I said. "See how many candidates there are. Nothing too personal."

"I have so many ideas. Tell me everything you know about him." She whipped out her phone.

This was okay, right?

"He can't know," I said. "We can't do anything to tip him off."

"I am the master of stealth."

I scoffed. "You're as stealthy as Dai with an army of robotic pigeons."

"Okay, I will apply my talents to attempting to be stealthy. Start with what you know."

"He's staying at our hotel. I think he's part of our group, because the only other people I've seen are older and German."

"We can confirm that at the desk. He speaks English?"

"Yeah."

"Accent?"

"Nothing obvious."

"Height and build?" She was typing my answers.

"Um." I held a hand over my head, trying to remember. "About six feet. Not too big and not too skinny. Ugh. This feels like a police lineup."

"The height rules out several guys," she said, ignoring my worry. "The accent eliminates Sanjay. We'll have to check into the guys from the other schools. Hair color? Skin?"

"I can't see his skin. He wears gloves and a full mask. His hair is dark brown or black."

"Any chance he's wearing a wig?"

"I doubt it." Angelo didn't seem that paranoid.

"Hmm, okay, what else? Ooh, shoes."

"Shoes?"

"People pack light on vacation. He probably didn't bring many pairs of shoes, so maybe we can match them." She leaned sideways to scan the footwear present in the room.

"They were black, I think." I wasn't sure how valid that theory was, but it was something easy to check without revealing I was spying on him. I tried to recall other details. "His phone case was black too."

"Good. Was he wearing cologne?"

"It's not like I intentionally smelled him. No," I added when Natasha opened her mouth. "I'm not smelling him tonight."

"I'm just saying, that could be helpful."

"Then I'd have to go around smelling our classmates too, and that's weird."

"Okay, okay. Keep it in mind. Anything else he said that might give a clue?"

"We mostly talk about the Elven Realms. But I don't want to ask every guy here if he likes them. That would be way too obvious."

"We'll start by eliminating the easy ones. In our group, based on what you've said, Dai and Matthew are too short, Nathan is too tall, Sanjay has an accent, and unless your guy does have a wig, Scott is too ginger."

We looked at him, sitting by the window, light glinting off his very orange curls.

"From our school, that leaves Tristan and Bryce," I said.

"And Gabriel," Natasha added.

I laughed.

"It seems unlikely, but we can't eliminate anyone yet." She made another note in her phone. "What about the others?"

We scanned the students who had arrived early for breakfast. Based on who was here, there were already four or five possibilities among the guys we didn't know.

"We'll have to talk to them," Natasha said.

"That will be hard since we're supposed to spend the day with our partners."

"I can see if they have accents." She rose and I grasped for her arm, but she was too fast.

She strolled to the food line and started chatting, confirming my fears about her extreme lack of stealth.

When she returned, she let out a *hmph*. "No good. We can't eliminate them yet. That's okay. I have other ideas. I could stake out the halls tonight and see what floor he comes from."

"No stakeouts. If he sees you, he might figure out you're my roommate. I mean, the roommate of the girl he's hanging out with."

"I'm insulted that you think I'd get caught."

"You'd totally get caught."

"Morning," Dai said as he took a seat at our table. "What are you thinking?"

"ROUS-es," I said at the same time Natasha said, "Infrared binoculars," and I groaned.

"Ooh, ROUS-es would complement my pigeon army."

"Hey, was Bryce in the room all night?" Natasha asked Dai.

"I don't know, I guess so? I was sleeping. Why?"

"No reason."

I rolled my eyes. Not smooth at all.

When Bryce came down, I watched as he filled his plate with eggs, chatted with other people in line, and filled the room with his loud laugh.

I had trouble seeing him as a possibility for Angelo. I'd known him since the first day of freshman English. We'd served on committees together; I'd helped him through sophomore-year geometry. I thought we were close enough that I'd know if he liked fantasy books and dressed up in costumes, and if I'd been talking to him all night. He wasn't shallow, but going deep with him was rare, and Angelo and I had talked about a lot of topics from the beginning.

Then again, I was different in the mask and the darkness, so I couldn't rule Bryce out. With his conspiracy theories, he was quirky enough that he might have secret hobbies.

Gabriel was the last to arrive, entering right before Mr. Owens. Natasha had listed him as a candidate, but that was even harder to imagine than Bryce.

Mr. Owens stopped him. "Mr. Martinez. I didn't see you last night after dinner. I hope you didn't wander off alone."

It took me a second to recall that part of last evening, the shopping and the lack of my partner's presence, before the club adventure.

The expression on Gabriel's face revealed that *wandering off alone* was a rather accurate description of his evening. And that he intended to say something sarcastic or straight-up admit his wrongdoing, and then I might get in trouble too.

I darted to my feet and joined them. "He was there. He was excited to buy one of those sailor hats that say Venezia."

Gabriel's blank expression shifted to me.

Mr. Owens's face relaxed.

"It was one step toward fulfilling his lifelong dream to be a sea captain," I added.

"I do love the sea," Gabriel said.

Mr. Owens's brow wrinkled. "Right. Good. Thanks for looking after your partner, Evie."

I smiled, and Mr. Owens moved on.

"Why'd you do that?" Gabriel asked, a faint wrinkle on his forehead.

I gave him a solemn stare. "Because I sensed your inner sailor the moment we met."

He waited, eyebrows expectant.

I shrugged. "Like he said. Partners. Where were you last night, anyway? Never mind. But I'm not making a habit of covering for you."

Gabriel was here. It was project time. I needed to focus on that, not on finding my mystery guy or understanding Gabriel's tendency to escape.

I waved at Natasha, refilled my coffee, and sat with Gabriel. He looked at me, blinked, and started eating. I pulled out my phone to search for places we could write about today.

"Are you sick?" Gabriel asked a few minutes later.

"No, why?"

"You haven't asked me a personal question, and it's been half an hour."

"Aw, did you miss my questions? I have lots more. Should I break out the list?"

"There's a list?"

"Technically it's in my head." I tapped my temple. "Mental notes."

His mouth twitched the slightest amount. "I'm just glad I don't have to find you a hospital. That sounds like too much work."

"Not to mention explaining why you brought me there. 'Yes, doctor, my friend took a break from digging into my personal life, and I'm worried she's dying.'"

"I like how you believe I would call you a friend." He was smirking.

"Give it one more day, and I have no doubt you will."

Will I, though? asked his raised eyebrows.

As he continued to eat, I tried to access that mental list of questions, to annoy him, but my brain wasn't working. I was tired, and half my thoughts remained in the club, recalling every nook and corner. And my best friend was playing PI, chatting up two more guys who had arrived, and I was trying not to watch the impending disaster. I should have been helping, not only to find Angelo but also to ensure she was more discreet.

Instead, I held up my phone. "I found some places for us to see. If you want to let me know what you think."

Gabriel nodded once. "I wrote up notes on what we saw yesterday. Not a full report, but details so we don't forget."

"Cool. Thanks."

He looked at me steadily, his eyes clear brown in the light. I'd learned that him holding eye contact without his frown getting worse basically equaled him smiling and nodding, so I took the expression to mean *you're welcome*.

I'd been staring at him too long. I cleared my throat and held up my phone again. "Since we saw churches yesterday, today we should focus on a different type of building. I found a famous opera house that you can tour without having to see a whole opera."

"Maybe I love opera," he said. "Maybe that's the one thing I wanted to do in Venice."

"Do you? You never answered my question about whether you liked music."

"I guess we'll never know since you're not taking me to a show."

Our eyes met again, and my neck warmed.

Was he being nicer since I had covered for him with Mr. Owens? Like by being dishonest, I'd proved I was semi-trustworthy, in some weird, twisted Gabriel Martinez logic?

I forced my gaze away when Sanjay approached and said he'd heard I had allergy meds.

After I handed some over, Gabriel was watching with one of his unreadable expressions.

"Ready?" he asked.

I fought the urge to ask what he was thinking. "Yeah."

Leaving the hotel with him was strange as Natasha, Bryce, and Dai headed the opposite direction. Feeling like a gondola set loose from the bank without anyone to steer it, I waved at them and set my chin. I would have a good day with Gabriel, no matter what.

Gabriel took over navigating the emptier morning streets, where a chill emanated from the stone buildings and crowds didn't yet fill the walkways. Depending on whether they were in sunlight or shade, the canals we crossed were pale aqua or dark green. People ate pastries and sipped coffee under café umbrellas.

We found a decent-sized plaza with an unassuming white stone building with columns on its porch.

"Neoclassical," Gabriel said, then as we approached the building, added, "Check out the bird."

A golden carving that said GRAN TEATRO LA FENICE guarded the entrance.

"Phoenix," he said.

"How do you know?"

"The name."

Apparently *Fenice* wasn't an alternate spelling of *Venice*. I really needed to stop underestimating him.

Inside, the opera house's plain exterior gave way to a foyer of gleaming marble. Dusty pink carpets stretched up broad staircases, and fancy sconces glowed against pale peach walls. Twinkling light from a chandelier reflected on every surface.

We joined a family on an English-speaking tour, learning about the building's history, famous shows and performers I'd

never heard of, the fires that had destroyed the theater and re-
sulted in its being rebuilt multiple times, leading to the name.

Gabriel didn't even gloat at having been right.

The private boxes were overwhelming, with candelabras
and gold embellishments that reflected off shiny mirrors.
Below were the stage, orchestra pit, and rows of upholstered
guest seats, and the curving walls held other boxes, evenly
spaced and glowing with rosy light.

I made notes on the art while Gabriel pointed out details of
the wallpaper and floor and murmured, "Baroque," before the
tour guide said the word.

I wanted to know what Gabriel was thinking, but he didn't
seem inclined to share. He hadn't made a snarky comment in
ages, and I considered asking if he was sick, as he had me,
except I knew he would answer sarcastically and break his
streak.

An upstairs room held a smaller stage, and before the guide
could stop her, a small girl from our group in a sparkly purple
tutu scrambled onto it and darted to the center.

She immediately started belting out an opera.

Kind of. It didn't sound like actual words. More like howl-
ing meant to imitate an opera singer, in no language I'd ever
heard.

"Excuse me," the guide called. "You can't be up there."

"Apparently she heard opera house and thought karaoke
bar," Gabriel said, a strange, gentle light in his eyes.

"Easy mistake to make," I replied.

"I myself have mixed them up several times."

"Oh, me too. My rendition of 'Phantom of the Opera' was a huge hit at the last student council party."

"That," he said, "is almost enough to make me join student council."

"But not quite," I guessed.

"But not quite."

"Miss, you have to get down," the guide said, which made the girl sing even louder. "We have a tour to finish."

The girl's mom held a phone and had begun to film.

Gabriel sighed loudly enough for me to hear. That unfamiliar expression still softened his features. Before I could ask what was up, he neared the stage.

As soon as the girl paused for breath, he clapped. "That was excellent. You should take a bow."

The girl went into a series of exaggerated bows, so I clapped as well. Soon, her family joined in.

The girl beamed, and Gabriel lifted her to the floor and gave her a high five, his face the softest I'd ever seen it. *Stop staring, Evie.*

The guide concluded his talk and dismissed us, glaring at the girl as she waved at Gabriel and skipped away.

As we exited the building into the small plaza, I was at a complete loss for words.

I knew Gabriel well enough by now to know that asking how he'd become so good with kids would shut him down, so instead I chose, "Where do you want to go next? I have another theater, a palace with a museum inside, and a museum of musical instruments."

"The opportunities are truly endless," he said. "Like this morning." But his lips were almost smiling, and his eyes glinted.

"I know you enjoyed the opera, don't deny it."

"You said we weren't getting a show."

I laughed. "I thought you liked it when people put themselves out there. Yesterday was okay because the cellist was good, but today wasn't because that girl was clearly confusing opera with yodeling?"

"Nice try," he said. "You're hoping I'll say that people shouldn't do things they're bad at, the way your mom does. But if that girl wants to create a new musical genre, good for her."

"I sense there was an insult to my family hidden in there."

"Oh, was it hidden? Should I have been more obvious?"

I shot him a look, and he raised an eyebrow. Then I imagined my mom's reaction if she'd been on the tour, if that singing girl had been Maddie or me, and I couldn't help but laugh. Loud and uncontained.

Gabriel appraised me.

"What?"

"Why'd you do it?" he asked. "For real?"

"Do what?"

"Lie to Mr. Owens this morning."

My laughter faded, and I looked at the buildings around us rather than at him. "I'd rather you not phrase it like that."

"Like the truth?"

"I don't like lying to teachers."

He studied me. "But you did it anyway."

I fought the urge to squirm under his inspection. "I didn't

want either of us to get in trouble. I was protecting my partner. My friend," I added, the word a challenge.

"You use that word liberally."

I started walking, slowly, and he fell into step. He meant it in a negative way, but I gave him a serious answer. "My definition might be different from yours, but that doesn't mean it's not genuine. I like to believe almost everyone has the potential to be a friend. Maybe not a best friend, but if we hang out, we talk, we generally like each other, what else would you call someone?"

"I prefer not to call people. Phone calls are evil."

I rolled my eyes. "What qualifies as a friend to you?"

"I'm surprised you believe that I have any."

"Who knows, you might be very popular outside of school. I don't appreciate you making assumptions about what I do or do not think."

He held my gaze. "A friend is someone you can rely on. Someone trustworthy and loyal. Someone you can be yourself with and who's honest with you. They make you better but don't try to change you. In my experience, those people are hard to find."

"Maybe you don't know where to look."

"So that describes your friends?"

"Of course."

Mostly, anyway. Other than the fact that I wasn't being honest with them, and that implied I didn't trust them. They didn't try to change me. I might've changed myself, though. . . .

Gabriel must have read something in my face or voice that revealed my doubt, because his eyebrows lifted in question.

"I love my friends," I said. "We have fun together, we help each other. And I trust them."

He nodded and left it at that, unaware of the tempest inside me.

But now I knew what it took to be Gabriel's friend. I'd prove myself trustworthy, like when I'd covered for him this morning. I'd be myself. And I would show him . . . something. I just wish I knew what.

Chapter Eleven

Apparently, the tiny opera singer hadn't scared us away from music altogether, because we ended up visiting the museum of instruments. It was housed in an old church and contained everything from three-hundred-year-old clarinets to decorated guitars, to a giant harp and cellos, to violins and old music books. Everything was situated throughout the church, with instruments under statues of Mary and paintings of biblical scenes and giant metal organ pipes.

"I'm not sure if this counts as an art form for our report," I said.

"Music is art."

"Yeah, but it's, like, separate. From art class. We were going to focus on the interplay of art and architecture."

"We can talk about the contrast of the church as a setting for instruments."

"Yeah, but what will Mr. Owens think?"

Gabriel started to say something, then seemed to switch gears. "He's an art teacher. He'll appreciate the creativity."

"I guess so. . . ."

"Blame me. Say I made you put it in."

I narrowed my eyes playfully. "Haven't you learned by now that I don't let friends get in trouble?"

He rolled his eyes. "Plus, the craftsmanship counts as art."

Many instruments had pearl inlays or intricate sculpting or decorations or were made of multiple types of wood. There were also hand-drawn music sheets, not to mention the classical religious art on the walls. I supposed he had a point.

In one display, a cherub statue reclined next to old clarinets on a swath of red velvet. I didn't try to stop my laugh from erupting.

One of Gabriel's eyebrows quirked.

"Your name," I said. "It just occurred to me. I wonder if that's the angel Gabriel. Clearly your parents didn't know what they were getting when they picked the name."

"Wishful thinking," he said, and I snorted. "Plus, Gabriel the angel is bigger and grander than that guy."

I studied the cherub. "Nope. I'm now imagining that's exactly what you looked like as a baby."

"If you think you're seeing my baby picture to confirm or deny, you're out of luck, Whitmore."

"Don't need one. That's you. I see it in the eyebrows."

I was possibly acting goofier than usual. Gabriel responded better, talked more, when I let that side of me out. He was showing more interest, discussing the museum's contents. We pointed out instruments with odd shapes, and tiny mandolins that could have been played by a bard in a tavern. Then we came to an old piano.

"You should play it," Gabriel said.

"I'm pretty sure you're not supposed to touch the valuable historical items."

"I'm pretty sure you aren't supposed to go onstage at the opera house either," he said dryly. "Rules are boring."

"Rules keep you from getting in trouble. Breaking them makes people mad."

"Interesting." He drew the word out in a way that implied he wanted me to ask what he found interesting.

We moved on to a display on the history of violin making, which, okay, that was art.

I would resist. I would.

Oh fine, I would not.

"What's interesting?" I asked.

He smirked as if he'd heard me lose my mental debate. "That you didn't say you dislike breaking rules because it's wrong."

"Of course it's wrong." My recent nighttime activities gnawed on my stomach.

Gabriel angled his head. "But that's not what you said. You focused on how others react."

"I don't like getting in trouble. Are you psychoanalyzing me, Martinez?"

"I wouldn't dare, Whitmore." His eyes glinted.

A not-unpleasant shiver went through me, and I held his gaze before looking away.

This new, nicer side of him was dangerous. Friends was one thing, but the way my heart thumped extra hard when he looked at me meant trouble.

I should have been thinking about finding Angelo, who had seen the real me, who was easy to talk to and asked me questions. The opposite of Gabriel.

I didn't know why I cared so much about Gabriel's friendship. Like I'd told him, I had lots of friends and lots of people I was friendly with. But it would mean more coming from him, like I had to earn it, therefore making it more valuable.

We stopped for a late lunch, and sitting across from Gabriel was weird. Normally I was comfortable eating with anyone and could make conversation, but he defied the usual rules since he didn't like personal questions. And personal questions were the kind I most wanted to ask.

The menu offered standard Italian fare and was written in multiple languages. White tablecloths covered the tables, and Frank Sinatra crooned in the background.

It felt like a date.

After I poured us both water from the bottle the waiter brought, my phone buzzed, revealing a text from my mom. One of her clients wanted social media ads. I helped with graphics, and this was a company I'd worked with before. What time was it at home? The middle of the night? I turned my phone over. It wouldn't take long. I'd do it later.

"So what did you think about what we saw?" I asked.

He groaned. "Enjoy the moment, Whitmore."

"What do you mean?"

"We don't have to discuss the project every second."

"What else can we discuss? You want to tell me your hobbies or your favorite childhood memories? No? Didn't think so. Besides, you seemed to like the museum—don't worry, I won't tell anyone—so I thought it was a good topic."

"It's not."

The food arrived, and he began eating in his slow, deliberate way.

I sighed and dug into my lasagna.

"Do you always eat so fast?" he asked, setting his fork down. "Can you even taste the food?"

"I can taste it. Why?" I clutched my fork.

"You're in Italy. You should savor your meals. Not devour the food like you haven't eaten in weeks."

"Are you saying I'm unladylike?"

"I don't care if you're ladylike, whatever that means. I'm talking about not rushing through something that's meant to be enjoyed."

"So you enjoy the meal? Have I found one thing in the world that you like?"

"Yes, you caught me," he drawled. "I like Italian food. Happy?"

I beamed. "This definitely means we're friends now. I told you it would happen today, and it only took until lunchtime."

He reached across the table. "If we're friends, I'm helping you." He plucked my fork from my hand and set it down. "A ten-second pause is now mandatory between every bite. And the count starts after you swallow, not when the food enters your mouth."

"That's so not a thing."

"Be grateful I didn't make it thirty."

"But the project."

"Will be there waiting if lunch takes an extra twenty minutes. Why are you in such a rush?"

"I'm not."

I forced myself to slowly take one bite and set the fork down again. Huh. More flavors exploded on my tongue. Garlic and rich cheese and fresh tomato. The pasta was thin and soft and infinitely better than the store-bought lasagnas I was used to.

Gabriel's mouth twitched as if he could read my thoughts.

Before picking up the utensil again, I spun my glass. Whether he cared or not, I wanted him to understand.

"My family is big on meals together, but more as . . . business meetings, I guess. My mom believes it's important that we take time to sit together, but everyone's so busy that we don't have long. I guess we do eat fast since we're always on the way to somewhere else. We eat at different times every day, depending on our schedules, and we give updates."

He gazed at me. "On your day?"

"More like status reports. The progress we're making on projects, events we have coming up, grades we got on tests. My sister, she's fifteen, she'll talk about her latest business endeavors, and I'll discuss student council events and whether I've heard from the colleges I applied to, update the college chart."

My brother, before he left home, had avoided these meals at all costs, and when he'd been forced to sit, had given updates on how many clean socks he had (usually none), what his video game stats were, and how many homework assignments he'd skipped, until our mom stopped asking. The meals offered a sharp contrast to before our dad died, when we'd talked about art and books and movies and dreams instead of numbers, goals, and achievements.

"The college chart?" Gabriel asked.

A pit formed in my stomach. "Big colorful thing on the wall that my mom updates when acceptances arrive."

Because that didn't add to the pressure of not having a plan for my life.

Gabriel didn't say anything, but his brow was doing its furrowed thing. His eyebrows did more talking than his mouth.

"Does your family enjoy long meals?" I asked before he could offer commentary on my home life. Before I could agree with his eyebrows that it sounded tiring and rather dreadful and not much like a real family meal.

"If we're home at the same time," he said. "Which rarely happens. They're generally very loud."

"You said you have three siblings. If we're friends, can you tell me how old they are?"

His eyes said he was humoring me. "My older sister is twenty-four, my brother is twenty-one, and my younger sister is sixteen."

Nothing in his expression or voice revealed whether he loved them dearly or loathed being related to them. Would it kill a guy to share anything?

Ohhh. Younger sister. His adorable ease with the opera girl suddenly made sense.

"My brother's also twenty-one, but he moved out three years ago. Your younger sister isn't at our school?" If she was, I hadn't been asked to give her a tour.

"No."

I barely stopped myself from asking why not, since he obviously would have elaborated if he wanted me to know. But he was driving me crazy.

I continued the slow eating, timing my bites to Gabriel's.

A man bumped our table as he passed. "Scusi."

Gabriel replied in what was not English.

This time I put my fork down willingly.

Gabriel blinked. "Why are you looking at me like that?"

"You speak Italian?"

"A little."

"You're not Italian, though, are you?"

His mouth did the slight dimple smirk. "Only Italian people are allowed to speak the language?"

"No, that's not what I meant, just . . ."

"You didn't expect someone like me to know it."

"Not like that. Just, in general. If by *someone like you*, you mean a high school student at a school that doesn't offer Italian classes. Oh, I guess your last one might have. Sorry."

He was fully smirking now, but then it faded, and his expression turned contemplative. He held my gaze, and I didn't breathe, like I was preparing for something but I didn't know what.

"I learned at a library," he said. "A public one. Conversation classes. I went to Japanese and French also."

He'd offered the information willingly. I was making progress. Something fizzed inside me, like I'd opened a can of shaken soda and bubbles were escaping.

"Wow. That's cool."

He waited like he was bracing for more, and when it didn't come, he asked, "Are you done? Didn't it taste better my way?"

"Maybe . . ."

"You're welcome."

Our lunch had left me with a desire to know more about him, different from my usual curiosity. His reluctance to talk about himself, which most people loved to do, made the small facts mean more. How many hidden depths did he have that no one suspected? I was hoarding clues to the real Gabriel, storing them up, guarding them like treasure, and what I had wasn't enough.

As we left the restaurant, I glanced at him and stumbled. Where had that uneven rock come from?

His hand grasped my elbow, but he quickly let go. "Ready to get back to that project you were so eager to work on?"

I groaned. "I'm ready for a nap after that meal." And only three hours of sleep.

"Why don't we?" he said.

"What?"

"Take naps."

"But the project. We just ate a leisurely meal."

"No, we ate a normal meal. A break will be fine. We have all week. And we're not far from the hotel."

It felt as much like sneaking as going out at night.

"We'll say we're taking time to write up what we've seen." Gabriel said it like a concession, like he couldn't care less if Mr. Owens caught us napping and he would sleep on an outdoor couch in plain sight, but he knew I needed the excuse.

"Are you going to write while I sleep?" I asked. "You don't have to do it all. I was joking."

"I don't plan to do it all."

We walked in silence, and I focused on not tripping. A nap was smart so I didn't stumble over a cobblestone, hit my head on a gondola, and plunge to my watery death in a canal. Natasha would have made me push on. She also would have completed the meal in half the time. The food really had tasted better eating more slowly.

When we entered the hotel lobby, Mr. Owens was there, talking to Valentina.

I was preparing to blurt out a lie, but Gabriel nodded and kept walking, tugging me after him up the stairs.

"What are you doing?" I asked, and he immediately released my arm.

"He wasn't suspicious, and you were about to invent a story about how we're here to write a research paper. Saying nothing is easier, especially if no one asks you a question."

"But—"

"Take a nap, Whitmore. I'll meet you in a couple of hours."

He left me in the hall, blinking after him as he climbed the stairs. I stumbled to my room and collapsed.

Chapter Twelve

When my alarm woke me, I had a problem—I felt loads better. Which meant I was going to have to admit to Gabriel that he had been right. Again.

I sensed his ego didn't need the boost.

I freshened up and joined him in the lobby.

"Feeling better?" he asked.

"Aw, were you worried?"

"Wondering if I should prepare myself for more questions."

"I do feel better," I said.

"Great, so more questions." His eyes glinted in the light, and it sent a flutter through my chest.

I never would have let myself rest without his encouragement. "Thank you."

He gazed at me. Nodded. Didn't tease me about the forced rest. He sat at the end of the sofa I'd nearly demolished with my face the first night, and I took the wingback chair next to it. He handed me his laptop so I could read what he'd written the day before.

"You didn't write today?" I asked.

"I told you I'm not doing all the work. I wanted a nap too."

I laughed. "Fair enough."

I typed up thoughts from the opera house and museum, including the things he'd said earlier about instruments as art, and handed the laptop back.

He leaned to take it, causing his calf to bump mine. He didn't move it and studied me, and it required effort to keep my focus on his eyes when every nerve in my body was screaming about our legs.

"You keep looking at me like I'm an alien." I smoothed my hair. I'd touched up my makeup before coming downstairs. Had I missed pillow wrinkles on my face?

"Your hair's fine, Whitmore." He nodded at the computer. "This is good."

"Oh. Thanks. Wait, is that your surprised face? You didn't think it would be good?"

"Can I add something about music, not just the artistry of the instruments?" he asked.

"Yeah, of course. Partners, remember? And you didn't answer my question."

"No, I didn't." He smirked and typed some more.

"No, you didn't answer, or no, you didn't think it would be good?"

He kept typing, lips pressed into an almost smile.

I shook my head, fighting my own smile.

And fighting the bubbly sensation that had resumed in my chest.

This was easier than it would have been with Natasha, who would have rewritten everything. When Gabriel handed me the laptop again, I found a surprisingly poetic paragraph describing the art found in music. My attention jumped to his face, but he was staring out the window, not at me.

It sure sounded like he liked music or had some personal connection with it.

I returned the laptop. While he typed, I took out my phone and did the graphic for my mom. The work was easy; it just took time. My mom and I hadn't actively discussed me not helping for a week, but I had sort of assumed she wouldn't ask while I was in Europe. I saw now that had been shortsighted of me.

"You look focused," Gabriel said.

"Yeah, sorry, side project for my mom. I help with graphics for some of her clients. Logos, branding, ads. There are lots of free apps you can use, but they pay her for it."

"And your mom pays you." It wasn't a question, but the words somehow conveyed that he wouldn't be surprised if I said no.

"A flat rate each month." Which my sister had negotiated for me in exchange for my doing her laundry for two weeks— including every hand-wash-only piece she owned.

"You should be getting overtime for working while you're out of the country," he said. "Actually, you should have gotten the week off. They honestly can't wait one week for a logo?"

"This one is social media graphics for a sale the client's having next week."

"Someone else's emergency doesn't have to be one for you."

My stomach wriggled. "It's not that hard. I'm almost done. I'll work on our project now."

His hum said the project wasn't what he'd been thinking about, but I didn't want to dwell on his opinions about how my mom took advantage of—no. She didn't take advantage. She paid me. It was a job.

I swapped the phone for my sketchbook and focused on using photos I'd taken to draw the places we'd seen, details I'd liked of the chandelier in the opera house, a fancy violin, sculptures in the church.

Peace enveloped me, warm and relaxed and nice. Both of us were engrossed in work—and it was work I enjoyed. I was with someone, but there were no expectations. Gabriel didn't want anything from me. I didn't have to be alert for ways to help him or figure out how to act. We could just *be*.

Some of our classmates trickled in, and I greeted them. Gabriel, of course, didn't acknowledge their existence.

We received weird looks, but I just smiled.

Lina stopped next to me. "Hey, Evie. Sanjay said your allergy meds saved him. Any chance you have aspirin?"

"Sure." I fished some out of my bag and gave her a small pack.

"You're a lifesaver."

She trudged off, and once again, Gabriel watched. His expressions had become slightly more readable, but I couldn't nail this one down. He was confused, or analyzing me, or possibly in need of aspirin himself but refusing to ask.

Natasha texted to ask if I'd confirmed the latest round of job fair RSVPs. I set down the sketchbook and dashed off several emails. Then saw that my mom had responded to my graphic and asked for one more, so I finished that, ignoring Gabriel's gaze and the foreign desire to tell her no. I didn't tell people no. I couldn't. She and her client were counting on me.

A while later, Bryce and Dai came in and paused by us.

"Hey, guys, how was your day?" I asked.

Dai told me where they'd been, and as soon as he finished, hoping to catch him off guard, I asked, "Great, so what are you thinking about?"

"The Easter Island statues coming to life," he said.

Bryce fist-bumped him. "Those were definitely made by aliens."

I laughed at their impressive subject change.

"Hey, did you ask your mom about that rec letter?" Dai asked.

"Oh, right. I'll do that now." I dashed off one more text, then asked, "Where's Natasha?"

"On the patio, working."

"You're not helping?"

"She wouldn't let us. Can you get her when it's time for dinner?"

"Yeah, I'll go when we're done here."

"Later."

When they left, it was quiet again.

Gabriel finally looked up. "Is the word *no* in your vocabulary?"

"No," I said.

He snorted, and I grinned.

Then my smile faded. "What do you mean?" I knew what he meant. But for some reason, I wanted his thoughts.

His eyes were dark. "Everyone relies on you for everything. You don't have to do it all. Especially while you're in Venice. Can't this wait until you're home?"

"Natasha is here and still working on the job fair. I promised I would help. And Dai needs that letter. I meant to ask my mom already, but I was worried about the time difference."

"When does Tanaka need it?"

"This week."

"When did he ask?"

"On the airplane."

Gabriel scoffed.

What was he thinking?

But he didn't say anything else, just went back to work, leaving me unsettled, like he was seeing too much.

My eyes felt like they were full of dirt, and a dull ache had taken up residence behind my temples. The nap was wearing off. But tonight I'd have hours to explore the club, so I would ignore the tiredness and press on. After dinner, I put on my costume from the first night.

Natasha sat on the bed. "How's your project going?"

"Okay."

The project had honestly fallen way down my list of issues of importance. The food, the city, the art, the club, Angelo . . . Gabriel. Those held so much more appeal.

"What about you?" I asked.

"We saw lots more places." She held up her wrist, wrapped in a black watch. "I got fifteen thousand steps today."

As I got ready, she described their report and complained about the crowds and the scent of cigarette smoke in the public places. Our opinions about this city were very different.

When she finished, she said, "Remember, you need to check his shoes and cologne. Oh, and see if he's right- or left-handed."

Right. Finding Angelo. How had I let Gabriel distract me from that goal today? "Okay."

"I met two candidates from Westview," she said. "One is a horrible person, but sadly we can't rule him out yet."

"Why is he horrible?" I frowned as I secured my belt. "The guy I met is nice."

"He's captain of their Model UN team."

Pieces clicked. Our rival school. The team Natasha led. The competition she had lost last year. Before I could ask if *beating her* was the full extent of his horribleness, she said, "Jewelry."

"Jewelry?"

"Check for earrings. The other guy from Westview wears two small gold hoops. Anything else would be good too."

"I don't know if I'll be able to see anything. He wears gloves and a collared shirt. Plus the mask. But I'll try." Only if there was a good opportunity. I didn't want Angelo to suspect I was snooping.

"Sure you don't want me to stake out the hall? I studied the staircase earlier. If I stand at the top, I can see three floors, and we can learn which one he's staying on."

"What if he's on the top floor and sees you watching when he leaves? No stakeouts."

Now that I knew the club—and Angelo—was worth it, I had an easier time shoving aside my nerves. Rather than waiting for any distractions, I strode quickly to the breakfast room. No acting required, no suspicious cats.

I was breathing hard anyway. Breaking rules would never come naturally. Sneaking out shouldn't have been so simple. I wasn't doing anything particularly bad, but who knew what else people might get up to late at night. If crime was too easy, anyone might do it.

Lax security was good for me, though, so I slipped out into the night.

Angelo was a few minutes behind me.

"What do you want to do first?" I asked as we moved through the empty streets. "Not that we have to do it together. Just, what are you most excited about?"

"I wouldn't mind studying the palace itself. See what's original and how they restored it before integrating the Elven Realms elements."

"Really?"

"It sounds nerdy when I say it that way."

I laughed. "No, not at all. I mean, it does. But I'm curious too. Besides, isn't everyone at the club nerdy? You're in good company."

"By land or by boat tonight?"

"Boat was fun. I wonder if it's the same guy every night?"

"I guess we'll find out."

We walked at a leisurely pace, perfect for enjoying the evening.

Halfway there, I remembered to check his shoes. They were black low boots with laces, not particularly memorable. No jewelry was visible, but I didn't want to stare. I didn't smell anything except the city's sea scent, and I had no intention of leaning closer to sniff him.

My detective skills were pathetic. Although, if I figured out who he was, then I had to decide what to do about it. One reason I wanted to keep the search simple was, if I learned his identity before our official reveal, I would have to tell him. I couldn't pretend not to know.

We chatted easily about our favorite books other than Elven Realms. The conversation was so different from the ones I'd had with Gabriel. Angelo opened up more readily, asked as many questions as I did.

"What are your favorite book tropes?" he asked.

"Found family," I said immediately. "People you love and trust despite different backgrounds."

"That's a good one, especially in Mask of Souls."

"It gets me every time, people who don't have to love you but who choose you." I sighed. "Now I'm wishing I had that."

He huffed softly.

"What? Do you have that? Sorry, never mind, that was too personal."

"No, it's okay." He was silent, but like he was thinking. "I don't have it. If you'd asked me a week ago if I wanted it, I would have laughed."

"And now?"

"Now I'm reevaluating."

My chest tightened at the admission, the wistfulness that echoed my own. He couldn't possibly mean he saw Fantasma as family after two nights, but I'd had the thought after discovering the club, so maybe that's what had made him reconsider. He sounded like a loner, which fit with Gabriel's vibe. But then, I'd been contemplating recently how I wasn't as close to my real-life friends as I'd thought. Could Bryce be having the same doubts?

Or was Angelo someone else altogether?

"I don't know if this is a trope," he said, "but I like it when people who are underestimated or overlooked end up being the heroes. The underdogs, I guess? The world sees them one way, but that's not who they are. It's especially satisfying when they beat the bad guys and bring justice to those who deserve it."

"That's all the Mask of Souls characters, isn't it? The appearance versus the reality of a person. And found family are the ones who see the truth." I bit my lip. "I've been thinking a lot about masks this week. The ones we all wear."

I stopped there, too close to revealing my true self, and he didn't press me.

In a way, we had revealed ourselves. As we'd discussed, the outer face didn't always provide a true picture of a person, and Angelo and I had talked about real stuff despite hiding our faces. The thoughts I shared with him were more personal than facts about my family or school would have been, especially because they were things I hadn't shared with anyone else.

The more time I spent with him, the more tempted I was to follow through and meet for real, regardless of the results of Natasha's and my investigation. Surely finding someone you could talk to this freely was rare and special.

Tonight's gondolier was a different man, shorter, with less of an accent when he greeted us. Same boat and similar costume, though.

We took the short ride in silence, and the person waiting inside to greet us was the same.

He must have recognized our masks, because he said, "Welcome back."

"No trivia questions tonight?" I asked.

"You're in now. Enjoy the evening."

I was in. A secret club. A thrill shot through me.

We made a slower circle tonight, inspecting the details of the tavern. I stopped to admire costumes and let other people admire mine, showing off the belt and letting them inspect my mask. No one questioned my commitment or my right to be here. Energy was zinging around inside me. This was too amazing.

When we headed upstairs, we heard voices coming from the weapons room. A woman at the door in an elven scout costume and an impressive metallic half-mask waved at us.

"Would you like to join?"

"Join what?" I asked.

"Sword lessons. And a mock fight."

"Ooh, yes." I turned to Angelo.

"I'm in."

Chapter Thirteen

We joined a dozen others in front of the wall of weapons. The swords matched ones described in the books—solid, plain blades that the city guards like Luca used, ornate ones like the nobility carried, and beautifully crafted, elegant blades with elven runes decorating the metal.

I ran my hand over a leather-bound hilt. "Who made these?"

"A few craftsmen," the woman answered. "The ones up high are the quality ones. The lower ones aren't sharp, and they're lighter. We use those for lessons and mock fights."

Sure, made sense, so no one ended up getting stabbed. Keeping this place a secret would be challenging if they had to call an ambulance. Wait. Venice had no cars. Did they have ambulance boats? I'd better be careful. Riding in a boat to a hospital sounded dreadful.

I wanted to sketch the weapons. I'd researched swords before drawing any, to capture the overall shape, but I could learn more to make my sketches more detailed. Ideas formed

in my mind, from Luca wielding his blade against a dark elven
3creature to the elven armies lined up for battle.

"Everyone, select a weapon."

Angelo opted for a guard's solid blade, while I chose a narrow elven sword that reminded me of one Ana had stolen during her escape from the elven prison.

Yet again I was hit with longing for my dad's presence. The role-playing games and reenactments transported me to childhood. He would have thrown himself into this. Missing him created an odd pressure, a burden to ensure I made the most of this whole experience not only for me but for my father too.

The woman in charge had us watch while she and a man engaged in a mock battle. They were fast, blades whirring, feet dancing across the floor. It looked like a movie scene.

When they finished, we applauded, and they switched to demonstrating the basics: how to position our feet, what angle to hold the blade, how to step forward and thrust or swing. Then we paired off to practice.

Angelo faced me with his sword in his right hand. Natasha would be disappointed he wasn't a lefty because that would have narrowed our pool of candidates.

The lights in here, like everywhere else in the club, were bright enough to see but not too bright. So as I faced my mystery friend, I was no closer to seeing details about him. His eyes looked dark, but that could have been from the shadow of his mask.

We moved closer as we swung our weapons, which collided

with a *thwack* that reverberated up my arm. We went back and forth until the instructor told us how to move forward and backward while we swung.

Angelo lunged and I blocked, then stepped forward. He didn't move, and we ended up close, our blades crossed between us forming a barrier, his eyes right above mine. I thought they were brown.

My heart skipped before I laughed. "You're supposed to move."

"Maybe you weren't supposed to move." Humor laced his voice.

We lingered, bodies inches apart, and my pulse tripped before I made myself back away so we could start again.

"I can't believe I'm here, doing this," I said.

"Attacking a stranger?"

"With a fake sword. *Are* you a stranger?"

"I guess that depends on your definition."

His words reminded me of Gabriel talking about what defined a friend.

"Comrades in arms?" I suggested.

"I can live with that."

Our weapons clacked. If anyone from school saw me now . . . If my *mom* saw me now, what would she think? Probably that I should be taking this lesson so seriously that in the next hour, I'd become the best swordswoman in the room and defeat everyone single-handedly in armed combat.

A tiny part of me felt guilty for simply having fun. I rarely got to do that. I always had something to keep me busy, chores or school or work or helping Maddie. Fun was a luxury. But I had vowed to ignore the guilt during the nights I spent in the club, so I pushed aside thoughts of everything I had to do this week, and Angelo and I fell into a better rhythm.

I wanted to ask if he played sports, but that seemed too personal, so instead I asked, "What role would you play on the book team? Fighter? Brains behind the operation? Lockpick, since you like Pietro?"

"Hmm. Maybe Bastian."

He didn't elaborate, so I didn't ask what he meant. Based on Bastian's character, there were multiple ways to interpret that answer. The protector? The observer? The wise counsel? The magical skills and deadly fighting ability?

"And you?" he asked. "Are you Ana?"

"I don't know." Ana was more like Natasha, with the planning and the take-charge attitude. I wished I was that way, but I was more the one who made sure everyone was happy and having fun, while handing out snacks. "I guess there are some ways I relate to her, but I love the books because I see myself in all the characters."

"People aren't simple."

"Exactly. Different parts come through at different times. We have layers."

"And masks we wear."

He meant more than the physical ones. "That makes it sound deliberate."

"It is, for some people," he said.

"Yeah, but doesn't context matter? You're different at school or work than with your family or friends. You adapt to fit the situation."

"Maybe, but shouldn't you still strive to be yourself?"

I didn't have an answer to that. Not one I wanted to say aloud. To reveal that my life was a constant string of masks, and that I prided myself on knowing which one to wear in each situation. That here, now, with a physical mask, I might be finding the real version of me.

"All right, everyone, weapons down," the instructor called.

Angelo and I lowered our swords and faced the woman in charge. A thin layer of sweat coated my skin.

"Now it's time for the battle."

Battle? I bounced on the balls of my feet as curiosity and excitement sparked in me. I glanced at Angelo, wishing I could see his face.

People rushed to the edges of the room and rolled out objects designed to resemble trees and rocks, which they spaced throughout the room.

The instructor split us into groups and moved everyone into positions to re-create the scene from *Bay of Phantoms*, the final book in the trilogy, where the dark elves fought the army of humans and friendly elves. More people had arrived. It was exactly one in the morning, which must've been the designated reenactment time. Some people wore homemade plastic armor or carried shields of foil-covered cardboard. The mix of costumes was colorful and random.

The man who took charge of our group, organizing us and

assigning roles, had clearly done this before. Was it the same battle every time, or did they do different scenes?

Another man did some deep lunges, causing me major concern about the durability of his tight pants.

When people stopped to watch, he said, "What? I'm old. Last time I did this, I pulled a hamstring."

Music blared, and I jumped. A dramatic instrumental score poured from speakers.

A thrill was overtaking me. The music definitely set the mood. I wanted to laugh, and yet I also felt ready to fight. With my unimpressive new sword skills. I took my position behind a tree.

Wait. I knew what this was.

I was LARPing.

I could never mention this to anyone, ever.

And yet.

It was kind of amazing. Everyone else was having as much fun as I was. Or more, like the guy with the too-large broadsword who kept trying to twirl it and ended up smacking himself in the face. No phones were out. No one was recording. We were just adults running around pretending because it was fun and we loved the world of the books.

The battle began. My side was supposed to fight the group that wore black cloaks, the dark elves. I swung at anyone who came near, ducking and dodging, using props for cover.

When I spun away from someone and bumped into a tree, the movement dislodged my mask. It came partially off, exposing one side of my face. I scrambled away and hid behind the tree, tugging the mask into place. I was breathing hard.

No one was looking. Angelo was across the room, and no one else knew me. Probably. Still, panic clawed at my throat. Even in a room of strangers, the fear of being exposed lurked.

It should have been fine. If I was safe anywhere, it was here. But my heart took a moment to settle.

What did I think was going to happen? These strangers would take a picture and report me? My world wouldn't end if someone saw half my face. Maybe I could relax while I was here, at least.

Still, I made sure the mask was secure before readying my sword again.

A man in an elven cape nearby raised his blade in a question. We charged forward together, my fear forgotten. Two people in black met us, and I swung at one while my friend took on the other.

"Alas, I am slain," my new friend cried.

His mask had come off, revealing a man of about fifty. He made no move to fix his mask, and I wanted to avert my eyes at the sudden face-nakedness in a room of anonymity.

He fell to the ground, and red spurted from his jacket. He muttered in French, something that sounded like a curse as he fumbled with his jacket. "Too much. Stop. Stop."

I defeated the person who'd slain him, and she fell to the ground also, with less fake bleeding. At least, I assumed it was fake, considering the amount of blood was more indicative of slicing open a major artery than getting smacked on the arm with the flat side of a plastic blade.

"Thank you for avenging me," my bleeding friend said as he tried to cover his chest pocket that thick red liquid was sporadically oozing or spurting from, coating his hands and seeping across the floor.

"My pleasure. Should I find you a towel?"

"No, thank you." He was on his hands and knees, using his cape in an attempt to mop it up, but only spreading the blood around. It looked like a crime scene.

A figure emerged from the shadows near the door. Multiple people were dressed as a fake monster, like Ana and the others fought.

"To me," our team captain called, and we scrambled toward him, including my dead friend, who slipped in his puddle of fake blood before catching himself and following me, leaving red footprints on the floor. He skidded again and crashed into a fake tree, sending it toppling over. I hauled him up.

Together, our group charged the monster. It was made of plastic, likely so we wouldn't destroy it and they could use it again. Half the people held up the plastic shell, while the ones between them waved pool noodles like tentacles. The music swelled.

"Oh no, not again." My friend was spurting blood once more, this time from his pants pocket. "They cannot kill me!" He continued fighting, sliding along the trail of red he was leaving.

I felt bad for whoever had to clean the floor. Hopefully fake blood didn't stain.

Angelo appeared next to me, and we hacked with our swords, dodging pool noodles. One of the fighters who'd done the initial demonstration was twirling and dodging like an action hero. Someone next to him yelped when her sword broke in half.

Finally, the monster collapsed as the people manning it dropped to the floor. My team cheered and congratulated each other. We hadn't been good, but it was rewarding, completing the task together as a group.

Who were these people? Had I passed them on the street? Had they served me dinner or gelato or driven a boat or taken my ticket at a museum? Were any of them the people who'd given me clues?

With masks, the brilliance of this place was, you could be whoever you wanted to be. For a night, for a week. Like, in hiding yourself, you were finding yourself. Or new parts of yourself. Nothing outside these walls mattered as long as we were here. Here, the world was what we wanted it to be.

And that was magic.

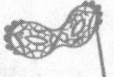

Chapter Fourteen

After we finished, my shirt was clinging to my skin and my sword arm was tired. As everyone returned the weapons to the wall and exited, I retrieved my bag, took out my notebook, and stayed to sketch the swords.

I looked up when I sensed someone watching from the door and saw a girl from the battle, in a blue elven tunic and blue-and-silver mask.

"Hi," I said. "Do you speak English?"

"Yes. You like to draw? Have you seen the gallery?" I couldn't place her accent.

"In passing. I wanted to look more." I stowed my supplies and followed her into the hall, where the art was displayed.

As I'd noted the first night, the walls contained everything from black-and-white sketches to paintings and colored pencil drawings to prints and masks. Character art and scenes and custom book jackets, like I had made for myself, were displayed.

I lingered in front of a color sketch of a sea monster attacking the fort. "I like this one, the way they envision the monster.

I always saw it more armored than scaly, but these details are excellent. Do you draw?"

"Yes, but I am not very good." The girl showed me character sketches with detailed outfits.

"You are good! This is exactly like I pictured the elven guard uniforms."

"There is an artist online I like, on the RealmScape forum. Are you on there?"

"I am."

"Her name's ElfFriend109, and she does lots of great pieces, but I really love her scenery."

My heart lodged in my throat. Did she just say Elf Friend109? As in . . . me? Surely I'd heard wrong, and this girl from around the world didn't know my artwork.

Did I dare confess? I checked my mask. Straightened my spine. "That's, um, me. I'm ElfFriend109."

"No! That is so cool. Have you added anything?" She waved toward the wall.

I shook my head. "How does it work?"

She shrugged. "You find a space and hang a drawing."

"I'll have to add something this week," I said. "Have you been drawing long?"

"All my life, but it is for fun. I study history. Where did you learn? Are you in art school?"

"No, it's just fun for me too."

She grabbed my arm and dragged me down the hall, chattering about drawings—*my* drawings—and what even was happening?

The girl stopped us at the bar in the tavern. "Let me buy you a drink. What do you want?"

The menu offered sweet wine, ale, and chilled cider. I was thirsty after the fight. "A cider, I guess, but you don't have to."

"Two ciders, please."

The bartender handed us heavy stoneware mugs, and she clinked hers to mine.

"Thanks," I said. I took a sip of sweet, rich liquid and leaned against the bar to face her. "Do you come here a lot? Do you live here?"

"I live in Munich. I take a train down one time per month, stay for a few nights with a friend. Come. You must meet the others." She hauled me to a table where three people sat. "This is ElfFriend109."

Surely they didn't all know—

"The artist?" one asked.

Well.

They spoke over each other to offer compliments, and I was frozen.

I felt like a celebrity. They talked about my vision, my style, specific drawings they liked.

Was this real?

I had stepped outside my body and was watching from above. This couldn't possibly be happening, the most unbelievable thing, while I was literally standing inside a setting from my favorite book. My art had always been something I'd kept private, to guard it. But I felt safe, even excited, to share with these strangers.

"How do you come up with your ideas?" one asked.

"When I read, I see the story as a movie in my head. I start with a basic outline of a scene, then use details from the stories to focus in. Whatever isn't described, I think of what would fit the setting, the characters, the overall feel of the Elven Realms universe. Sometimes I just go with whatever would look the coolest."

"Would you do something for the wall?" my new friend asked.

"Sure." It would be amazing to leave a piece of me here. "I don't have many art supplies with me now, but I can bring something tomorrow."

I felt so anonymous behind a screen. When people liked my posts or commented on a drawing, it was hard to picture those clicks as real people, as much as I enjoyed their praise. But these were actual fellow fans who had immediately recognized my name.

Two of them also posted art on the forums, and we talked ideas and styles and the mediums we liked for different types of pictures, and this might have been more surreal than fighting a fake elven monster.

When they left, I settled into a table alone with the rest of my drink. I was already wondering if this evening had been real. I'd never entered art shows. Outside of class, my art was for me, a way to express the images in my head and share my love for the books. Art was like reading. I could immerse myself, get lost in it.

I liked the idea of contributing to the gallery. My art

wouldn't be judged or analyzed. This was a chance to share with others who appreciated the subject matter. I didn't interact much online, beyond posting and thanking people who gave me compliments. Could I have found this community sooner if I'd put myself out there more?

Angelo joined me. "Apparently I've been sneaking out with a famous person."

"Hardly. A few people know my art. Are you online?"

"Not really. But I'd like to see it. If you don't mind."

Showing someone in person felt different from posting anonymously. He was seeing it for the first time, and I would be sitting right next to him while he did.

I opened the folder on my fan forum account and set my phone on the table.

Angelo scooted next to me, our knees bumping, and he left the phone in place while he scrolled, like he didn't want to overstep by picking it up.

We sat in a quiet, dark corner, our own little piece of Venezari. I watched the screen as he went through the images slowly, sometimes zooming in. The pictures showed my takes on whatever had caught my fancy. Scenes around Venezari or the elven realms, close-ups of outfits, boats, the ball scene, masks. Some were more polished than others.

He paused on a scene of the Dreaming Forest and looked at me. "These are amazing. They're like . . . how I imagined things without knowing that's how I imagined them, if that makes sense."

"Thanks."

"Do you—?" He stopped himself.

"What?"

"Never mind."

"What were you going to ask? No promises I'll answer," I said lightly. "But you can ask."

"Do you study art, outside of this?" He nudged the phone toward me. "Not that this isn't enough."

"I'm not in art school." That was safe enough, not admitting whether I wasn't old enough for art school or simply wasn't in it. "I don't know if I want to make it a job. Like, if I have to do it, have to draw certain things at certain times, instead of doing it when the mood strikes. Besides, then people might tell me they don't like my work and offer critiques."

"You don't like criticism?"

I shuddered. Were there seriously people who didn't hate it? Who didn't feel like anything less than perfect meant you'd failed someone by not meeting every expectation?

But what I said was, "It makes it so official."

I had never shared this out loud. Or shared at all. These were thoughts that circled in my brain, without an outlet.

"It's great to have hobbies," Angelo said, and left it at that. "Are you ready to go? Or do you want to join the trivia contest?"

"Tempting, but I'm tired." And I would get way too into trivia. "Unless you want to."

"No, that's okay."

We listened as a moderator asked questions and teams wrote answers on chalkboards. They weren't messing around. Many questions referenced obscure facts from single sentences.

Which, okay, I knew a lot of them, but I hadn't lied. I was tired after the fighting. And it was getting late. I waved to my new art friends, and we left.

"Not into trivia?" I asked Angelo.

"Nah. I know I don't remember all the details like some people do." He didn't sound bothered. "I'm not that level of fan."

"You can be a fan without knowing everything or quoting every chapter. I hate it when people think you have to be an expert to appreciate something. You can know you like it, or appreciate how it makes you feel, without having a PhD in it. What level even defines a *true fan*? How much do you have to know for it to count?"

I stopped myself.

"Sorry," I said. "That's a soapbox for me. Which means now you must share one too."

He laughed. "Okay. Hmm. I guess mine is that it's also okay not to like everything about something you love. You can think critically, admit there are elements you might change, and that doesn't take away from the overall enjoyment."

"That's fair. True fans can look lots of different ways."

It was a subject that hit close to home. I considered myself a big fan. I did know lots of details, and I made art. But many people knew more than I did or talked about it in their normal lives rather than hiding. Some might not consider me *enough* simply because I didn't share openly.

"I'm just happy to find other people who like the same thing," I said. The club was making me question if I'd been missing out by not sharing this with anyone in my everyday life. I glanced at Angelo. "I hope you've enjoyed finding friends this week."

My heart gave an extra hard thump. And possibly beyond the week?

He slowed and faced me, and I sensed that under the mask his gaze was lingering, solid.

"I have indeed," he said.

Chapter Fifteen

I swallowed a groan as I rolled out of bed. Who would have thought that swinging a plastic sword would be so much work? Muscles I didn't know I had were sore. Yesterday's nap had helped—I was tired but functional today. But between the time difference with home and not allowing my body to adjust to a normal schedule here, I had no idea what time it actually was. And I didn't know how long I could push through with a few hours of sleep each night.

Still, last night's high continued to hum in my bloodstream, the thrill of LARPing, my apparent celebrity, and the idea of drawing something today to leave in the gallery. Hopefully I'd find inspiration. Our whole group was touring two nearby islands, then I'd have the rest of the day with Gabriel, who didn't care what I did, which meant I could take time to draw.

"What did you do last night?" Bryce asked as I joined him for breakfast.

"What? Nothing!"

"You disappeared right after dinner."

Oh. Right. "Jet lag, man. What are you thinking?" I asked to distract him, before remembering he was a candidate and I should be questioning him about his night.

"The world in a box," he said.

"I'm afraid to ask."

"What if the world is just a ball inside a box, and the stars are holes in the box letting in light from outside?"

"What's outside the box?"

"I dunno, God or aliens or cosmic scientists watching us like lab rats. And earthquakes happen when they shake the box."

"But the whole earth doesn't move in an earthquake."

"It's a working theory," he said. "What are you thinking about?"

"Why capuchin monkeys are so creepy."

"How dare you! Monkeys are cute."

"Nope, they look too human. Definitely creepy."

"I'm with Whitmore on this one," Gabriel said as he passed our table. "Disturbing."

"Thank you," I called.

Bryce shook his head. "How's it going? With . . . everything?"

He meant with Gabriel, but I was choosing to ignore that. "Okay. I love Venice."

"Me too. Tanaka and Natasha don't care if I help with the project, so I'm mostly walking around taking pictures."

I laughed. "Yeah, I don't know why Natasha is taking this so seriously. I mean, I do, because it's her. But it's not for a grade for either of you."

"I'm just glad to be here. See cool stuff. Feels like another world, doesn't it?"

That sounded like something Angelo might say. Was Bryce thinking about the other world of the Elven Realms? Or just the historic, unique vibe of Venice in general?

Mr. Owens gave instructions about sticking together while we walked to the north edge of the city to a water-bus stop, where we'd take a boat to the other islands. We marched through quiet residential streets, less touristy than the center of town, with flower shops and markets and homes, until we reached the water and the dock.

The large vaporetto had a central open deck for standing and a cabin with seats. As I sat with my friends, my gaze met Gabriel's when he passed us. I felt bad abandoning him, which was dumb, because he certainly didn't mind. I wanted to ask him to sit with us, but he moved away to the small area at the back of the boat. Okay then. I'd thought he'd agreed to the label of friends, but apparently we hadn't reached the level of hanging out when it wasn't mandatory.

Part of me wanted to follow him.

Natasha leaned in close. "Did you learn anything new last night?"

How to sword fight. That my art was known in other countries. That fake blood was extremely slippery. "No visible jewelry," I said, "but that doesn't necessarily mean anything."

"Yeah. What about his shoes?"

"You're strangely committed to this shoes theory. They were black with laces."

"Like combat boots? Those would weigh a lot. Someone might have worn them on the plane. I can look through Bryce's video."

"Not exactly combat. Regular ankle boots."

My gaze dropped to people's feet. Sheesh. This was ridiculous.

Natasha stood and strolled down the aisle between the seats, then into the open area, keeping her head down. Because that wasn't weird at all. I took a second to check my phone. My mom had asked for another graphic. A spike of annoyance lanced through me, swift and sharp. I shoved it down. Helping her was a job. I shouldn't be upset that she was asking; I should be grateful she trusted me.

"No one's wearing shoes like that," Natasha said when she rejoined me. "It's mostly tennis shoes or skate shoes."

"They're part of his costume. I'm not wearing my stuff today."

"I'm going to keep watching," she said. "I maintain this is a valid theory. Did you smell him?"

"No, I did not smell him." Well, not intentionally. I hadn't noticed a particular cologne.

"Any facts about him?"

I didn't want to tell her anything too personal. What happened in the masks, stayed with the masks. "He's right-handed."

"I can work with that."

I was afraid to ask.

Natasha rubbed her hands. "Time to step this up."

"How?"

"Talk to the candidates more in depth. Hey, Bryce," she called over her shoulder to where he sat behind us, "was Dai in the room last night?"

"What? Dai's not a candidate," I hissed quietly.

"Reverse psychology," she murmured before twisting back toward Bryce. "I had to go down to the front desk and I thought I saw him in the lobby."

Bryce frowned. "I don't think he left? We went up after dinner, and I played games, went to sleep."

He seemed to be telling the truth, and Bryce was generally a terrible liar. But then, so was I.

Natasha turned to me. "Let's tackle the Washington High guys today."

"Not literally, I'm assuming?"

"Why would we tackle them literally?"

"With you I'm never sure. Tackle them, sit on them, force them to tell us their secrets."

She made a face like she was considering the idea. "I meant talk to them. The ones that fit the profile. Ask how they're liking the trip, maybe hint at that book stuff."

"How is that supposed to help?"

"Something might click, his voice or a phrase he uses."

"Or he'll recognize me," I mumbled. I wasn't asking every guy about Elven Realms, but talking to some would be easy.

After a ten-minute ride, we unloaded at the dock and faced Mr. Owens.

"Welcome to Murano," he said. "This island is known for its glass, and we wanted you to experience the local craftsmanship.

We'll watch a demonstration, then you'll have an hour to look around. Stay with your partner. Be back here at eleven."

A wide sidewalk led along a broad canal, giving the place a more spacious feeling than Venice. The lighter crowd helped too. We passed restaurants and multiple shops selling colorful blown-glass creations. I wrapped my sweater tighter against the breeze off the water.

As we walked along the canal, Natasha sidled up to a guy I didn't know.

I studied the other candidates, the ones I knew and the ones I didn't. I felt like Angelo and I had connected enough that I should be able to tell who he was, but I had no idea. I kept trying to picture Bryce or Tristan or even Gabriel dressed up, in a mask, playing with swords, but I couldn't see it.

I found a guy about the right height and introduced myself. His name was Elliott, he was from Washington High, and he wanted to be a graphic designer. He had a quiet voice and was wearing a Starfleet Academy shirt. After chatting about the trip and art, I pointed to his shirt and asked if he was a fan.

"Yeah, I love science fiction," he said with no hesitation.

"Cool. I'm more into fantasy. Do you like that too? Lord of the Rings or Elven Realms?"

"Nah, I prefer stuff with spaceships."

He could have been lying, but unless the quiet voice was a cover and he was better at projecting while wearing a mask, I didn't think it was him. He didn't mind admitting he liked nerdy things, so he probably wouldn't lie. I debated what else to ask to cover my guilt over approaching him to find out if he was someone else.

Before I could speak, he looked at me sideways. "Are you carrying a phaser?"

"What?"

"Because your beauty stuns me."

I blinked at him.

In his soft voice, he continued, "Beam me up, hottie."

"Um. No thank you?"

"I'm going to ask you out. Resistance is futile."

"Excuse me?" What was happening here?

"Everything okay?" Gabriel asked, falling into step with us.

Elliott eyed him, then me, then sighed and strode ahead.

I was not sad to see him go. "Yeah, fine, why?"

"You didn't stay with your partner."

"Aw, did you miss me?"

He angled his head toward Elliott's retreating form. "Working on that lack of a boyfriend issue?"

"What? Oh, him? No. Besides, it's not an issue. Wait. Are you jealous that I'm being friendly with other people too?"

"You said friendly is your natural state."

Was he jealous? Why did I want him to be? Especially when I was searching for another guy.

"Friendly is natural until someone breaks out the *Star Trek* pickup lines," I said. "Then I'm done. Thanks for the save."

He snorted. "I have so many questions."

"Don't we all, Martinez."

Our group went through a courtyard and into a workshop that resembled a big garage, where we clustered at the edges to watch a man at work. He introduced the art of glassblowing, telling us about its history, which dated back to the thirteenth century on the island.

Then he lifted a long pole with a glowing ball at the end that he heated in a furnace so hot the air around it shimmered. He dipped the ball in colored powder, blew air down the long tube to make the melted glass slowly expand, and used metal tools to twist and shape it, reheating the taffy-like substance often.

It was fascinating. I should have taken notes, but I just watched. Gabriel would understand, with his whole live-in-the-moment vibe.

Many of our classmates were talking, barely paying attention to the impressive work. My gaze met Gabriel's. He quirked an eyebrow. What did that expression mean? Was he saying hello? Acknowledging me? He immediately went back to watching the man intently.

The look, and his focus, made my blood feel like that glass, melted and stretched and hot.

After the demonstration concluded with a blue-and-green vase fully shaped before our eyes, we funneled into a shop, where glass creations were displayed, from tiny beads and miniature statues, to bowls and vases, to chandeliers and elaborate sculptures of flowers, animals, even people. It was either very brave or very foolish to allow this many teenagers free run of a place full of breakable items.

Sanjay and his notoriously giant backpack were an accident waiting to happen. He was known to tip over desks if he set that thing down wrong. I caught Natasha's eye and pointed to him, and she quickly steered him out of the store.

I lifted a bowl to check the price and almost became the accident. The piece was heavier than I'd expected. I caught the bowl before it slipped from my hands.

"What's wrong?" Gabriel asked.

My muscles are sore because I spent hours pretending to be a warrior fighting dark elves, don't mind me. "Nothing, I'm good."

"Be careful. Partnership doesn't extend to paying for stuff you break."

"What about friendship?"

"We're definitely not there yet."

I grinned at him. "Your use of *yet* gives me hope."

Too bad these items were impossible to transport home safely. My sister would've loved them. I checked a small dolphin sculpture and choked at the price.

"More shopping?" Gabriel asked.

"Not with these prices. I'll wait until later."

"That's a lot of gifts. I know you have lots of friends, but . . ."

I carefully put the dolphin down. I would not be touching anything else here. "They're for my sister."

"Did you do something terrible?"

"What do you mean?"

"You must owe her a big apology."

I laughed. "No, it's not like that. Do you know Summerside Bazaar?"

"It's like a marketplace for lots of small businesses?"

"Yeah, women-owned ones. My mom founded it. Plus a consulting and marketing program for the businesses that participate. They mostly sell crafts or homemade or homegrown items. My mom's crazy successful. Started her own business and then grew big enough to help others too. She's always looking for ways to expand, to grow, to network. She's kind of intense. Like Natasha but more."

"Wow, no wonder you're . . ."

"It's probably best for both of us if you don't finish that sentence."

His lips twitched before pressing together. "Excellent call."

"Anyway." I gave him a pointed look. "She's awesome. I'm not being negative. Like, she built it all. She loves to teach us lessons she learned from business. Go after what you want. Manage your image. Do everything with excellence. Competence eventually silences doubters."

Gabriel's eyebrows dipped in a way that said *yikes*, as clearly as if he'd spoken aloud.

Yeah. "My sister loves it. She has what I guess you'd call entrepreneurial spirit or whatever. She's always finding ways to make money. As a kid, she wasn't the one mowing lawns or washing windows or walking dogs or babysitting. She's the one who unionized every kid in our neighborhood and acted as a broker for those services through the neighborhood message boards. Everything's a negotiation."

"And the gifts?" Gabriel asked. "Let me guess. She plans to resell them at a markup?"

"Yep. I have to keep my receipts. I know she'll somehow use the exchange rate against me, despite our written contract stating the percentage I get from her profits."

He let out the loudest laugh I'd heard from him. I twitched and almost bumped the nearest shelf.

If his scowl was a dark cloud, that smile was the sun breaking through. It transformed his face. Every feature softened, his eyes crinkled. I wanted to stare, to bask in it, to make a sketch to capture this moment. Time was suspended, like that taffy glass slowly being drawn out, stretched, thick with potential.

"Yeah, yeah," I managed. "It's funny when you don't live with her."

But I was smiling. Now that I knew making him laugh was possible, doing it again would be my mission for the week. My new one, on top of the drawings I was supposed to do today and the school project and the fan club and the graphics for my mom.

Possibly, my mom had rubbed off on me and I had too many missions.

But this one suddenly seemed vital to my happiness.

"What's your dad like?" Gabriel asked.

I didn't like talking about Dad, burdening others with my sadness. But considering how rarely Gabriel asked questions, I had to reply. I settled for the short answer I always used. "He died when I was twelve."

His brows softened at the edges. "I'm sorry, Whitmore."

Before he could comment, I hurried to ask, "What about your parents? Or the rest of your family?"

He paused so long I wasn't sure if he would answer or if I'd pushed too far, brought up another seemingly harmless subject that he found overly personal.

"My mom's an office manager, and my dad's a building inspector. My brother's living at home while he goes to college—he's studying psychology—and my older sister has a house with three friends but they come over to eat our food. Then my younger sister."

"Wow. That sounds . . ."

"Busy? Loud? Exhausting?" His eyebrows settled into their thoughtful position. "Your house sounds tiring too."

It was, especially the five-plus years since Dad had gone. Did I sometimes wish I didn't have to step up and do everything? Did I wish my brother hadn't bailed? Did I wish I'd been able to keep doing piano or soccer because they were fun, instead of quitting because I wasn't great at them and there were more important ways to spend my time? Yes.

But my family needed me, so it was worth it.

Maybe it wasn't completely pointless to imagine life could be different, though. I'd be in college soon. I could find hobbies or clubs. But since I couldn't picture myself at college at all, that wasn't helpful now. Plus, I'd still need to make sure Mom and Maddie were okay.

"What are you doing next year?" I asked. "College?"

Gabriel looked at me.

"It was connected in my head. The question wasn't as random as it sounded."

"I'm not sure we've reached the friendship level required for hopes and dreams, Whitmore. That's a step above paying for things you break."

I rolled my eyes. "Plans in a few months and deepest longings in life are hardly the same."

"Nope, keep trying."

"Oh, I will."

He didn't sound mad or annoyed. More like he was enjoying the game and knew I was relishing the challenge.

And it was a game I planned to win, without knowing exactly what winning looked like.

Chapter Sixteen

We moved outside and rambled down the main street, until we neared a church tower and Gabriel circled the building. A vivid blue sculpture caught my attention, a giant spiky star made of glass. Our steps slowed and, without talking, we studied the piece. It resembled a giant sea urchin, too modern for the old buildings around it.

"I like it," I said. "It's unexpected."

"Smart to have a fence around it. Your friend Tanaka would impale himself."

That was an extremely fair point.

We moved on to a side canal where houses of pink and orange sat close to the water, with awnings tilted downward and small boats lined up along the bank. I stopped and took out my sketchbook, seeing the floating market of Venezari take shape. I did a basic sketch for the club that I could add color to later.

Gabriel waited, watching the view. "For the project?"

I angled the page so he couldn't see that my version had a

Sentinel on the bridge and a sea monster in the water. "Just for fun."

"Good."

"What?"

"I'm glad to know you're capable of that."

"Shut up," I said with a smile.

I wasn't sure why we stayed together. We hadn't even discussed our project.

I also wasn't sure where Natasha or the others had gone. She was likely interrogating guys. I should have been helping find Angelo, the guy who understood me, who didn't criticize my family, but I'd gotten distracted by Gabriel. Again. I'd get back on mission later.

Since Gabriel had waited for me while I drew, and since I enjoyed his relaxed attitude and the lack of stress I felt around him, I trailed him when he stepped onto an old wooden dock.

"Are we allowed to be here?"

"I like to take the road less traveled," he said. "You find more interesting things by going places no one else does."

"Or you get lost or end up trespassing or are late and miss the boat."

"I have no doubt you'll keep me on time. And have I gotten us lost yet?"

"I probably wouldn't know the difference."

He huffed a laugh. Not the full-on one from earlier, but still. My chest swelled.

I tried to picture Gabriel exploring LA. It seemed unlikely

that he'd found places no one else had in a city that big. "What interesting things have you found at home?"

He lifted a shoulder. "Cool architecture, random museums, hidden restaurants."

"And Italian classes?"

"And those."

We wandered down another side street.

"Getting your steps for the day?" I asked.

"My what?"

"Your steps. You know, like counting them. Natasha says she's getting lots this week."

"Why would you count those?"

"Her watch does it. For fitness." That made me remember his watch and how I'd been curious. Now that we were friends, I could do this. I snagged his arm and held up his wrist, exposing the leather band. "Yours doesn't do that."

"It does not."

"Where'd you get it?" I ran a finger over the dented metal rim, and my fingers brushed the bare skin of his wrist. He didn't pull away.

"Gift from my sister because I'm always late. She bought it at a thrift store."

"Did it make you start being on time?"

"No."

I snorted. Figured. My insides softened at the fact that he wore it while in another country and his sister wasn't here to see it.

When we made our way to the boat, most of the group was waiting for the water-bus.

Natasha was throwing things at people.

"What's she doing?" Gabriel asked.

"It's usually safer not to ask."

We edged closer. She held a sack in one arm and was taking out one item at a time—and chucking fruit at people. Were those oranges? She slung one at Sanjay, who snatched it and immediately started peeling it. Then one at the *Star Trek* weirdo, who dropped it. Then Olive, then a guy I hadn't met, who wasn't paying attention and it bounced off his shoulder.

"Sorry," Natasha called.

I was certain she had a plan that went beyond assault by oranges; I just didn't know what it was.

She continued tossing, switching to an underhand throw because the last guy was scowling at her.

When we boarded the boat to our next island, I left Gabriel and sat next to Natasha. "What was that about?"

"I was checking to see who caught with their right hand versus their left hand. I think Jason from Washington High is left-handed. I'll get him to write something for me later to confirm so we can eliminate him."

"But you were throwing fruit at everyone."

"I couldn't look like I was singling anyone out, could I?"

She really was an evil mastermind.

"There's another guy from Westview who has potential," she said. "But I ruled out the terrible one."

"The Model UN guy?"

"Yeah, he said he doesn't read fiction. Can you believe it?"

"*You* don't read fiction."

"Yeah, but I don't say it with a judgy tone."

I sniffed a laugh. "I eliminated someone too, from Washington High. He doesn't like fantasy."

"That only leaves a couple more from the other schools. Let's hope they're better than Alex." In her mouth, Model UN Guy's name sounded like a curse.

A few left, plus three candidates from our school. Pressure squeezed my lungs. The final night was creeping closer, and I was no nearer to deciding how I felt about removing my mask.

The ride to the next island took thirty minutes. We disembarked near a wooded park and walked into the small town, and soon I saw why Mr. Owens had said Burano was one of his favorite places. Brightly colored houses lined the main canal in a rainbow of green, rose, teal, yellow, orange, periwinkle, and red. The colors were cheerful and charming, and the town was quaint and vibrant at the same time.

Shops lining the sidewalk sold the island's local product, lace. There were shirts and dresses, handkerchiefs, scarves, shawls, tablecloths, lace umbrellas, all delicate and intricate.

Off a square was the lace museum, where we explored rooms displaying dresses, veils, and other examples of the work, plus information about the history of lace making in Burano. In one room, three old women sat in wooden chairs, bent over projects. Their nimble fingers worked tiny needles and spiderweb-thin thread. I was surprised they could see after staring at the patterns for decades.

After exploring the streets, we went to a café for lunch. Natasha devoured her meal before I'd finished half of mine. The pizza came whole, so I had to cut my own slices. The outer crust was thick and pillowy, the middle paper thin. It was the perfect combination of chewy and soft, with gooey cheese that stretched and giant bright-green basil leaves. I took my time cutting small slices and savoring the flavors.

Bryce paused in cutting his pizza to flex his hand.

"You okay?" I asked.

"Hurt my hand last night. Playing games."

I froze before continuing to eat. Did he mean video games with Dai? Or was there a chance he meant playing with swords in a LARP battle?

"Did he beat you?" I asked Dai, hoping I sounded casual.

"I was getting my beauty sleep. I think he played online."

My grip on the kinfe tightened. Bryce had brought his laptop to play games, and he was acting normally, not like he was hinting at secret activities.

Natasha's eyes lit up. "What game? Who'd you play with?"

Her interrogation didn't seem to make him suspicious. "*Fortnite*, with the baseball guys."

That could track. Nighttime here was morning at home, and it was spring break.

Natasha studied him and grunted, apparently, like me, not a hundred percent sure if he was telling the truth or not.

If I asked him directly . . .

My heart stopped briefly. Nope. Too soon.

Natasha tossed her napkin onto her empty plate. "Are you still eating?" she asked me, and I was, because without meaning to, I'd been counting to ten between each bite. "I'm going to check out the town."

"Go ahead without me," I said. "It's fine."

Gabriel smirked at me from his table where he was eating alone, his eyebrows saying, *I see what you're doing there.* My face went hot.

Natasha stopped at a nearby table, where a Latino guy was eating with his left hand.

"Jason, right? Are you ambidextrous?"

He looked at her like she'd asked if he was an alien. "No, why?"

"That would be cool. I could get twice as much done."

"I don't think it works that way," he said.

"It would for her," I said.

"Um. Okay." He returned to eating.

Natasha widened her eyes at me. She was crossing him off the list. I shook my head as she left.

I was almost done when Mr. Owens rushed up, looking worried.

"What's wrong?" I asked. "Can I help?"

"Tristan is sick. I need to take him to the hotel immediately."

"Oh no. Is he okay?"

"Motion sickness combined with all the walking, I think."

"I have medicine. What do you need?"

Tristan was one of our candidates. Was there any chance he was tired and trying to fit in a nap? He probably wouldn't do it in so dramatic a fashion. Good thing Natasha wasn't here to take advantage of this.

"Will you be in charge of our group?" Mr. Owens asked.

"Counting, getting everyone on the boat. Tristan and I will catch the next vaporetto, but we'll never round up everyone else in time."

"Why can't Ms. Reyes do it?" Gabriel asked from his table.

"She didn't answer my text. I trust Evie."

Gabriel opened his mouth again, so I hurried to say, "I'm happy to help."

"Thank you, Evie. I knew I could count on you."

He moved off, and I ignored the weight of Gabriel's gaze that said he had thoughts I wouldn't like and all it would take to set them loose was basic eye contact.

I'd been looking forward to exploring with Gabriel again, drawing, soaking in the atmosphere, but now the weight of responsibility pressed down. If we wandered off like earlier, I'd be constantly worrying that everyone else was doing the same, getting lost or getting in trouble, and worrying that I'd be late.

We did roam, but in the direction of the water-bus stop.

"This whole place is like art," I said as we paused to admire a row of colorful houses whose twins were reflected in the canal below. "I wonder what it's like to live here. You'd always have to keep your paint fresh so you're not that one person who stands out."

"You would be on the committee checking for fading or peeling and telling people when it was time to repaint."

I nudged his arm. "You'd be my most frequent offender."

It sounded like a meet-cute for a rom-com, the cheerful small-town committee member and the grumpy rule-breaker. My neck flushed.

When I returned to the dock, to my surprise, Gabriel came with me. I'd expected him to ditch me and be the last one back. His presence at my side was becoming too familiar. And I liked it too much. When we were home in a week, I probably wouldn't see him again. He'd go back to ignoring everyone, giving single-syllable replies—if he even used words—not participating in the things I loved. I shouldn't get used to this. Better to focus on Angelo.

The first few people arrived, including Natasha, deep in conversation with a dark-haired guy I'd seen this week and I thought was the rival she hated. I didn't have time to wonder, because I was checking the time on my phone. Olive and Sanjay had been here, but where were they now? The boat was boarding, and the other school's teachers were counting their students.

"Guys," I called. "Get in line. Let's go."

My friends did as I asked, but several others ignored me, taking pictures or joking around.

"Guys, please, come on. You'll miss the boat. Matt! Sanjay? Olive? Please, guys."

"Hey," Gabriel barked. "Everyone line up now, or we're leaving you here and you can swim back."

His tone said it was not a joke but a real possibility. They could wait for the next water-bus, but then Mr. Owens would worry and I'd feel guilty.

They shuffled forward. Several shot scowls at Gabriel. He, naturally, ignored them.

I smiled. "Thank you. Sorry. Please line up here. I hope you had a good day. I think there are seats left inside."

The boat attendant was looking impatient and said something in Italian.

"No more room inside," Gabriel said to Lina, who was shoving her way on board. "You'll have to stand."

Lina stopped. "But—"

"No point arguing with me." He pointed to the boat guy.

She glared at Gabriel but went to the railing.

I sagged. "That's the last. Who would've thought fifteen people were so hard to manage?"

"Me," Gabriel said.

"You didn't have to be so mean."

"Sometimes nice doesn't work, Whitmore."

"Nice always works."

"Yeah? How was it working for you there?"

I grunted. "Okay, fine. It could have been better." I eyed him. "Thanks."

His head bobbed once, and he offered a hand to help me board. I blinked at it for a second, then grabbed it before he changed his mind. With the cabin full, we found a place to stand by the railing on the open deck area. Gabriel didn't speak, so I didn't either, just watched the water and the other islands as the boat cruised to the port we'd left from.

Tension eased from me, with the breeze and the lapping water and Gabriel's undemanding silence. The deck's gentle vibration and the rocking boat had my eyes drooping. Gabriel's shoulder was right there, looking solid and warm and comfortable. I shook my head to erase the too-tempting idea of leaning against him and forced myself to stay awake.

I was the first one off and planted myself on the sidewalk, reminding everyone they had the rest of the day with their partners and giving directions to the central part of town.

As Olive passed us, she wrestled to get her windblown scarf back in place. I reached out to help.

"Thanks, Evie. You were right about the color. A guy in Murano said I looked nice."

"You do look nice." I finished adjusting the scarf. "Glad I could help."

When only Gabriel and I remained, I sighed. I liked being useful, but it was exhausting. What would have happened if I'd refused, told Mr. Owens to wait for Ms. Reyes or ask another teacher? My stomach clenched at the mere thought.

Gabriel glanced at me and started walking.

"Where are we going?" I asked.

"Somewhere to sit and work on the project."

"Who are you?"

"I figured you had lots of thoughts. I'd rather you write them down so you don't talk all day." His eyes glinted, and I knew he was joking. Mostly. "And you looked like you needed somewhere quiet after dealing with that."

"We should add the glass and lace to our report. And the town. I can do some drawings too." I'd taken pictures of the products and could do a detail of a lace pattern.

"Do you show anyone your art?" he asked. "The stuff you do for fun?"

My heart stutter-stepped. "Not really. Why?"

"Just curious."

"Art is art, whether you share it or not." I flashed back to the night before, when I'd had the same thought about fandom.

"That's true. But art shared across time and place teaches us so much."

His words came out passionately, and he blinked. I saw the shield of distance start to come up in his eyes, like he hadn't meant to be so real. Now I had to chime in so he wouldn't shut down. I liked the open, reflective Gabriel.

"So it doesn't count if it's not in a museum?" I asked.

The shield paused. His expression hovered somewhere between *I shouldn't have said anything* and *Possibly I'll continue this conversation.*

"It can't just be for fun?" I pressed.

"It can be. Art can fulfill lots of purposes. Maybe it's museum quality. Maybe it's technically average but people like it enough to hang on their walls. Or maybe it made the artist happy to create it."

His pointed glance hinted that he might have meant my drawing.

"I agree," I said softly.

I almost told him about sharing my art online but chickened out.

My phone rang, and I broke eye contact that I hadn't realized we were holding so intently.

Nora, a friend at home.

"Hey, what's up?" I asked.

"Evie, it's a huge disaster, you have to help."

Chapter Seventeen

"Slow down, Nora," I said. "Start at the beginning. What's the problem?"

She sounded like she was hyperventilating. "It's the Shoreview. A pipe burst, and the ballroom flooded, and it won't be fixed in time."

The Shoreview. That was the hotel hosting our prom. "Tell me everything."

"We have no place to hold prom. What are we going to do?"

Gabriel was watching me. Nora's voice was so loud, he probably heard every word.

"You should have that email I sent months ago with location options," I said. "Find it and call the others on the list. See what's available. Has the hotel refunded the deposit?"

"I didn't ask."

I fought the urge to massage my forehead. "Call them, make sure they do. Be firm. When you check the other places, give them our budget and don't negotiate. We can pay what we paid the first place, nothing more."

"Right. Okay. I can do that. Thanks, Evie."

She hung up. My phone rang again.

"Charlie?" I answered.

"Hey, Evie. Did you talk to Nora? Wait, are you in Europe?"

"Yes, Venice. It's fine. What's up?"

"Nora's calling the places, but what about the caterers? And the DJ? And—"

"As soon as Nora has a new location, call the vendors. The list is in the shared document. You may need to meet them at the new spot so they can see the space."

"I was hoping you could do that."

"I'm in Venice," I repeated. "You need to get on this fast, before everything is booked."

"But you're better at this stuff."

I clenched my jaw and kept my voice friendly but firm. "You can do it, Charlie. I trust you. I'll be back next week."

"Right. Okay. Can you send me those files again?"

Trying to keep my breathing level, I hung up, opened my files, and emailed him. I sensed Gabriel watching the whole time.

What if they messed this up? What if there was nowhere else to hold prom? I was the committee chair, so it fell on me. What if—?

My phone rang again.

Blood was pounding in my ears. My nostrils flared. I clenched the phone and inhaled slowly. If I chucked it into a canal, no one else could call me. But then, prom might be a disaster and I would get blamed and everyone would be mad and—

Gabriel took the phone from my hand. "Evie is busy right now. She'll call you back. Or maybe she won't. Figure it out yourself. And don't call again."

Wait, who had that been? What if it was important?

Gabriel shut my phone off and guided me to sit on the steps of a nearby church.

"I told them not to call me this week," I said. "They're perfectly capable of handling this. I left instructions in case there was a problem. Can no one else make a stupid phone call? What if they mess it up? I have to email our advisor and then check on—"

"Hey." Gabriel's voice was sharp. "You don't have to do any of that. Breathe."

"Easy for you to say. You're not the one who will get blamed if prom is held in a murder barn in Simi Valley. Not like you care anyway." I dropped my head. "Ugh. I'm sorry. I'm not mad at you."

"Even though I stole your phone?"

"Keep it. I was about to throw it in a canal." My heart was throbbing, and my hands shook.

Gabriel's hand rested gently between my shoulder blades, as if he wasn't entirely sure touching me was a good idea.

"Do you . . . want to let it out?" he asked.

"What?"

"Scream. Yell. Whatever."

"Is that how you deal with things?"

"You don't want to deal with things the way I do. Go on." He spread his arms. "Let me have it."

I chuckled softly.

"I mean it. What's bothering you?"

"Other than the murder barn? And the graphics my mom wants? And all the competitions, the responsibilities, the expectations, and I can't quit anything or my mom thinks I'm slacking, and she freaked when I mentioned giving up tutoring, never mind that I'm not even great at math. And Natasha's making me help with the career fair, which keeps reminding me that I have to *find* a career and I have no idea what to do with my life."

I was breathing hard but feeling lighter. Then it hit me, everything I'd revealed, to a guy who didn't want to be friends and hated drama.

"I'm sorry." I straightened and leaned away. "I shouldn't have said any of that."

"No wonder you're always stressed. I'm honestly surprised you've made it this long without snapping."

Gabriel seemed so unbothered, so dryly amused, with his eyebrows in their usual position of general indifference, that I actually laughed, though it sounded shaky.

My face was warm, and I didn't want to meet his gaze. "I don't know why that happened now. I'm tired from the travel." And the sneaking out at night. I rubbed my temples.

He shrugged. "It happens."

"Not to me. I've never done that before."

"Don't be embarrassed for having emotions. Those people should be ashamed for calling you while you're out of the country and for not stepping up. And Mr. Owens should be too for making you help today instead of asking another teacher."

I *was* embarrassed about having emotions. Or, about show-ing them. I didn't like adding to anyone's stress. I was grateful he didn't bring up my family, my best friend, or my lack of a future. And I was mortified that anyone had seen that, let alone Gabriel, who cared about nothing and no one.

Except . . . he was being nice. Who else in my life would have been so calm, so nonjudgmental? My mom would have told me not to let it show, to suck it up and deal. Natasha would have made a quick escape to avoid excessive emotion or imme-diately made a plan for me.

"I think I know your problem," Gabriel said.

"What?"

"You said you've never done that. You need a good melt-down every once in a while. Clear the system. It's been building for so long, it was bound to happen."

"I don't know if that's comforting."

He shrugged again.

But . . . it was comforting. He wasn't trying to solve my problems or brush them aside or telling me to ignore them. He was saying it was okay.

And that made me feel like I was okay too. "Thank you. For being cool about it."

He waved a hand. "Don't mention it. Really, I mean that. I don't want others coming to me with problems just so they can break down and I can hang up on people for them."

I laughed again. "I bet you love hanging up on people."

"Good point. It was fun."

"Does this make us friends now?" I asked. "Would it be so terrible? To call me a friend?"

He held my gaze. Something in it sparked, and my stomach flipped over. "Okay, Whitmore. You win. Friends."

My stomach flipped again. Why did that word, in his low voice, sound like the promise of something so much bigger?

"I would have freaked out the first day if I'd known that was all it would take," I said.

His lips quirked.

"But don't worry, I won't make a habit of it."

He helped me to my feet, and we walked on, slow and unhurried.

I bit my lip. "What did you mean about not handling things your way? You don't have public meltdowns in foreign cities?"

"I try to keep mine local."

I snorted.

He scuffed his shoes.

"Sorry, you don't have to answer that. I keep forgetting you view questions as personal threats. But if you want to share . . . we're friends now, right?"

He studied me. "As a friend, can I tell you that you're too nice?"

"There's no such thing as too nice."

"There is if you let others take advantage of you."

"They don't take advantage. I just don't like to disappoint people. I don't want them to think they can't count on me, that I don't want to help them."

"Setting limits is good. You can't take on everything."

"That feels like failing," I admitted. "Them, and myself."

"It's called being human, Whitmore."

"I don't believe in that," I said in a breezy way to show I was joking. "Only superhumans around here."

His turn to snort.

We walked half a block, and my breathing was returning to normal when he said, softly, "I almost got into a fight."

"What?"

"At my old school."

"Why?" I made my voice quiet like his, not like I was judging.

"My sister. The younger one. She's a musical genius, but she's not the most socially aware. She hums all the time, carries her flute to play when she has a free minute or wants to practice."

I recalled the guy playing the cello and how Gabriel had appreciated it, the museum of instruments and his interest.

"It can make her an easy target. The kids at our old school weren't nice. Kids at most of our schools have sucked. We moved a few times, so we've gone to several. But at the last one, there was a group that was especially bad. The popular crowd, who acted like my sister was talented and special. Only to set her up and make fun of her publicly."

"That's awful. I'm so sorry." I grabbed his hand and squeezed. Then immediately dropped it, heat flushing my neck. "Sorry."

What had I been thinking?

He flexed the hand I'd grabbed, then scrubbed it across his face. "I was ready to fight the leader, but my sister stopped me. I don't know what I was thinking. I wasn't. I just couldn't keep listening to them tease her. Even though I hate fighting. You know, use your words."

His voice was wry.

"Did they kick you out?"

"No. You shouldn't listen to rumors." He poked my arm. "I didn't do anything except yell at them. But my parents decided to move us both. Get us out of there."

"Is your sister okay?"

"Yeah, she switched schools too, to a private one with advanced music classes. We've never had the money for it, but they decided it was time."

"She's lucky to have a brother like you."

"If I were a good brother, I would have stopped things before they got that far."

"You can't prevent everything."

"Like you can't do everything?"

I narrowed my eyes at him, and he lifted an eyebrow.

Pieces were fitting together. Why he'd liked the music, why he'd been so good with the tiny opera singer. The idea of him standing up for his baby sister, the genuine affection in his voice when he spoke of her, was causing a warm weight to settle in my chest. This protective side of him was new. He didn't hate all people. He had someone he was willing to fight for. The heaviness in my chest was twisting, twining, reaching toward him.

"You are a good brother," I repeated. "Trust me, coming from someone who knows what an utterly indifferent one is like."

Gabriel waited, his eyebrows in their *go on* state.

"Let's just say mine has no trouble arguing with my mom but certainly never would have stood up for my sister or me. When my dad died and Mom needed help, with us and the business and the house, he was fifteen and wanted no part. We've barely seen him since."

"I'm sorry."

We stopped at the edge of a square. Gabriel studied me. I held his gaze, his eyes a clear and warm brown. I felt like he was trying to dissect my soul. I felt like I didn't mind.

His head ducked, and he bit the corner of his lip, drawing my focus to his mouth.

"I . . . have a confession," he said. "I judged the popular kids—and you—from the moment I arrived at Central. I assumed you would be like the people who mocked my sister. You were so friendly, like they were, and I thought it had to be fake. They weren't my first bad experience. People eventually prove that they can't be trusted, that they don't really care. Like I said, we moved a lot, and kids would act like your friend, but as soon as you left, no one noticed, even ones you thought were close. In my experience, most people only like you when it's convenient."

My lungs constricted at the fact that so many people had let Gabriel down. "It makes sense. All you saw was those kids pretending to be nice to your sister so they could betray her."

"Yeah. But . . . you aren't like them. You aren't like that."

Pleasant tingling swept through me. I took a tiny step closer. "I would never do that. My friends wouldn't either."

"I know that now." His gaze locked me in place.

My fingers twitched, wanting to reach for him. "I'm sorry you've met so many awful people."

The air between us was doing that slow, stretchy thing again, my heart twisting and pulling.

He blinked first and sniffed. "Now I sort of wish she'd transferred with me. I have no doubt you would have made her popular."

"I like that you think I have that power."

"Whitmore, there are people who are popular because others fear them and want to be like them, people who have power and money and status. And there are those who are popular because they're nice people and others see that. The second type is rare."

He thought I was a nice person. A rare one. Coming from him, that sent a hot coal straight through me.

We walked on, the silence not uncomfortable.

"Thank you," I finally said. "For telling me. I won't say anything. Unless you want me to spread rumors about an actual fight, how you took on four guys and sent two to the ER for looking at you wrong, so it makes people leave you alone."

"You're the only one who doesn't leave me alone. Everyone else already does."

"Too bad for you that we're friends now."

"Yeah," he said. "Too bad."

The look he gave me, a golden tint to his eyes, his brows softened, said the opposite and lit my insides on fire like the golden sunset.

Chapter Eighteen

There were no set dinner plans for the evening, so when we passed a restaurant that looked warm and cozy, I asked, "Want to eat?" before I could consider the invitation.

I was reluctant to leave our new, tentative friendship. It still didn't feel like enough. I hoped this meant that we could talk more, that I could learn more about Gabriel, go deeper and uncover it all. The crumbs had made me want a feast. To understand how he thought and hear his dry humor and insightful comments, figure out what made him passionate.

To my surprise, he agreed.

To dinner, not the feasting on personal information.

The evening would have been a good opportunity to investigate other candidates and work on finding Angelo, but I'd see him soon. I allowed that to fade from my mind and dashed off a text to Natasha telling her not to wait for me. Gabriel and I ducked inside a small place with romantic lighting and the tantalizing scent of baking bread.

As Gabriel studied the menu, I examined him. From the

shiny dark hair, to the way his jacket fit his shoulders, to the watch peeking out from his sleeve. The long, slender fingers that gripped his menu, the way tendons moved in his hands. The set of his eyebrows, which seemed more relaxed.

"What looks good?" he asked, and he meant the menu, not his face, so I hurried to hide myself behind it.

"Pasta, probably."

When the waiter brought a bottle of water, I reached for it, but Gabriel's fingers had closed around it first. He didn't let go.

"Don't think I didn't notice," he said.

"Notice what?" I hadn't released my grip, so both our hands were wrapped around the bottle, our fingers touching.

"The way you always serve. It won't kill you to let someone else do something small for you." His gaze held a challenge.

I didn't let go. The act had been instinctive all week, and I suspected he was the only one who'd noticed. He was certainly the only one who would call me on it.

"I have all night," he said, not moving.

It might actually kill me to have someone insist on doing something for me, if the electricity zinging around inside me was any indication. I reluctantly removed my hand and let him pour.

After we ordered spaghetti, I flipped through my sketchbook and showed him drawings I'd done for our project, careful to keep the Elven Realms one hidden. We ate partly in silence, partly discussing today's islands, more in terms of what we liked than in terms of the project. Then Gabriel left to find the bathroom.

"Don't stay in there for hours," I said, and he raised an eyebrow at me.

The gesture expressed humor, I thought. Those eyebrows needed a translator. They spoke their own language, and I wanted to be fluent.

A phone buzzed. Not mine. Gabriel had left his face down on the table. It stopped, then immediately buzzed again. When it happened once more, I reached out. Hesitated. He might hate this invasion of privacy. He could call the person back. But what if it was an emergency and someone needed help?

Caller ID said *S*.

Was this testing our new friendship too soon?

I grabbed it and answered. "Hello?"

"Hello? Gabe?"

"No, this is Evie. His . . . classmate. He stepped out, but the phone kept ringing and I was worried."

"Oh. Cool. Tell him to call Soph."

"Is everything okay?"

"That's what I was going to ask. Gabe hasn't called yet today. Wanted to make sure he didn't fall in a canal."

"He hasn't, not as of ten minutes ago. I'll tell him."

"Cool. Thanks." The line went dead.

And of course, Gabriel returned while I still held his phone. His eyebrows were flat, saying nothing.

"Soph called. Multiple times. I answered because I was worried. I didn't look at anything, I promise."

He dropped into the chair and held out his hand. His face

wore its usual carefully neutral expression, so I couldn't tell if it bothered him.

I handed the phone back. He had a black case, but that didn't mean anything. Probably eighty percent of guys had black cases.

"Gabe?" I asked.

"That's what my family calls me. Sophia is my sister. The younger one."

"Do your friends call you that too?" My hands clenched as if his answer held great importance.

"Is this you asking if I have friends? Or if you can call me Gabe?"

"It's me asking what you prefer to be called."

"What's Evie short for?" he asked. "Or is it long for Eve?"

"If I tell you, can I call you Gabe?"

"Depends if I can call you your real name." He maintained eye contact, didn't even look at his phone.

"Uh-uh. Evie is my nickname, Gabe is obviously yours. So if I tell you it's Evangeline, we're on nickname basis."

"Evangeline." He said it slowly, the syllables rolling off his tongue.

I hid a shiver at the way my name sounded in his low, unhurried voice, like each syllable was significant. Its echo reached every cell in my body.

Wait. Was that the first time he'd said *Evie* too? It was always *Whitmore*.

"No one calls me that." My cheeks were hot. "I suspect my

mom thinks it takes too long to say, so I have no idea why she picked the name. My sister is Madeline, and we call her Maddie. Strangely, my brother was always Jonathan, though."

Our eyes locked. His were warm, nearly amber in the light. He didn't seem annoyed about the phone, or maybe he'd forgotten.

"Is Evie what *you* prefer?" he asked.

I froze. Clutched my cup. "I . . . never really thought about it. When someone calls me Evangeline, it's reflex to say, *Call me Evie.*"

Did I prefer the nickname? It was easier for others to say. But Evangeline sounded grown-up and mysterious.

Gabriel continued to watch me as I had a mental debate.

I was the first to look away. "You should call you sister. *Gabe.*"

His eyes glinted, and he raised the phone, still watching me. He didn't bother leaving or asking me to leave as he said hello, which sent a pinball rocketing around my chest.

I grabbed my phone and stepped outside to give him privacy anyway. I had a text from Natasha, which I returned. This was a good time to check in with my family too. And to escape this new awareness between Gabriel and me. It might have been an accomplishment to be able to call him friend, but I was aware how precarious that was, how it might not survive the rest of the trip, let alone going home.

"Evie, how is everything?" my mom answered.

"Good, just checking in."

"Any more college emails?"

Ugh. "No. We had some prom excitement, though. I handled it."

"Of course you did. Have you seen my latest email?"

I knew exactly what Gabe would tell me to do—tell her I was busy and would do it when I got home. The words hovered on my tongue. But I chickened out. "Yeah, but I've been gone all day. I'll do the graphics before bed."

They shouldn't take long. If we went to the hotel now, I could get them done before leaving for the club. So much for a nap.

"Thank you."

Her voice faded at the end, and my sister's voice came on. "What are you buying?"

"You wanted cheap stuff, right?" I asked. "I'm making sure everything says *Made in China*."

"Ha ha."

"Are you paying for a massage when I get home? Because this stuff's making my backpack heavy. My shoulders hurt."

"You're welcome to use your profits on that," she said.

"Isn't that, like, unsafe working conditions or something?"

"Should have put it in your contract from the beginning."

I rolled my eyes. "You're worse than Mom."

"Thanks," she said.

When I rejoined Gabe, he was off the phone.

I slipped into my chair. "Everything okay? Sorry if I overstepped."

"She was just checking on me."

"To make sure you hadn't thrown yourself into a canal? Does she know you have a tendency to do that?"

"That's a more recent hobby. Since meeting you."

I stuck my tongue out at him.

"What about you?" he asked. "You look stressed again."

"Ah, yeah. Mom, college stuff, my sister treating me like hired help, all that."

"Do you want to talk about the college thing? Wait, what am I saying? You always want to talk."

My heart fluttered every time he took an active step to get to know me. Too bad I hated the topic. "You might regret asking. But that's my least favorite subject. I haven't told anyone."

"I don't talk to anyone else, so your secrets are safe."

"I'll keep that in mind."

I didn't want to ruin the evening. And although I thought I knew Gabe well enough to be confident he wouldn't judge my lack of direction, I was more afraid of the honest and insightful commentary he might make on my life. Being him, he didn't press. But his silence didn't feel like other people's, always wanting me to listen and not listening to me. His said he was respecting my desire to avoid the topic.

We wandered slowly toward the hotel. I ignored the graphics project that awaited me and stopped at the end of a narrow alley to sketch Ana jumping across the roofs.

I was reluctant for this night to end. I hoped Gabe wouldn't change his mind in the morning and decide that he didn't want to be friends after all or that I was too much work. I took my time, clinging to the evening's last moments.

We reached the hotel door. He hesitated with his hand on the doorknob.

I paused at his side and looked up at him. "Thanks."

"For what?"

"Being my friend," I said, in a soft voice to convey I meant it.

His brows softened, and his head bobbed once before he let us in.

My friends were hanging out in the lobby when we entered.

"Evie!" Dai called and spread his arms. "You're alive."

"Where have you been?" Natasha asked.

We'd returned before Mr. Owens's curfew, but I guess it was strange that I'd willingly spent my free time with Gabe.

Gabe kept moving toward the stairs rather than the seating area.

"Good night, friend," I said.

He paused. Turned his head enough to make eye contact. "Good night, Evangeline."

His soft voice sank into my bloodstream with a gentle hum.

I joined my friends, listening to them discuss their day, though half my brain lingered on Gabe. I tried to imagine telling them about my freak-out, or about how much there was to do and how people couldn't let me enjoy a week off, but they were as busy as I was, and none of them complained. So I said Gabriel and I had been working, and no one asked anything else.

When Natasha and I went to our room, she said, "Okay, spill."

My heart stuttered. Surely she hadn't read my interest in Gabe, right?

"Any progress on the secret-friend front?" she asked.

Oh. That.

Yes, I liked Angelo. But becoming friends for real with Gabe was exciting too. I didn't want to tell her about him, though. Not because she'd be mean. Because she'd remind me of truths I was trying to ignore, like the fact that he was hanging out with me because he had to, and that we were in different worlds at home. And if she mentioned his supposedly shady past, I wasn't going to betray his trust by telling her the truth.

A tug-of-war was taking place in my mind. I was riding the high of the evening with Gabriel, but I was also excited to see Angelo and go to the club.

Part of me just wondered what it might be like with Gabe.

A combination of tiredness and the ease of the previous night's escape had relaxed my alertness. That night, I crept downstairs like usual, but I didn't stop to listen as I retraced the path to the breakfast area—where the lights were on and three of my classmates sat, talking.

I froze.

Which was a rookie mistake, because it gave them time to study me and ask questions.

"Is that an Elven Realms costume?" Matt asked.

"What's that?" asked Sanjay.

"They're books, man."

"Cool costume," said Lina.

"Do we know you?"

They were staring at me.

I was wearing a mask. I'd be fine. Right?

"Scusi," I said. "Buonasera."

That was the official extent of my knowledge of Italian phrases, and my terrible accent probably hadn't fooled them, so I lifted my chin and marched straight for the door.

"Where are you going? Can we come?"

"Is there a party?"

"Ooh, I want to go to a party. Do we need costumes?"

"You don't really speak Italian, do you? Say something else."

Nope. I let the door shut behind me and strode across the patio, debating whether I should run. A beam of light pierced the darkness.

"Wait for us!" Sanjay called.

"Do you go to Central?" Lina asked. "Do we know you?"

"Or Washington? We must know her. She sounds American, and no other Americans are staying here."

"Who are you?" Matt asked.

Seriously? I helped them, and this was how they repaid me?

I couldn't stop—they would recognize me. So, like the bold, brave criminal I was . . .

I ran.

Straight for the gate, into the street, skidding around the corner.

Laughter and footsteps followed, despite the fact that Matt was in pajama pants. This was a game to them, like I was intentionally leading them on a chase, not a life-or-death social situation. I could dive into the canal to hide, except the ripples in the water might give me away. My bag with my drawings slapped against my hip.

I skidded around the corner. Angelo was waiting, leaning against the wall. He straightened when he saw me running.

"We have company," I said. "Sorry."

Voices carried on the breeze, coming closer.

"This way."

He immediately took my hand, and we dashed off. Through the dark, quiet streets, along the water. Down narrow alleys, then one where motion sensor lights came on, giving away our location.

I felt like Ana escaping the city guard, except Ana knew Venezari's hiding places, and I had nothing but the possibility of checking every door and letting myself into a stranger's unlocked house.

We emerged into a square, cavernous and empty at night. The usual tables, chairs, and umbrellas had been stored, making it feel larger. Angelo aimed for the round cistern in the center, about three feet high. We scrambled behind it, crouching to keep our heads down.

I clapped a hand over my mouth to muffle the sound of my breathing. Angelo kept a steady grip on my other hand. His reaction to this situation offered another clue about him—he stayed calm under pressure.

But then, I might have seemed collected, when actually I was barely managing to control my desire to panic, fighting the urge to puke on the cobblestones.

"Who do you think that was?" Sanjay's voice sounded close.

They must have entered the plaza. Would they cross it and check the whole area? Our hiding spot was hardly secure. I shivered.

"I don't know," Matt said. "But the costume was cool."

"Where'd she go?"

"What are those books again?" Lina asked.

"Elven Realms. It's this long series with lots of different shorter series. My sister loves them."

"Was she meeting someone? Do we know her?"

"Dunno."

"Come on, man, we should go. Mr. O will freak if he learns we went out so late."

"That girl didn't care."

"Did you run all this way in pj's, bro?"

Their voices faded as they moved away.

Angelo and I stayed hidden until it had been silent for several minutes. Then we stood and stretched. The square was dark and empty again.

I gulped air, feeling shaky. Checked my mask.

They hadn't identified me. This might be fine.

I dashed off a text to Natasha asking her to cover in case anyone came looking.

But I needed to be more careful. What if that had been Dai and Bryce in the lobby, who would've recognized me? Or Mr. Owens, who would have wanted to make sure I wasn't a student sneaking out?

"How'd you get out?" I asked Angelo.

"Front door. No one was at the desk."

He was smarter than I was. Or more observant.

"You okay?" he asked.

"I will be. Once the minor heart attack is over. Sorry I wasn't more careful."

He waved a hand. "It ended okay."

He didn't ask if I knew them, and I didn't comment on who they were.

We walked in silence, allowing me to catch my breath. And contemplate how complicated tomorrow was going to be for me.

Chapter Nineteen

For tonight's main event, the Dreaming Forest room was prepared for an elven feast. Silver light infused the space, and ethereal music played. My heart gave a wistful twist. The year before he died, Dad had introduced me to the Lord of the Rings movies. We'd watched the whole trilogy in a day, complete with a full spread of hobbit meals. He would have approved of this evening.

A gray wood table, matching the description of the one in the scene in the second book where Ana dined with Bastian in the elven realm, filled the room, covered in dishes.

How did they pay for this? Donations? Fundraisers? And who had set it all up? Was there a crew or committee or something?

Of course I was thinking in terms of committees I would love to join. Gabe would make so much fun of me.

Gabe. Our discussion earlier about what we preferred to be called was making me contemplate names. I shivered again at the memory of my full name on his lips.

In the books, Andriana de Rossi used the nickname Ana when she was on the streets. Ana was her real self, more than the daytime persona. Which name suited me? If she got to choose, shouldn't I? Instead of accepting the one everyone else chose for me? I had no good answer.

Dinner didn't have a program. People chatted and passed around dishes that matched the meal served in *Bridge of Echoes*—a sparkling fruity drink, airy pastries, fish with herbs, fresh berries, vegetables, warm bread.

Most people's masks allowed them to eat. Some, like Angelo, had to shift theirs. I focused hard on not staring at him across the table to catch a glimpse of his face because I didn't want him to think I was trying to figure out his identity, even though I was, and even though this might have been my best chance.

The meal was friendly, with conversation centered on the books. I would have eaten less at dinner if I'd known this was waiting. Was there an official schedule for this place? Did people show up each night unprepared, like I was? Or did everyone whisper about the events, putting nothing in writing? It was impressive that they'd managed to keep this so secret.

Near me, a British woman and an Italian man were discussing casting for the Elven Realms series that was rumored to be in the works.

"I'm just saying, unknown actors are better," said the woman. "They can become this role, instead of you always wondering what else you've seen them in."

"But you never know if they will be good enough. Inexperienced actors are risky," said the man.

"Plenty of people without huge résumés have talent," I said. "Yeah, some aren't great, but that's on the casting director to make sure."

"Exactly," said the woman.

"Fine," the guy said. "As long as we agree a television show would be better than a movie."

"Absolutely," I said. "Movies always leave too much out."

"And then viewers get confused if they haven't read the books, and if they have, they're upset at the changes," the woman added.

"Hopefully they choose Mask of Souls," the man said.

"I hope so," I said, "but I'm worried they'll go with the Exiled King since those books were the first."

"Yeah. Shame. I'd love to see the dark creatures brought to life."

"And the heist at the duomo," I said.

"For me it would be when the crew takes refuge in the garden, but the dark elves show up, and Bastian is injured but fights them anyway," Angelo chimed in as he took a third helping of fish.

"Really, all the Bastian and Ana stuff," the lady said, and we both sighed dreamily.

"I wonder if they'd film here in Venice," the man said.

"Might be hard with so many tourists," I said. "But it would be perfect. I've seen so many places that remind me of scenes from the books."

That made me wonder if there were other cities with canals

that could serve as a setting, which made me think of Gabe, and I needed to get my brain under control.

After the meal, we were slow to move on, people rising a few at a time and drifting away.

"Do you come here often?" I asked the British lady.

"This my third time."

"It's amazing. How does it work?" I waved a hand toward what remained of the food.

"Volunteers donate food or time. People take turns setting it up. Some regulars live here, and others come often and help."

She seemed knowledgeable, so I pressed on with other questions I had. "How'd they build it? How long did it take?"

"I heard it was partially financed by the author herself. She helped a group purchase this old palace that was sitting empty, then assisted with renovations."

"Wow, really?"

"She loved the idea, apparently, when she saw fans discussing it online, and she wanted to help make it happen."

"I love that. Do you think she's ever been here?"

"The beauty of masks, correct? No one knows."

How amazing would it be to talk to C. M. Patricks and not even know it?

As the woman left, I retrieved my bag from the floor and took out the drawings I'd done. They weren't as fancy as ones I'd done at home, but I'd added color after reaching the hotel, before doing the graphics for my mom and getting ready for tonight.

Sleep was for the weak.

And for people who knew how to say no.

In the art hall, I took out the floating-market sketch, inspired by Murano, with a sea monster, and one of Ana and Bastian on a bridge, and hung them on a blank patch of wall. It wasn't a museum, but taking one more step beyond drawing for myself felt good.

A few people moved closer to look, but I kept going, through the market, where people browsed, and the tavern, where a card game was in full swing. I blended in, my costume and mask making me normal in a place like this.

If anyone was normal. Were human beings too complex, too layered for that? Maybe we all had secret habits and interests and quirks that made us unique.

This was breaking my brain. I didn't know why I was contemplating such deep subjects right now. Maybe because I was surrounded by the idea of parallel realms, each part of a whole but also distinct, layered on top of each other.

"Having fun?" Angelo greeted me when I joined him downstairs.

"Does that question need to be asked? If I lived here, I would never sleep. Ooh. If you lived here, would you want to help? Making food or running events or games?"

He considered. "Creating the place would have been fun. Converting it from an abandoned shell into something unique and new. Your art could have helped create the vision."

The compliment lit a star in my chest. I had a sudden urge to move up our agreement, to ask who he was. Had he been trying to guess during the day, like I had? The idea of him knowing me was less terrifying than before.

We chatted about light topics on the walk to the hotel, and then he paused and shifted toward me.

I waited.

"Fantasma." The low rumble of his voice vibrated through me. "I'm looking forward to our last night."

I shivered. I was too.

Natasha had a hit list waiting for me the next morning. Before I had a chance to tell her anything about my evening, she presented me with a list of every person on our trip, with red X's through most of them.

"If any of those people go missing, I'm denying all knowledge of this," I said.

"We're down to six." She didn't acknowledge my valid concern. "Bryce, Gabriel, and Tristan, two from Westview and one from Washington. Time for the next step."

"I'm afraid to ask."

She tapped the paper against her hand. "What are your thoughts on hidden cameras in the halls?"

"The better question is, what are the Italian police's thoughts on hidden cameras in the halls?" I said. "Oh, we had a meal last night. I did learn that he likes seafood."

She rubbed her hands together like she was contemplating force-feeding our candidates fish and recording their reactions.

"How did you get this?" I nudged the incriminating list.

"First I confirmed at the desk that we're the only American guests who arrived in the right time frame. Then I talked to the teachers from the other schools and got names. We needed a visual aid."

So I could clearly see that six options remained.

I'd known that in my head, but the visual drove home how close we were. I had just been thinking about how I might want to meet him. Would the result of our search change that, or confirm I was making the right choice?

Breakfast was lacking in seafood options, so Natasha's nefarious plans would have to wait.

Despite another night of far too little sleep—my mom was going to wonder why I needed two weeks to recover from this trip—I was determined to do more art today. Leave my mark at the club. Which might be tricky during the group visit to the Guggenheim museum.

Matt and Sanjay arrived, holding an animated conversation.

The night before flashed through my mind, them chasing me through the streets. Last night's panic clawed at my throat. I patted my hair. I looked different. They had no way of suspecting the costumed girl had been me, and they would certainly never guess that model citizen Evie Whitmore had been sneaking out.

They went to the front desk. Were they conducting a Natasha-style investigation? I strained to listen as they asked Valentina about people leaving the hotel at night. Her refusal to check the security cameras unless a crime had been committed was comforting.

The guys entered the breakfast room, and I forced my attention to my plate as they circled the room slowly. They were definitely searching for someone—for me.

Wait. Ignoring them would be suspicious, coming from me. I took a steadying breath as they passed.

"Hey, guys," I said. "Excited for the museum today?"

"Sure. Hey, when did you go to bed last night? Did you see anyone in the lobby?"

"We were down here kind of late with Dai and Bryce, but when we went to bed, no one else was up. Why?"

Sanjay leaned closer. "We saw someone sneaking out!"

My heart slammed to a stop before hitting the gas and racing off again. "No way. Who?"

"We don't know. She was wearing a costume."

"Like a Venice one?" Did my voice sound casual enough? Or did it reveal my panic?

"No, a fantasy one."

"Like cosplay," Matt whispered as if he were sharing a juicy secret.

"Wow." Natasha did not sound casual.

I stopped myself from kicking her under the table.

"We didn't see anyone," I said, "but I'll keep an eye out."

"She had a Tigers patch on her bag, so she must go to our school."

I was doomed.

Chapter Twenty

Busted by a backpack. I nudged my bag farther under my chair and put my feet on top of it. I hadn't considered that it might give me away.

Matt and Sanjay moved on. If they questioned everyone, was there a chance they could find out the girl they'd seen had been me?

"I have to switch bags," I hissed to Natasha.

Her gaze darted to the guys. "Go now. Quick."

I snatched my bag and kept my body between it and the rest of the room as I ran upstairs.

I met Gabe coming down.

"Going the wrong way," he said.

"I'll be right there," I called as I raced past him.

How had it not occurred to me not to use my usual bag? Oh, right. Because this was my first dip into the criminal under-world.

In my room, I paused. I hadn't exactly brought extra back-packs. Oh. I had bought some cute purses for my sister. I dug one out that was large enough to hold my sketchbook, transferred my stuff, and hurried back downstairs. Hopefully I looked stylish rather than guilty.

There was nothing more I could do, except be careful today.

Our group left and walked south through town. A window full of metal masks caught my eye, and I wanted to point them out to Angelo. But Gabe was there instead.

"What's up?" Gabe asked.

I blinked. "You're asking me a question. What's happening?"

"You looked like you wanted to say something, but then you didn't, and it was making me worried about the hospital again."

I sniffed.

"Go on, I won't judge you. I'm your friend now, remember?" His eyes held a spark of humor and a hint of challenge.

"I was worried you'd change your mind about that. I was looking at the masks."

"Yeah, they have a steampunk feel, don't they?"

I wouldn't have expected him to know what that was.

We spent the rest of the walk finding things we found interesting—a window full of colorful cannoli, a light fixture shaped like a dragon, a display of flatbread and pizza crusts with faces cut into them, framed wall hangings that were 3D miniature bookcases.

Since Gabe seemed to share my enjoyment of small things, I didn't hold back, and we spent the whole walk side by side.

So much for not acting weird today—walking with him instead of my friends surely looked suspicious.

We didn't stop until our group reached the largest bridge yet. It crossed the Grand Canal, and everyone paused to take photos of the broad expanse of water and numerous boats.

Dai and Bryce came to stand by us.

"What are you thinking?" Dai asked.

"Pineapple on pizza," I said.

Dai shuddered. "That's an abomination."

"A crime against humanity," Gabe agreed.

I gasped and clutched my chest. "How dare you."

"I think it's delicious," Bryce said.

I high-fived him. "Thank you."

"Did you hear Sanjay saw someone sneaking out?" Dai asked. "Who do you think it was?"

I darted a glance to Bryce, who didn't appear overly interested or overly worried by the question.

"I dunno," I said.

"He said it was a girl." Dai scanned the people walking nearby. "I can't see anyone from our class breaking Mr. Owens's rules, though."

Nothing to see here. She's not standing right in front of you. I tried to keep my voice calm. "Maybe he was wrong, and it was someone from another school."

"Maybe."

This side of the Grand Canal was less crowded, and we approached the museum, saving me from having to continue a conversation I did not want to have.

Leading to the museum entrance was a courtyard with an abundance of vegetation and sculptures nestled throughout.

Under a round white gazebo with a dome roof wreathed in ivy stood a stone table. I immediately wanted to grab my sketchbook and drop the gazebo into a scene in the elven forest.

I lingered toward the back of the group as everyone entered the building, reaching for the sketchbook in my new and less incriminating bag. Surely I could do a basic sketch.

Gabe stayed with me.

"What are you doing?" I asked.

"Keeping an eye on my partner," he said. "Usually I'm the one wandering off. What are *you* doing?"

"Just a quick drawing."

I lingered long enough to sketch the basics, branding my idea into memory to finish later. Gabe stood with his hands in pockets, studying the nearby sculptures. When I moved to close my book, he asked, "For the project?"

"No, I just liked the scene."

"You can finish if you want."

"But . . ." I waved a hand toward where the group had disappeared.

"They won't leave without us. You're appreciating the museum."

He had a point. . . .

I added more details before I sensed his attention on me. My face, not my sketchbook.

"What?"

"You get into your drawings. It's like you're somewhere else." His look and tone were warm and approving.

I swallowed hard.

"What do you draw when you draw for fun?" he asked.

Scenes from fantasy books. Oh, and that costume and mask that our classmates saw me wearing last night. "Whatever strikes me."

"Glad to know you're not completely without hope."

I shoved his arm, and his mouth tucked into a small smile.

The museum interior was bright white with pale wood floors and lots of modern art—abstracts, geometrics, some images I couldn't begin to identify. It had the wrong feel entirely for the Elven Realms, and I should have been appreciating the actual art, but it was too modern, too new. I craved tapestries and mosaics and age-darkened stone, shadows and pillars and statues worn by time.

We found the group, but soon it was Gabe's turn to lag behind as he took his usual unhurried pace through each room, examining every piece of art. He studied them with an angled head. His expression, though not much different from usual, contained more interest. It wasn't the first hint that he enjoyed museums. But he didn't seem inclined to talk today, like he had when we were alone. Still, I found myself hoping he'd drop a sarcastic comment or discuss the art, and I stayed with him as he had with me in the garden. I couldn't stop yawning—not that the museum bored me, just that I needed sleep.

"Aren't you worried about getting left behind?" he asked. The others had moved on to a second building that housed a special exhibit.

Yes, I was. "I'm keeping you company like you did for me."

"And making sure I don't wander off?"

"How far can you go? They won't leave without us." I repeated his words.

His eyes glinted. "We could test that."

"Stop involving me in your delinquency, Martinez."

That earned a lip quirk.

I was reminded again that he was a possibility for my nighttime friend. They were so different, though. I couldn't see Gabe dressing up and LARPing and joining all the reindeer games. The height and dark hair were right, but Angelo had been so open from the beginning, the complete opposite of Gabe. I wasn't sure which I liked the more, the ease or the challenge.

"What do you think?" I asked.

"Why, what do you think? Not into modern art?"

"I don't always understand it. Not to knock those who make it or like it."

His attention was on a painting when he answered. "It shows a different way of seeing the world. A glimpse into someone's imagination."

I might not have been as interested, but for him, I would happily linger, slow the group down, take as long as he wanted.

When we caught up with the others, Natasha was talking to the dark-haired guy she claimed to hate. Her eyes were flashing, but she didn't look as angry as she kept claiming. I smothered a smile.

Since I was comparing candidates to Angelo, and since I'd barely seen my friends the past few days, I left Gabe to join Bryce.

"Having fun?" I asked him.

"Yeah, but I like old art better. Especially in Venice."

"Me too."

"The modern art doesn't fit."

He sounded like Angelo, with his interest in old buildings, but that was too vague to confirm anything. Asking specifically about building restoration like Angelo had mentioned seemed too direct.

Sanjay came over and pointed to my purse. "Hey, you know that stuff."

I raised an eyebrow.

He waved a hand. "Like, fashion or style or whatever. Have you seen someone with a black or brown bag that goes across their chest?"

"You mean like half the people here?" I asked.

"Yeah, but I haven't seen anyone with it today. It had a Tigers patch."

"Maybe you saw it wrong or the person wasn't with our group."

He frowned. "I guess it was dark."

I made a quick escape to rejoin Gabe. I hoped Sanjay's detective skills weren't any better than Natasha's.

We walked back over the bridge, following Mr. Owens to a restaurant in a large plaza, and everyone took seats under umbrellas for lunch. I was itching for my sketchbook, to find more hidden gems like the little garden. A meal with this many people was going to take forever.

I sighed and stared across the square.

Gabe appeared. "Mr. Owens? I'm not feeling well. Can I go back to the hotel?"

I squinted at him. He'd been fine all morning.

Mr. Owens turned from the stand where he'd been trying to order for everyone. "Do you need a doctor? Or anything from the first-aid kit?"

"Just rest. Can my partner walk with me? So I don't get lost?"

He was the one who kept us from getting lost. What was he doing? I fought to keep my suspicion off my face.

Mr. Owens looked at me. "If you don't mind, Evie?"

"Of course not." I stood.

I waved to my friends and pointed across the square, not like they would know what that meant. Natasha frowned. I shrugged. I felt bad. She also would probably prefer not to sit here, although she'd use the time to work on her report or other school projects, especially if I left.

Gabe trudged away, and I trotted after him. His shoulders were slumped, and I was preparing to ask what was wrong. But as soon as we were around a corner and out of sight, he straightened and smirked, miraculously healed.

I narrowed my eyes. "Wow," I said. "My company must be excellent medicine."

He stuffed his hands into his pockets and faced me. "Where do you want to go? You looked like you didn't want to be there."

"So you lied and left? And took me with you?"

"Yep."

I shook my head. I should have been upset. It was something my brother used to do, simply leave whenever he didn't like something, regardless of who was around or what was expected. But today I wanted to smile.

"You're welcome," he said. "Why didn't you want to stay?"

I debated denying it, but he read me too well. "There's so much to see. I like hanging out with everyone, but I don't know, today I was in the mood for . . . exploring."

"So let's explore. Where are we going?" he asked.

"This was your idea."

"No projects, no schedule."

"We do have a project to work on."

"By getting you out of lunch, I'm getting us extra time that we wouldn't have had. Consider it a chance to see or do whatever you want."

I should have been thinking about the official project. I should have been at lunch with the group. Apparently today was a day for throwing *should* out the window.

I bit my lip. "I'd like to do some more drawings."

"Of what?"

"I don't know. Anything that strikes me."

"So we'll walk. You want to stop, say the word."

"What about lunch?"

He raised an eyebrow. "I'm told Venice has more than one restaurant. I'm fairly confident we can find another."

When we were moving again, I asked, "Why are you doing this?"

"Long, loud lunch with a big group or go rogue? You have to ask?"

"I thought you liked slow meals."

"I like enjoying my food rather than swallowing it whole. But not with dozens of people making small talk."

"Oh, come on, no one tries to talk to you anyway. And you like it that way."

"I don't mind talking if someone has interesting things to say."

"Do I count, since you asked me to come? Ooh."

I stopped at a pretty bridge, and a scene filled my head, of Clio at night, secretly practicing with her forbidden elven weapon. I sat on the sidewalk nearby and took supplies from my bag.

Without me asking, Gabe moved so he couldn't see my sketchbook. Light gilded his profile, his hair gleaming, skin golden, face contemplative. I had to focus not to draw him instead.

I glanced at him occasionally, but he seemed content to sit in silence.

Soon, art enveloped me the way I loved, until nothing existed but the scene in front of me and the image in my head that was taking shape on the page. My only connection to the real world was the feel of paper under my hand and the pencil nestled against my calloused finger.

When I was pleased with the drawing, I put my stuff away.

"Done?" Gabe asked.

"Yeah. Thanks."

"For what?"

"Waiting, I guess."

He shrugged.

The silence was comfortable. I didn't feel rushed or pressured. Gabe was there if I needed him, but he didn't expect anything of me.

We made one more stop at a water fountain that was meant for people to fill a bottle from, except the water poured from grotesque faces that made me want to draw dark elven beasts.

"We could write about that for the project too," Gabe said.

"Right. Sorry. I know we need to work on that."

"I assure you I'm far less worried about it than you are."

Before I could reply, my phone interrupted. Nora. Again. Was there another prom problem?

I sensed Gabe's attention on me.

I stared at the screen. And shut it off.

He examined my face leisurely, inch by inch. The warmth in his eyes melted any guilt I might have experienced. If I had answered, he would have stolen my phone anyway.

"See anything else you want to draw?" he asked.

You. I gave the far safer answer. "I'm good right now."

His attention jumped from me, and his eyebrows lifted. "Then it's my turn to choose."

The window in front of us had a sign that said MASK-MAKING CLASS.

I had to admit, I was intrigued.

"Can I cover your face in glue?" he asked. "We should do that."

"This doesn't seem relevant to the project."

"Sure it is. Masks are classic Venice. If it makes you feel better, we can learn how to make them and then compare it to how they were made in . . . medieval times. Or whatever."

Why had I thought, for a second, that he was going to finish that sentence with *in the Elven Realms*? What would happen if I asked him if he knew the books?

For one, he might connect me to Sanjay and Matt's investigation. Better to keep quiet.

Making masks did sound fun, if potentially messy. Gabe expected me to say it might ruin my makeup. "Fine."

"Really?"

"Why, scared it will mess up your hair?" I reached out as if to touch it.

He swatted at my hand. "It takes a lot of work to look this good." He opened the door. "After you, Whitmore."

Chapter Twenty-One

An explosion of color covered the shop walls. Rows and rows of masks watched me in a variety of colors, shapes, and patterns. Some had sparkles or enormous feathers or beaks or rhinestones.

"Buongiorno," I said to the older man behind the counter.

Gabe repeated the greeting with a better accent and pointed to the sign advertising classes in both English and Italian. He asked a question in Italian.

Was it warm in here? It was definitely warm in here.

The man responded in English, "Yes, we start soon. We have room for two more."

He led us toward a door at the back, past the multitude of colorful masks.

"Did you make these?" I motioned to the walls.

"Yes, they are all handmade."

"Wow."

His own gallery, something he'd built, after years of work. Like my mom and her business. The familiar chasm opened inside me, with a voice screaming from the depths that I was never going to have this, never going to figure out what my *thing* was, my way to make a mark on the world.

Through the door was a workshop, with shelves of plain white masks that were slightly disturbing. Their blankness represented my future. They had the potential to be anything, to be beautiful, but were currently awaiting inspiration that might or might not come.

Since that depressed me, I shifted my thoughts to Gabe. Was he also used to wearing a mask? This was a perfect place to drop hints and figure out if he was the guy I'd been hanging out with at night. If I wanted to. I wasn't sure if I wanted to risk messing up whatever relationship Gabe and I had established. Friends. Partners. Maybe more? The way he looked at me sometimes felt tangible and sent shivers through me.

We joined the other people in the room and sat at a worktable covered in newspapers.

"Can you read them?" I asked Gabe, pointing to the papers.

He tilted his head to see and rattled off Italian.

This place needed AC.

"What does it mean?" I asked.

"I don't know all the words. I can just pronounce them."

The older man faced us, letting me hide my flushed face. "Today we will learn papier-mâché and create a mask and then decorate it."

I eyed the vibrant paint colors and brushes, the canisters of glitter and cups holding a variety of sparkly and metallic decorations, fake jewels, rhinestones, feathers, and trimming.

"Do we get to papier-mâché each other?" Gabe asked.

The man laughed. "No, we have molds."

"That's disappointing."

I jabbed him. "You don't want to do that. It might mess up your hair. What's up with that, anyway?"

"What, my fantastic hair?"

"Yeah." It really was, dark and shiny and soft-looking.

"My sister. The older one. She works in a salon, and I let her experiment on me. I should introduce her to your mom. She wants to open her own business one day."

"My mom could definitely help. Did your sister ever conduct a failed experiment?"

His lips pressed in to contain a smile. "There are no photos, which means it never happened."

I felt drunk on the fact that not only had Gabe volunteered personal details, he'd also implied he might continue talking to me once this trip was over, if only to help his sister. I would cling to that hope.

The man, who had donned a paint-splattered apron, introduced himself as a master artisan and shared the history of masks in Venice, their meaning and uses, the various types over the centuries and how they were made.

Gabe shot me a smirk. "Is this educational enough for you?" he murmured. "Do you need to write this down?"

"I'm trusting you to take mental notes. And I know you're joking, but yes, we should add this. It's art, and like you said, it's classic Venice."

"Mental note-taking has begun."

After the talk, the man showed us round molds with a face imprint on one side. He explained the different styles, from basic half-masks to full-face ones, masks with elaborate head-dresses or plague doctor noses or cat ears.

Gabe and I both selected half ones. Did that mean any-thing? They were the most common, the easiest. Was Gabe tired of wearing a full-face one at night? Or had he never worn a mask before?

My brain needed to stop and rest.

We took bowls of a sticky mixture of paper and glue and followed instructions on layering the paste into the molds. The substance was messy and wet. Gabe reached over and poked my cheek, leaving goop behind.

My heart fluttered. I narrowed my eyes at him. I knew he was waiting for me to freak out and wipe it off, so I ignored the itching and left it.

He sighed loudly.

"What?" I asked.

"I'm actually impressed." He moved closer and lingered, hovering a damp rag by my face. I blinked up at him. His eyes, almost black and framed by thick lashes, were inches above mine. His eyebrows were soft.

I froze. My heart did too, before beating again at double speed. He gently wiped the mess off my cheek, and even though no part of his skin touched mine, only the rag, it felt like he was trailing his fingers over every inch of my face.

My insides had turned to papier-mâché, gooey and melting.

When Gabe moved away, out of my personal space, he left a hole.

We put our masks into a machine that dried them quickly, then moved to the worktables to decorate them.

"You have an advantage here," he said.

Really? Because I felt the opposite, like that moment of proximity had left me unbalanced, at an extreme disadvantage compared to him, who appeared unaffected.

"I thought you were taking art," I said.

"I didn't say I was passing it."

"How do you fail art?"

"Okay, fine, I'm not failing. And I'm taking art history."

"Is that how you ended up on this trip?"

"Yeah. There was scholarship money left from a group the school works with, and Mr. O invited me."

"And you had a passport because you like to visit canals?"

"Because we visit family in Mexico."

"Do they have canals there?"

His lips twitched.

The teacher showed us common patterns and explained the symbolism and meaning. Then the family near us descended on the decorations like pigeons on a person offering food. One kid knocked the feathers over. Another grabbed a fistful of rhinestones and immediately started gluing them all over her mask with no plan or pattern.

"You can never have too many rhinestones," Gabe murmured.

"I'm putting that in the yearbook as your senior quote."

"I like that you think I intend to include one."

"I like that you think you have a choice. I'm on the yearbook staff. I'll make sure you don't get left out." That was why I'd joined in the first place, to make everyone feel included.

"If I'd known the full extent of the benefits of your friendship—"

"You would have tried harder to resist it?" I asked.

His mouth tucked in.

We studied the options that the scavengers had left behind.

I held up my blank mask. "I love these. They're so beautiful and unique. We should make masks fashionable again."

"I bet if you started it, the trend would catch on."

Our gazes snagged and held.

I blinked first. "What color should I use? Blue and gold for you. The navy one."

"The brighter blue for you," he said. "And white."

The cobalt blue he grabbed for me was the one I'd been eyeing. I took it, and our fingers brushed, and I twitched and almost dumped paint into his lap.

What was happening? Was this flirting? It felt different from when Bryce and I joked, more loaded. Less like friends and more like . . . something else.

I focused on painting, replicating one of the designs, starting with the base colors, then adding delicate gold swirls.

"How'd you do that?" Gabe asked.

"Want help?"

He slid his mask to me, and though he hadn't specifically said, *Yes, Evie, please help me, I happily accept,* that was what my heart heard.

I added geometric shapes to his.

"Nice. You're good."

"I won't bring your grade down," I said. "Although it sounds like that might not be possible."

He pretended to wipe paint on my nose, and I wrinkled it at him.

A kid shrieked, and a second later, a light coating of something landed on me.

Silver glitter sprinkled over us, though more landed on Gabe than on me.

It looked like stars sparkling in the black of his hair, dusting his face, his gray Henley, the denim jacket on the back of his chair. I barely contained a laugh.

"If you take a picture, Whitmore, we're done."

"Ooh, thanks for the idea." I pretended to reach for my phone.

He gave me a mock glare.

I brushed off my arms, but tiny pieces clung to my skin no matter how hard I rubbed. I glanced at him, reached toward him, then paused. "May I?"

"Yeah."

I ran my hand through his hair, feathering it, trying to brush the glitter out. As I'd suspected, it was soft and silky, and I possibly continued longer than was strictly necessary. "Bend down."

He ducked his head and shook, and I brushed more.

"It's not rhinestones," I said, "but I hope you feel the same way about not being able to have too much glitter, because that's never coming out."

"I had been thinking it was time for a change. I guess this will have to do."

He pointed to my head.

I let him return the favor and run his fingers through my hair. The gentle pressure on my scalp sent tingles dancing from the top of my head all the way to my toes.

His hands moved to my face, and his thumbs brushed my temples, my cheeks. One hand lingered, cupping my face as his thumb swiped carefully below my eye.

We hesitated, eyes locked, not breathing, until he cleared his throat and backed away.

My face burned with the memory of his touch as we tented our clothes in a futile effort to clean off the world's most stubborn substance.

When our masks were dry, if more sparkly than we'd intended, we attached ribbons and put them on.

Gabe faced me, his navy and gold mask hiding his forehead, cheekbones, and nose. I tried to evaluate his eyes, the way his hair looked when squished by a mask. This one was a different color and shape than Angelo's, and his eyes looked different in the bright workshop. He could have been Angelo. But I wasn't sure.

"You look . . . ," he started.

"Be careful how you finish that sentence."

"Cheerful and mischievous," he stated.

"*Mischievous* isn't a word people generally use to describe me."

"Probably because they don't know you well enough."

My heart somersaulted. "And you do?"

"I'm working on it."

The promise in those words, the potential, sent a shiver through my midsection.

Our eye contact broke when the horde of decoration fiends stampeded out in a flurry of voices, leaving chaos behind. Glitter covered the tables and floor, rhinestones twinkled from all corners of the room, and it looked like someone had defeathered a flock of rainbow birds.

The teacher was on his phone, his voice heavy and his shoulders slumped.

"What's he saying?" I asked Gabe.

"Sounds like he's apologizing and telling someone he'll be late."

I removed my mask. "We should help him clean up."

"It's his job," Gabe said.

"Yeah, but being nice is everyone's job." When the man pocketed his phone and grabbed a broom, I approached and reached for it. "May I?"

"No, no, it is not necessary."

"Please, we want to." I eased the broom from him. "Can you tell us more about becoming a master artisan? How did you get started?"

I swept, and Gabe fetched a dustpan and held it for me

without comment, while the man cleaned tables and talked. His face grew more animated and his voice lighter as he shared.

When the room had been restored, he kissed my cheeks. "Thank you. Tonight is my son's birthday, and now I will not be late."

I beamed. "I'm glad we could help."

We went into the main shop. The artisan had informed the class that we got discounts if we bought anything, and he offered to give me a mask. I selected a few extras for my sister and waited to get them wrapped.

"Too bad my sister wants receipts, or I'd claim I spent more," I said.

Gabe studied me, assessing.

"What is it?"

"Do you have allergies?" he asked.

"What does that have to do with anything?"

He waved a hand toward my bag. "The medicine you carry. The Band-Aids and aspirin and allergy meds. You don't use them, do you? You carry them for others."

His words were a giant spotlight, pinning me in place. I recalled him watching when people had asked for help, the times I'd wondered what he was thinking. I hadn't realized he'd paid so much attention.

"Aspirin and Band-Aids are always useful." I could imagine Gabe's reaction if he knew about the spare pens, gum, and extra phone charger I carried at school in case someone needed them.

He was studying me like I was a puzzle that was coming

together before his eyes, and the intensity in his face made me squirm. "I owe you an apology."

I blinked. The statement was so foreign coming from him that he might as well have been speaking Italian. I was at a loss for how to reply, as if he also expected me to respond in Italian. This whole conversation was making my head spin.

"What you did in there." He jerked his head toward the back room. "Seeing what he needed, seeing *him*, listening. Caring enough to act. That was . . . That's a unique gift. I'm sorry I said it was only to make yourself feel better."

Tingles swept through me at him recognizing something that I worked hard at and that was important to me, but I shrugged it off. "Taking care of others makes me happy."

"And you're good at it. But I hope you take care of yourself too."

Too much awareness filled his eyes. I ran my finger over the edge of a mask to avoid meeting them.

"When my dad died, I had to start helping. Look after my sister so Mom could run the business, make our lunches, do chores, keep track of school projects and schedules and stuff."

"That's a lot for a twelve-year-old."

I focused on a nearby gold mask, shifting away from the counter where a clerk was finishing wrapping my purchase. "I didn't mind. My brother was gone more and more, and if he was around, he and my mom were fighting. Someone had to do it."

A shadow crossed his face. "It didn't have to be you." His features softened. "Sorry. It's good that you wanted to help. I hope your mom and sister appreciated it."

Time to shift the topic away from me before he completely laid bare my soul. "What are your siblings like? The older ones?"

He held my gaze before giving in and letting me change the subject. "Active, outgoing. Involved in all kinds of activities. Always rushing from place to place. Most of the time, it was easy for them to forget about me, the one who didn't want to be busy. As soon as I was old enough, I stopped going to their games and performances and competitions, and they stopped asking."

His voice was light, like it didn't bother him, but he always sounded that way, so I wasn't sure if it did or not.

My heart sank for him. "Do you want to be asked?"

"Nah."

I waited.

He sighed. "Fine, maybe I like to be invited so I can say no. Even if I don't want to go, it's nice to be asked. I know that sounds dumb. People can't handle rejection forever."

"If you told them that, it might make them more willing to ask."

He raised an eyebrow.

"Right, sorry, I forgot. That would mean you talking to someone. My mistake." I vowed to invite him to eat with me every day between now and graduation until he gave in and agreed. "It's like . . . you don't necessarily want to be like them, but you want to belong. But you don't really know how to belong to people who are so different."

"Are you psychoanalyzing me now?" He was close, staring down at me.

"Maybe." The word came out as a whisper.

"How do you sound so knowledgeable about this?"

"Everyone in my family has goals, even if my brother's was to get out as fast as possible. Sometimes I'm jealous of my sister, which is silly. I'm three years older. It should be the other way around. But she has this whole plan, this drive. You've met my friends. I'm surrounded by people who know what they want and are going after it, and I . . ." I shrugged.

"Help them with what they want because then you don't have to figure out what you want?"

"Wow, okay, rude and accurate much?" I took the bag of masks from the clerk, and Gabe stopped me with a featherlight touch on my arm.

His eyes were intense and warm. "I just don't want you so focused on everyone else that you miss out on *you*. You work so hard to do what others want, and they never stop to ask what you want, which means you never ask yourself either. That matters, Evie. You matter too."

Chills spread outward from his touch on my arm to every part of my body.

Both of us had been left alone a lot. I had adjusted by making myself useful, while Gabe had chosen to embrace independence and keep away from everyone.

I felt that aloneness more often than I wanted to admit, the one that came from always wondering what everyone else needed and never admitting I might have needs. But being with Gabe made it feel less isolating.

We stepped outside.

"You still have glitter in your hair," he said.

"So do you. Glitter will survive the apocalypse and an ice age. Like cockroaches. It's inevitable."

I shook my shirt and brushed my pants, trying to get more off. Sparkles glinted on Gabe's neck, and I reached for it at the same time as he lifted a hand to my hairline. We paused with our hands on each other, faces inches apart. His gaze dipped to my mouth, and mine followed to his. His soft lips parted slightly. I raised my eyes to his.

He was slow to lower his hand, letting his fingertips trail down my temple, then my jaw.

I rubbed the glitter from his neck, feeling his pulse beneath my hand.

We stepped away at the same time, slowly, like gravity was forcing us together and we had to fight it. When we continued on, our arms bumped, then the backs of our hands brushed. We had to step aside on a small bridge to let people pass, and his hand ghosted across my spine. We were magnets, unable to stay apart.

His attention kept flitting to me, his brow creased.

The sky was the gentle gray of twilight, and golden lights glowed around us. Somehow Gabe had found lights that allowed him to see me. How did he understand more about me than I did? He'd sounded surprisingly nonjudgmental, his voice gentler and kinder than I would have expected when he said he wanted more for me, believed more of me.

How had I misjudged him so completely?

Chapter Twenty-Two

After changing out of the glitter-infested clothes that were going to contaminate my entire suitcase—and make me remember getting up close and personal with Gabe—I found another email from my mom.

Gabe was a bad influence because my first thought was *Why can't you give me one week off?*

I resisted the urge to type that, but after I read yet another request with a short deadline, I hesitated. My mom had other options. She could do it. Her assistant could do it. Even my sister was capable. But because I always agreed, always came through, beat every deadline, of course she kept asking me.

Natasha was ready and waiting for me to go to dinner. I desperately wanted a nap before visiting the club. And I was in freaking Venice.

I channeled Gabe and sent my mom a text that said I was busy with my project and wouldn't have time to get to her request.

My chest felt tight.

Had I really . . . said no? Like I'd ignored Nora's call earlier?

I didn't know if I wanted to laugh and dance out of the room, free and light. Or if I wanted to panic, immediately call my mom and take it back, and skip dinner to do extra work so she wasn't mad and knew I was a hard worker and—

Her response came: *Oh, okay, sure. Good luck with your project.*

How did she mean that? Oh, okay, I'm disappointed in you? Oh, okay, sorry I bothered you? Oh, okay, you will now be disowned as a shame on the family greater than your brother?

"Ready?" Natasha asked.

I stared at the phone, swallowing the lump trying to force its way up into my throat. I typed *thanks* and joined Natasha, telling myself again to channel Gabe and not give this a second thought.

The lobby was crowded, and after Natasha joined some of our classmates, Mr. Owens approached me.

"How's it going this week?" he asked. "I hope Gabriel is contributing."

I felt guilty that he had to ask, like I had betrayed Gabe by ever believing he might not contribute, when he'd probably done more than I had.

"Everything's going well," I said.

"Thank you again for working with him."

"Of course. I'm always happy to help." Help. As if that's what I'd been doing this week, helping a classmate. Lately our time together had felt way more like having fun than working.

"Thanks, Evie. I can always count on you."

If only Mr. Owens knew how I broke the rules each night. My stomach soured, but I tried to smile.

"Are you enjoying Venice?" he asked.

"It's amazing." That was one question I could answer honestly. "I love it here. Coming every year never gets old."

And seeing Valentina? I smothered a smile.

"Have you heard from any of those programs yet?" he asked.

I'd applied to a few art programs he'd recommended. Along with all the others. "Not yet. I'll let you know."

I didn't know if my applications were good enough. Some of the art I'd submitted was decent, but I knew I hadn't put the same passion into the school pieces as I had my fan art. Good thing I had so many other options.

"How did you decide on teaching art?" I asked.

"I always liked creating art, but even more, I liked sharing it with others. Helping them appreciate it, finding the spark inside, learning the value of creativity and expression, especially for students who need an outlet."

There was no career I could imagine talking about like Mr. Owens did teaching, confident it was the right path no matter what.

I had a sudden urge to show him my drawings and my online art, but others were approaching, so I stopped myself. Maybe later.

I smiled as my friends joined me. Mr. Owens greeted everyone before leaving us to eat on our own.

Bryce slung an arm around my shoulders. "We've barely seen you this week."

"I know. I'm sorry." I did feel bad. We'd been talking about this trip for months, and I hadn't spent much time with them.

After ditching everyone at lunch, I couldn't get out of joining my friends tonight. Wait. Why did I want to get out of it? They were my friends.

"Hey, man, you feeling better?" Bryce asked, and I turned to see Gabe entering the lobby.

Right. Because he'd claimed to be sick before spending the afternoon with me.

"Yeah," Gabe said.

"Want to join us?"

"You should come," I said, recalling my vow to make sure he was invited, whether he wanted to be or not.

He met my gaze, then eyed the others. "I should, should I?"

Bryce's arm was still around me, suddenly heavy, and I wanted to shrug it off. Why did I feel guilty? It didn't mean anything.

"What are you going to do? We're not supposed to go off alone." My voice challenged enough to imply that I knew he'd do it anyway.

His eyebrows lifted enough to say, *You think that's going to stop me?*

Fair point, eyebrows. Well argued.

But I wanted him to come. I wasn't inviting him to be nice so he could say no.

"It will be fun," I said.

His eyes softened. "I'll pass."

I tried not to flinch. I should have expected that answer.

He'd admitted an hour ago that he liked to decline invitations. And this wasn't family, but a group of near strangers. But as Gabe lingered in the lobby and I left with my friends, I peeked over my shoulder with a pang of sadness. He was watching me, and I smiled. He nodded in return.

What would he do, eat alone? Without me to pester him with questions? Order in? Or roam the city, trying not to get caught going off by himself?

I wanted to wander off with him. To hear his dry jokes and feel his unhurried calm and discuss anything and everything. Not just this week, but longer than that. Which was foolish to consider. When we got home, I would keep inviting him places, and he would keep saying no. I'd get busy with activities, so we wouldn't be able to spend much time together. Plus, we only had two months of school left. That was hardly a promising foundation for growing a friendship. Or, based on the way my stomach flipped when we made eye contact, a more serious relationship. I shouldn't have been thinking about it. We were too different.

I'd be meeting Angelo soon, and our deadline to remove our masks was approaching. I should focus on the person who had already indicated he was open to a future.

"What should we do tonight?" Natasha's question brought me back.

"Something that involves good food," Dai said.

Time to focus on my friends. "How was your day?" I asked Natasha.

"We ended up visiting Ca' d'Oro after lunch, and Alex had to follow."

The same Alex she claimed to hate and yet had been talking to all morning at the Guggenheim? "Oh yeah?"

She went on about everything he'd said and how annoying he was. Like I believed that.

The distraction was good, though. Wondering about Gabe was pointless. He'd be fine alone, the way he liked it. Except . . . he seemed to enjoy my company now. Or was that wishful thinking?

As we walked along the canal, the evening light perfect for drawing, all I wanted was a return to the afternoon, to stop and take it in, to enjoy the sound of water lapping the banks and the company of someone relaxed and unhurried and contemplative.

"What are you thinking about now?" Natasha's tone said that the question was genuine, not part of our game.

Kissing Gabe. "I just like it here."

"Too crowded and disorganized for me, but I'm glad. Is that glitter in your hair?"

"Long story."

We ended up at a place with tables right along the Grand Canal. Most of our classmates had come, and I managed to position myself so I was next to the water and could watch the twinkling lights and the boats.

"I'm glad this place doesn't have pigeons," Natasha said. "That lunch restaurant was infested. I swear one wanted to nest in my hair." She picked up the menu and nudged me and spoke louder when she said, "This place has lots of seafood options."

I didn't see how that helped, unless she planned to order for everyone and force fish down their throats, but I appreciated the sentiment.

I tried to act normal, chatting about the usual subjects—comparing our days, which I had supposedly spent in the hotel with an ill partner, how the projects were coming (Natasha and Dai had already written thirteen pages), upcoming events at school.

Natasha had heard from Nora that a new prom location had been found, lessening my guilt for ignoring her call.

Gabe was going to rub that in, tell me to say no more often and make other people step up. I had to admit, it was a relief that someone else had handled something for once.

While the topics were ones I liked fine, nothing excited me as much as the city itself or the club. But the pressure weighed on me, to play the role they expected—smile, laugh, give advice, be confident, encourage and help and always be *on*. Never be the one who needed anything. Not reveal that I was having trouble concentrating, my mind fuzzy from tiredness. It felt so much tenser than the afternoon with Gabe.

When the water arrived and no one moved to pour, I took over, thinking once again of Gabe.

"Okay," Sanjay said. "I have an important question. Who likes the Elven Realms?"

My heart plummeted to my toes.

"The books?" Dai asked.

"Yeah. I'm conducting a poll."

I made a strong effort not to look at Natasha. "I know about them," I said. "They seem okay."

"I've heard of them but never read them," she added, in a surprisingly chill tone.

"I read a couple, and I liked them," Bryce said in a confident voice. "But that wasn't me you saw."

Sanjay punched him good-naturedly. "I know, bro, I said it was a girl."

Was that why Bryce felt comfortable admitting it? He didn't say he hadn't sneaked out, just that he hadn't been caught. And since when had he read the books?

"Was it Olive?" Dai asked, probably because Olive wasn't here to defend herself.

Sanjay snorted. "Can you see her sneaking out? That's as likely as Evie."

I laughed with the others. What would I say in this situation if the girl in question weren't me, if I weren't keeping this secret?

"If she didn't talk to you when you saw her, maybe she doesn't want you to know," I said, trying to sound casual.

"But the costume was so cool. Where was she going?"

What would they say if I straight-up confessed? Sure, they said it was cool now, but would it change the way they saw me? Besides, if I admitted to sneaking out in front of most of my class, someone would slip and get me, and possibly Angelo, in trouble.

I might have told Bryce and Dai if we'd been alone, especially after Bryce said he knew the books. They were my friends. They wouldn't stop being my friends because I admitted this, and I could trust them to keep a secret. But with so many others here, the risk was too great.

The food arrived, and the waiter set a plate in front of Dai filled with spaghetti, except it was pitch black.

"What is *that*?" Natasha asked.

"Squid ink pasta," he said.

"Gross, dude," said Tristan. "I hate seafood."

Natasha's head whipped toward him. "All seafood? Not just because Dai's dinner looks like something that would leak from your car?"

The pasta definitely resembled motor oil.

"Nope, never." Tristan shuddered. "Too fishy."

I imagined Natasha making a big red X through Tristan. Our list was getting short.

Bryce dug into his shrimp pasta with normal cream sauce. He liked seafood and the books. He was one of our few remaining options. Maybe I could feel him out without straight-up asking. If he was Angelo, what was I going to do about it? Would it make me interested in pursuing something more with him? Or just deepen our friendship?

My mind jumped to Gabe. I had no good answer.

Maybe it was smarter to stop my investigation before Matt and Sanjay outed me.

For now, I would continue to be the Evie that everyone expected, even if the role didn't fit as comfortably as it had a week ago. Even if the costume and mask I put on at night felt more like me than this did and even if Ana's thoughts about masks letting you be your real self had never felt truer.

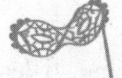

Chapter Twenty-Three

Despite my best efforts to stop her, Natasha was determined to become a spy.

As I was getting ready for the night, she announced that she had a plan and left the room.

Nothing good could come of that.

She hadn't told me what she was doing or where she was going, and I was nervous when I finished and she hadn't returned.

Where are you? I texted.

Are you leaving? Have fun!

That was not an answer.

Everything's fine, was her reply.

People only said everything was fine when everything was not, in fact, fine. But I couldn't do anything about it, so I slipped out.

There was no sign of Natasha in the hall. Was she setting up the stakeout I had told her not to? What if she ruined everything by getting caught or tipping off Angelo?

With a sigh, I tiptoed down the stairs and paused in the stairwell. Everything sounded quiet in the lobby.

I peered out. The cat was prowling. I narrowed my eyes at it.

But it didn't approach me. It leaped onto the freestanding pillar with the bowl of apples. The animal was staring down at something, and I spotted a small flash of movement.

A soft shushing noise came from behind the pillar.

Surely Natasha wasn't hiding in the lobby.

The cat headbutted the bowl, upending it and sending apples scattering.

Matt leaped out from the hiding place.

Apparently Natasha wasn't the only one planning a stakeout. As Matt fumbled his way through the apples, accidentally kicking them and sending them everywhere, I scanned the rest of the lobby from my hiding place. If Matt was here . . .

Yep, shoes peeked out from the curtains where Angelo and I had hidden the first night. I'd bet my mask that it was Sanjay.

I texted Natasha: *911 in the lobby, need backup.*

On my way.

I heard noises that sounded like Matt scrambling to pick up apples while cursing at the cat, and the night clerk asking him what was going on. Sanjay must have remained committed to his hiding place.

When footsteps came from the stairs behind me, I pressed myself against the wall. But it was Natasha—holding a giant armful of fluffy white towels.

I opened my mouth, hesitated, and decided not to ask.

"What's the situation?" she whispered.

"Matt and Sanjay were hiding in the lobby. Matt made a mess, and Sanjay is behind the curtain to the left."

"I'm on it." She marched onward.

"Watch out for the—"

I heard a big crash.

"Apples." I sighed.

I peeked again, to see towels scattered everywhere, along with fruit spread across the floor.

"What are you doing?" Matt asked Natasha.

"They brought us too many towels. What are *you* doing?"

"Bumped the pillar," he said, which was not an answer, and did not account for his stalker activity.

"Let me help." Natasha picked up a few apples, then kicked one toward the curtains. "Oops."

"Ow," came a voice, and the drapes rustled.

Sanjay emerged, pulling the curtain with him. He tugged, and I was afraid the whole thing might come down, but he managed to free himself, tripping over the hem and landing on the floor.

Natasha stood over him with her hands on her hips. "Sanjay?"

"Um. Hi."

She ordered the boys around, directing them to clean up the apples and fold the towels, and I used the distraction to make a run for the breakfast room.

Familiar eyes gleamed at me from under a table.

My feline nemesis.

Although knocking over the apples might have helped me.

It meowed.

Nope, it was still a jerk.

I ignored it and continued on. Outside, I paused on the patio, expecting the door to burst open behind me. The chaos in the lobby hadn't appeared to bother anyone here—the curtains in the windows overlooking the courtyard remained firmly drawn. I savored the quiet and the safety, calming my breathing, before hurrying out the gate.

Angelo was waiting in our usual spot. How had he gotten out without being seen, with all the commotion? Had he left early or climbed out a window?

"Hi," I said.

I felt awkward tonight, not only because I was investigating him. Despite the weirdness of liking someone whose face I hadn't seen, I found his geekiness adorable, I enjoyed spending time with him, and I was more attracted to him than I should have been. But now my thoughts were split between him and Gabe, so I didn't know how to act.

"No one chasing you tonight?" he asked.

"I eluded them like a master." With some help, but he didn't need to know that that was because my best friend was trying to go PI on him.

"Impressive. Shall we?"

As we walked, we chatted about what the main event might be tonight and what we would do if we were in charge of planning.

Inside the club, people were flooding from the tavern up the stairs, so we followed them to the fighting room. Tonight, instead of weapons, an odd variety of items and obstacles had been assembled.

"This must be someone's full-time job," I said.

Maybe I could move here and help at the club until I figured out the rest of my life. Too bad it probably didn't pay.

The group was dividing into two teams, and Angelo and I moved to the right side of the room. A man up front explained the competition—a group challenge with obstacles and puzzles that reminded me of *Survivor*.

This hadn't been on my list of ideas, but I was glad someone was more creative than I was, because it sounded fun.

There were multiple stations, and for each one, each team selected one or more people to complete the task. The challenges mimicked scenes from the books.

Two guys who were obviously many years removed from gym class did a rope climb, like when Luca sneaked into the fort. Three people from each team took slingshots and fired pebbles at cardboard cutouts of dark elven creatures—except one man, whose ammo kept flying backward, into his face. A woman from our team solved a puzzle to get a code, which let her open the lock of a box, which contained a book. Our team huddled close and pretended to be Pietro, solving the ancient riddles.

There was a table with cups of items on one side and buckets on the other, each labeled with the name of a bridge. I nailed that challenge, correctly matching the tolls that went in each bucket, like the objects I carried in my belt pouches.

Then it was Angelo's turn, to crawl under strings like he was sneaking through the Dreaming Forest, then crossing a narrow beam over kiddie pools full of water, like the crew returning to the human realm. He was surprisingly nimble and quick, reminding me of Bryce.

The whole group was cheering for each other, and my abs hurt from laughing so hard.

Our final task was surviving a Nerf gun battle with the other team, protecting one member while he gathered shiny metal balls representing elven artifacts and tossed them into a small tent before zipping it shut, sealing the breach between realms. Angelo and I pushed forward side by side, and the hope of maintaining this relationship felt too good to be true.

As we filtered out of the room, a woman mentioned that she was excited for tomorrow.

"What's tomorrow?" I asked.

"The monthly ball."

"Ooh, I might need another outfit."

She laughed. "There are some for sale."

Armed with that dangerous knowledge, I went to the market, straight to the racks of clothes. One held several gorgeous dresses.

"Did you make these?" I asked the woman sitting nearby.

"I did. I study fashion in Milan and sew these in my spare

time. I come as often as I can to sell them and enjoy time with other fans. I like your outfit. Do you study fashion too?"

"No, I draw. I designed this and had someone make it for me."

"I like the lines of the tails and the pattern."

"And I love this." I pulled out a rich blue gown with a lace-up bodice.

"Would you want to send me ideas sometime?" she asked. "We could work together."

"Maybe."

It might be fun to see more of my costumes come to life, not like I'd ever visit again. But giving a piece of myself to the club and other fans would be cool. We exchanged info, and I held up the dress.

"How much is this?"

The price she stated was beyond my remaining cash. I had my emergency card. Needing to dress appropriately for a ball certainly qualified as an emergency in my book. My mom would disagree, but I'd be home soon and could explain and pay her back.

After a brief hesitation, I said, "I'll take it."

I'd have to figure out how to fit a giant gown in my suitcase. My sister might be getting fewer items than expected.

Clutching a garment bag with my new outfit, I headed down the hall, passing the ballroom. It was empty tonight, but I could picture it full of people, music playing, romantic lighting, like in the first book in Venezari or the second book in Moravion.

I sat just inside the door and did two more drawings, first filling the room with the Venezari elite, then with elves in shimmering outfits.

When I finished, I sat in silence. I didn't have much time left here, and even if I decided to meet Angelo for real and had someone to talk to at home, nothing would fully recapture the wonder of this place.

Chapter Twenty-Four

Getting out of bed each morning was becoming harder and harder. I fumbled through my morning routine, and after two cups of coffee, I still wasn't coherent. Which meant my brain was too slow when Matt and Sanjay entered the breakfast room, animatedly reliving the excitement from the night before.

"Evie! You missed it. Where were you?"

"Um. Sleeping?" I asked brilliantly. "What happened?"

"There was a cat and a huge mess."

"And Natasha hit me with an apple."

"But we didn't see the mystery girl."

"Because you were too busy causing a scene."

"Me? You were the one who spilled the apples."

"I told you, the cat did that."

I supposed it was good for me that they were too busy arguing with each other to detect my lie or to ask more questions. It didn't sound like anyone else had shown up, which didn't let me narrow down the suspect pool further.

"Why is there an apple on the couch?" Bryce asked, picking it up on his way in.

"Dude, you missed it too."

Bryce smiled at me before asking them, "Missed what?"

"Nothing," I said, thinking about Angelo and the mini obstacle course the night before and Bryce's athletic abilities.

Gabe trudged in as breakfast was ending. He looked tired. Because he'd stayed up late?

My chest fluttered at the sight of his familiar denim jacket, his expressive eyebrows, his unhurried pace and relaxed posture. Despite the fun I'd had with Angelo, now, in the light, I was excited to spend the day with him—and share the idea I had.

Once groups left and Gabe and I were alone, I asked, "What did you do last night?"

"Stayed at the hotel, followed all the rules."

"Sounds exactly like you."

"Doesn't it? How was dinner?"

"Nope, you had your chance to go. You missed it, which means you don't get details."

He waited, and I narrowed my eyes. He'd already learned that if he waited, I would talk. Assuming I could remember dinner, prior to the club and Angelo.

"It was fine," I said as he smirked. "Dai ate black pasta that stained his mouth like a zombie. The view was nice. And you would have been proud of me." I recapped how I'd told my mom no and how Nora had handled prom after I ignored her call.

I expected another smirk, but instead, his eyes softened to a rich gentle brown, and the warmth made something simmer inside me.

"Good for you. What's next on Evangeline Whitmore's rebel tour?"

I wrinkled my nose. We had today for our projects, another group tour tomorrow, then one final day to finish writing and submit our reports. This was a bad idea. But we'd made good progress. And after our day together yesterday, I was feeling adventurous.

"I have an idea for today. I think you'll like it. Do you trust me?" I asked like a challenge.

Gabe's eyebrows lifted. "That question is generally a dangerous lead-in."

"It truly is. So do you?"

"You're not giving me any information?"

"If I did, it wouldn't require trust."

"Does it have to do with the project?"

"I'm sure we could find a way to make it apply. But not really. It's for fun."

His eyebrows twitched again, saying he was intrigued. That word, *trust*, hung between us.

"Fine."

The way my heart surged, you would have thought he'd promised he trusted me with his life.

Now, hopefully I could find the place I'd read about. Gabe was the one good at navigating. I checked the map. I'd been searching for unique places and stumbled across this, and it sounded amazing, and I suspected Gabe would be the one to appreciate it. My dad would have too.

We did a bit of meandering, me constantly checking to see if we were heading in the right direction. We had another of those fun detours where your path wasn't going to work unless you went swimming or could jump a long way across a bridgeless canal.

"Is your surprise that you're a terrible navigator?" Gabe asked as we stared at green water that we had no way to cross. "Because I already knew that."

"Shut up."

He smirked.

"My surprise could be pushing you into the canal."

"If I go, I'm taking you with me, Whitmore." He stepped closer and pretended to wrap his arms around my waist, though he didn't touch me. My skin tingled as if he had, as if it wanted him to.

We passed a bookstore, and Gabe veered off to enter. Who could say no to visiting a bookstore?

I followed him inside. The shop was sleek and modern, with books in Italian and also English and French and German. I ran my fingers over the colorful spines of a beautiful set of the Elven Realms series, the titles in Italian, with watercolor covers I'd never seen.

Over the past few years, I'd learned that it was small things that made you remember those you'd lost. The first few times I'd entered a bookstore after Dad died, and the smell of crisp paper hit me, tears had filled my eyes. Now, the stores had lost that extreme emotional punch, and I mostly just imagined him with me and which books he'd select. If he were here, he'd buy the whole set, then insist we learn Italian together so we could read them.

When Gabriel was done browsing, we wandered a little more and found the place I wanted, down a small street with a tree shading the entrance. Tables and racks outside contained hand-drawn posters, vintage postcards, calendars, and prints, and a glimpse into the building promised more books.

"Another bookstore?" he asked.

"Apparently we have similar taste."

His gaze was warm.

"I read that they keep the books in boats and bathtubs to protect them when the city floods."

We roamed the store, through multiple spaces with books stacked wall to wall. There was barely room to move. Books were piled on shelves and tables, some that leaned precariously. There were books in porcelain bathtubs and wooden and metal boats, even filling a gondola. Many were old, with faded leather spines, but some had bright, colorful covers.

It felt like an eccentric person's library or an old hidden-treasure stash.

A faded red-and-white life ring hung from the end of the gondola, boater hats dangled from shelves, and a cat slept on top of one stack of books. I thought of Angelo and peeked at Gabe.

The delicious smell of paper and old books was like a hug from a friend. Was there a better scent in the world?

One door opened directly onto a turquoise canal. FIRE EXIT was painted on a narrow stone wall with an arrow and a stick figure diving into water, which was exactly where the arrow pointed—into the canal.

"Solid plan," Gabe said. "Seems like a good escape from fire."

"And any other uncomfortable situation?"

"Exactly."

I lost track of time as we browsed books in Italian and English and a dozen other languages, books for kids, travel books, and classics, in no apparent order. We showed each other cool ones and pointed out interesting items or art mixed in throughout the shop. Once, I glanced at Gabe to find him watching me, and my insides turned to jelly.

Was I having the same effect on him?

Out one door there was a stairway made of worn, frayed hardbacks next to a stone wall.

"It feels wrong to step on them," I said.

He offered a hand to help me up, and his fingers tightened on mine. He paused at the top, and I stumbled. He pulled me close and caught me. I ended up pressed against him with his arm around my waist. We froze. My heart beat double-time.

My face was against his shoulder, and I was afraid to look at his face.

I cleared my throat and stepped back. "So? Are you glad you trusted me? I found interesting places I wanted to see, and I thought you'd like this one."

"I do like it." His voice was deep.

"Whoa, wait, stop. I need to add this to my short list of things Gabriel Martinez likes."

"What are the others?"

"You said you like Italian food and—"

"The other interesting places you want to see, Whitmore." The spark in his eyes said that he knew that I knew what he'd meant.

"How do you feel about crypts?"

"Surprisingly intrigued. Are you willing to do the same, and trust me?"

"Sure." The answer came easily, and the warmth in his gaze made me glad I hadn't hesitated.

"Great," he said. "My stop first, then we'll see your crypt."

"It's not *my* crypt. I have no intention of being buried there. Unless that was your idea, to dispose of me in a way more creative than drowning."

"Why would I dispose of you? Then I'd have to do the project alone."

"Also, you wouldn't have any friends. Ohhh. Is that why? Is that what happened to the others? They're buried in crypts?"

He rolled his eyes at me. We climbed down the book steps and exited through an alley, its walls lined with more frayed books. Leaving them exposed to the elements seemed equally wrong, but they did make a unique scene. Like art.

Gabe didn't need a phone to navigate, and soon the familiar Saint Mark's Square spread before us. He veered off again, this time into a gelato shop.

"This was your big idea?" I asked.

"Gelato is always a good idea. But no. This is a bonus."

We got cones and moved into the square, lingering when we heard classical music. Next to outdoor tables at a restaurant, a band was playing, complete with a shiny piano, a violin, and woodwinds. As we listened, a few older couples began to dance in the square.

I soaked in the rich music, the taste of chocolate on my tongue, and the palpable sense of joy from the crowd. Gabe wore the same faint smile I suspected graced my face. There was nowhere else I would rather have been.

And no one else I would rather have been with.

Gelato finished, Gabe aimed for the bell tower, its orange-red brick, pale green spire, and golden statue spearing the sunny sky.

"I suppose I should have asked how you feel about stairs," he said.

I stared up at the tower. I wanted to support his idea, but that was a long climb. . . .

"Actually," he said with a smirk, "there's an elevator. So I should have asked how you feel about heights. But I thought you'd like the view."

"Sounds awesome." I was already imagining what the city would look like from above.

After we waited in line, there was indeed an elevator, which they packed full of people, forcing us to press together. Whether I had claustrophobia would have been another good question to ask, but I was fine, although right next to Gabe. His arm came up to block me from strangers, but it felt like he was hugging me. His fingers lingered on my side, and his breath feathered my hair.

He was the right height for Angelo, but surely that was impossible. Right?

"You have glitter," he murmured, making the word *glitter* sound seductive. "Right there." He brushed one finger behind my ear, and my skin caught on fire.

"I told you it was never coming off." My voice was husky.

"Can I tell you a secret? I found something else I like. The thought of you sparkling."

My stomach dove into a canal and sank straight to the bottom.

As we ascended, Gabe grew tenser, his breathing loud in my ear. When the car stopped and people exited, he exhaled hard.

I twisted to see his face. "Are you claustrophobic?"

"No. I just don't love tight spaces."

I gave him a look. "That's literally the definition."

He rubbed the back of his neck. "I'm not afraid. I find tight places . . . unpleasant, that's all. We made it, didn't we? I never let fear stop me."

"I should have guessed."

"Guessed what?"

"Small spaces, uncomfortable conversations, classes, group meals. You don't want to be trapped anywhere you can't run away from. Anywhere you can't do your own thing."

"It's called liking independence, Whitmore. I didn't hear you complaining when we ditched lunch yesterday."

The elevator was now empty except for us, which meant we were standing closer than necessary, pressed together, our faces inches apart. The idea crossed my mind to stay here, turn fully into Gabe, and kiss him, but that was ridiculous.

My face hot, I got off.

Chapter Twenty-Five

The top of the bell tower had an enclosed area to walk around, with arched openings covered in metal grids that allowed a cool breeze to waft through. Large metal bells hung overhead, and views spread in every direction—the square, the basilica, all the way across the Grand Canal. From high above, the buildings and multiple other towers throughout the city resembled children's blocks.

Boats dotted the turquoise lagoon. The orange tile roofs were so close together that it was impossible to pick out streets. The colors were incredible. It reminded me of the scene in *Bay of Phantoms* when Ana climbed the tower to watch for her new elven allies, hoping their fleet would arrive before it was too late.

I thought of Angelo, and the odds that he was Gabe, and whether I should say something.

Gabe stood beside me, his shoulder almost touching mine but not quite, and I didn't have the courage to shift an inch toward him—or to speak.

"I like getting a sense of the city," he said. "Seeing it from above gives you perspective."

"Do you do that at home?"

"My favorite spots are Griffith Park and the Getty Museum."

"I love the Getty. I could spend hours there. I haven't been since freshman-year art class, though. There never seems to be time to go for fun."

He angled his head. "Do you want to draw the view?"

"Really?"

"Haven't you learned by now?"

"Right. You're never in a rush."

"Especially if you're taking me to the crypts next. And I have to ride the elevator again."

"We do have to return to the elevator. Sorry. I don't think they'll let us rappel down. But we don't have to go to the crypts."

"I was kidding, Evie. Evangeline. We're going."

The sound of my name, combined with the piercing look, sent goose bumps skittering across every inch of my skin.

The crowds offered limited space to draw, so I wedged myself into a corner of one window. Music and the crying of seagulls drifted on the breeze.

I sketched, staring out and imagining the fictional city. It wasn't hard, since other than the motorized boats, little had changed here in hundreds of years.

Gabe studied the view while I stowed my sketchbook.

"Why haven't you asked about my drawings?" I asked.

"If you wanted to tell me, I have no doubt I would already have heard more than I wanted to."

"Now I want to tell you everything to see if it annoys you."

His lips tucked in.

We studied each other. I . . . did want to tell him. Not the Elven Realms part, or the club, but partial truth?

"I kind of have my own project I'm working on this week," I said. "Drawings."

"Not for class?"

"No. For fun, but also for a purpose."

"Cool."

"You're . . ."

"What?"

"I don't know. Not going to pry? Or worry about it affecting our official project?"

"One, have you met me? Two, have you met me?"

I laughed. "You don't mind? Waiting?"

"Nope. But can I ask a question?"

"I would love it if you did."

His mouth curved. "You said you didn't know what to do with your life. Are you thinking about studying art? Not that it can't be a hobby."

His wording reminded me of Angelo asking something similar before the meaning of his question hit.

I froze. "I take it back. I don't love it."

He waited.

I stared at the light sparkling on the water, trying to recall how I'd answered Angelo and whether I wanted to risk giving Gabe a similar reply, in case they were the same person. "I like it as a hobby. I worry if it was a job, that might take the joy out of it."

"Or, it would let you regularly *do* the thing that gives you joy."

"Maybe. I don't know. Graphic design is one career I'm considering. One of many. I have no idea what to do."

"Do you have to know now?"

"Everyone does."

He snorted. "No, they don't. Everyone says they do, but how many people change majors or take jobs unrelated to their major or change jobs multiple times? There's nothing wrong with that. Try things, and if they don't work out, try something else. It's like with Venice. There isn't always a direct path. Sometimes you get lost, but then you find interesting stuff you weren't looking for."

When I didn't answer right away, he asked, "What are the options so far?"

"My mom thinks graphic design or marketing would be good choices. Natasha says politics or community service, and Mr. Owens encourages me to keep studying art and believes I'd be a good teacher. The guidance counselor said I should consider counseling."

Gabe made the slightest hum but didn't speak. I no longer needed a translator to tell me what his eyebrows were saying— slightly up in the middle meant he had something he wanted to say and it was taking all his self-control not to say it.

"Go ahead, spit it out," I said.

"Are you sure?"

I wasn't entirely sure, but maybe he had helpful insights. "Yeah. Hit me."

"Did it occur to you that you mentioned four people and every single one thinks their career would be perfect for you?"

Now that he said it, it sounded so obvious. But I didn't know what it meant. "So, they like their jobs and believe everyone else would too."

He barked a laugh. "I guarantee the guidance counselor would not recommend I pursue her profession. And I doubt anyone would suggest putting me in charge of a roomful of children."

"You don't think I'd be good at those things?"

"You would be good at any of them," he said confidently, making my insides warm. "But what do *you* want to do? Does one of them excite you?"

The possibilities I'd mentioned made me feel the same as always—nothing. "What do you want to do?" I asked instead.

"I don't know either." He studied the view. "I like museums. Art. Libraries. It started when I went to LACMA and got lost, and it turned into going all over Los Angeles in my free time."

"Your parents are okay with that?"

"They didn't neglect me, but since everyone else was so busy and I didn't ask for anything, they let me do what I wanted. When I was younger, I'd go to the nearest library. I liked the organization, the quiet, the idea of all that knowledge in one place."

He sounded okay with it, but was he really? His words about being the person who never asked for anything struck a chord. But I was also that person always rushing around. This week had forced me to slow down and appreciate life more—and that had allowed me to see him.

"And you'd learn random languages," I said.

"And personal finance and how to make kombucha at home—don't, it's disgusting—and LEGO night and helping old people learn how to use their cell phones."

"I definitely won't tell anyone that."

His attention remained locked on my face. "Other people's opinions don't bother me."

"They don't, do they? How do you manage that?"

"Have you met people? Do you know how many dumb opinions they have?"

"Not everyone has dumb opinions."

"True. The key is finding those few who matter and not listening to the rest." He was the first to break eye contact. "I also learned the free days at LA museums, and the bus routes to get there. Museums are like libraries, the peace and the idea of so much stuff in one spot, the peek into other cultures or ways of thinking, whether it's art or history or science. Always something new to discover. I made the mistake of admitting I liked art museums in Mr. Owens's class, and"—he spread his arms—"that was that."

"Mistake, huh? Still wish you weren't here?"

"I'm regretting it less."

As our gazes held again and time slowed and the cool breeze

ruffled our hair, a smile formed on my face. I gave his arm a gentle poke. "You're a secret nerd."

He lifted a shoulder, unconcerned. "I don't love school, but I do like learning. I think I want to work in a library or a museum one day. I'm waiting to hear from several schools, to see if I get accepted or get scholarship offers. I don't have a dream college. I figure I'll make the best choice from the options that work out."

That was so relaxed and chill and like him and unlike me that I wasn't sure if I wanted to smile or panic. "The job fair could help you."

His quirked mouth said it would be a major accomplishment if I could get him to attend. Then a slight crease wrinkled his forehead. "How do you do that?"

"Do what?"

"Make me laugh. Make me talk. Share things I never talk about with anyone."

Light shimmered in my chest, tenuous and delicate. "I'm very persistent."

He shook his head. "It's more than that. It's like you want to see me. To make me feel safe." He huffed and looked away as if he'd admitted more than he'd meant to. "I shouldn't be surprised. You do it with everyone. I just didn't expect it to work on me. Anything else you want to draw here?"

His admission had left heat bubbling inside me. "No, we should get the elevator trip over with."

"Or you could get me a rope and I could try rappelling."

My insides were jumbled as I thought about what we'd

shared. The things we had in common, like an appreciation for art. The way we both understood the peculiar way a person could feel lonely, separate, even when surrounded by friends or family. But there were also the ways we were incredibly different, like how we dealt with people. Were the differences too great?

I was starting to think they weren't. And based on the admiration in his eyes and the way they occasionally dipped to my lips, maybe a future wasn't as hopeless as it seemed.

On the elevator ride down, I informed Gabe that I would now be sharing all my dumb opinions with him and maintained a running commentary about movies for the whole ride, which made his brows relax and his gaze turn molten, like he knew I was trying to distract him from the small space.

At the bottom, I asked, "Lunch first? Are you hungry? What do you want?"

"What do *you* want?"

"Whatever sounds good to you."

He stopped, forcing me to as well. "Nope, not letting you get away with that. What do you like?"

"Anything's fine."

He waited.

I huffed. "I really do like anything."

"Good. Then you're picking today."

What if I picked something bad or that he didn't like or that—

"Stop worrying about me," he said.

I fake glared at him, and he gazed back, unaffected.

"Fine. I'll see what I can find." We started walking again. "You could explore this city for weeks and never see everything. There's always something new to discover."

"Too bad we don't have longer," he said. "I enjoy learning everything about the subjects that interest me."

The way he was watching me, the memory of the questions he'd been asking to understand me, made me shiver. Did he only mean the city? Being the object of his attention and focus was terrifying and thrilling, like rappelling down that tower would have been.

I selected a to-go counter with baguette sandwiches filled with salty meat and juicy tomatoes, and we took them with us as we walked. I should have been thinking about our project, but instead I enjoyed the moment. And the amazing sandwich.

I groaned. "Why is the food here so good?"

Gabe smiled, the genuine one that made his eyes sparkle and his face change and froze me in place. "No more calls from the incompetent party planners?"

"The what? Oh, prom. Aw, I didn't know you cared. No, nothing else. And they aren't incompetent."

He raised an eyebrow.

"Maybe mildly incompetent." I blinked. "I didn't say that."

He snorted. "I don't care. I was just willing to be mean to people if you needed it."

"I didn't realize you needed an excuse. Are you going to prom?"

"I've been looking forward to it for months."

I rolled my eyes at the sarcasm. I didn't know why I cared. I wasn't surprised. It wasn't like I'd thought he'd ask me.

Okay, fine, the idea had crossed my mind.

"I'm not committing until I know whether it's in a murder barn," he said.

"It won't be in a murder barn."

"Then I'm definitely not going."

I laughed. "Would you go to prom if your little sister asked you to be her date?"

"I'm not taking *her* to a murder barn."

I waited, watching.

He huffed. "Low blow, Whitmore."

"I knew it. There is a heart in there." I poked his chest. "You'd do anything for the people you care about."

"That's the trick, isn't it? Finding people I care about." His eyebrows held a challenge.

"Your sister." I held up one finger to count off. "Do friends make the list?"

He didn't answer right away. His gaze made a leisurely circuit of my face, the unhurried way he always moved.

"They might," he said, making the air between us suddenly thicker, or thinner, or whichever it was that sucked every ounce of oxygen from my lungs.

Chapter Twenty-Six

We eventually made our way to the church with the crypts. We toured the church first, from its imposing white facade to its ornate interior, with pews and grand columns. Tall Gothic windows let light in, and paintings covered nearly every inch of the walls.

"There you go. Project," Gabe said. "That's a Bellini. Now we can enjoy the crypts guilt-free."

"Are crypts something to enjoy?"

"Yes, those, and abandoned doll factories and ghost towns and cemeteries at night. This was your idea."

"I don't want to force you into a small space."

"It's fine."

"I won't let them lock us in."

He walked backward so he could look at me. "Why would that even be a thing?"

"It's probably not. But just in case."

"Thanks for watching out for me."

"What are friends for?"

"Something I constantly ask myself."

I shoved him, and he grabbed my hand and kept hold of it as we entered a side room with stairs leading belowground.

The crypts were flooded, so we had to stay on the brick walkway inches above the shallow water. The water was so calm that the reflections of arches, columns, and a monument looked real enough to touch. It was still and quiet, the damp air thick with a musty smell.

It wasn't fun, exactly, but it was kind of cool. Creepy and beautiful and haunting.

I liked the way the reflections were so perfect, like there was a whole other crypt beneath us. A parallel dimension, like the elven realms.

What would my friends say about this? Natasha would find it morbid. Dai would try to wake the dead or explore the corridors at the back, despite the fact that that would mean wading through dead-person water.

Gabe just soaked it in, holding my hand.

I shivered. Not from fear or cold. Just the atmosphere. I pressed closer, the contact spreading warmth from my hand to the rest of my body. Gabe felt like the one real, living thing here.

Talking seemed disrespectful, so we waited until we were outside again. The late-afternoon sunlight was bright and harsh after being underground.

Gabe still hadn't released my hand.

If I acted casual and pretended it wasn't happening, would he keep holding it?

"There's a unique beauty in creepy places, isn't there?" I asked.

"I like how you'd never suspect that was down there. Hidden."

I shivered again, and his fingers tightened in mine.

"You weren't afraid, were you?" he asked.

If he wasn't going to bring up the hand-holding, I sure wasn't. "No. I mean, I've never been to a cemetery at night, but I don't think I'm afraid of places. And I don't believe in ghosts."

"I'll take you to the cemetery next time I go. What are you—no, never mind. I don't have to ask."

"What do you mean?"

"What you're afraid of. I don't need to ask."

My stomach tightened. "Oh? Enlighten me."

"People being mad at you. Someone not liking you. Disappointing someone."

I tried to laugh to hide the fact that he'd nailed me, then slid my hand free and wrapped my arms around my stomach. "Those sound worse than an abandoned doll factory. Why would you mention such terrifying topics?"

His face was serious. "Don't be afraid of things you can't control, Evie." His use of my nickname sounded gentle, like he'd selected it for that reason.

I shuddered. "I can control them."

"Really?"

"I made you like me, didn't I?"

"Great, now I feel like an enabler." His eyes sparked with humor before he sobered. "But seriously. You can't control others' expectations, emotions, reactions."

"Isn't that the definition of fear? Concern about something you can't control? Like snakes or spiders or heights. Things that could threaten you."

"People's opinions won't kill you."

"They can make life extremely uncomfortable. Besides, I don't like letting people down."

"Why not?" His expression contained no judgment, no mockery, only intense curiosity.

Tightness gripped my throat. "If I stop doing those things, they might think I don't care. They might stop loving me." My voice came out small.

His eyes darkened, but his tone was caring. "People should love you for *you*, not for what you do for them."

"That's how I show love, show I care." I clasped my hands together, tight.

"Which is great. Others see that in you. But that can't be all it's based on. Love isn't something to be earned, Evie."

My insides were twisting into knots like my fingers. "But if I stop . . ."

"The people who matter will still love you, and if they don't, they aren't worth your time in the first place." His voice was kind but firm.

A full-blown hurricane was raging in my chest, sweeping me away as if his words had demolished the foundation I'd relied on for years. I was flailing, uncertain where to land, or if land even existed at all.

Gabe reached out and gently pried my hands apart, grasping them softly like he didn't want to break me. As if he hadn't already. He waited until I met his gaze, confirming I'd heard him, then squeezed my hands and let go. "Think about it, okay?"

I wouldn't be able to stop thinking about it. I studied his face. For someone who hated people, he was surprisingly insightful while imploding my entire worldview with a few short sentences.

"Since we're giving unsolicited advice . . ." I hesitated, and he waited, eyebrows slightly raised, amused and expectant like he was curious what I'd say. "You might find people you could care about if you give them a chance, rather than assuming the worst before you know them."

Shadows flickered in his eyes. "I did that once this week. That's my limit."

My stomach gave a jolt. He meant me, right? Asking seemed prideful. But the unwavering look in his eyes said my assumption was good.

"Maybe try to learn from that, then." My voice sounded breathy. "If I'm afraid of disappointing people, you're the opposite, afraid *they'll* disappoint *you,* so you avoid all of them. Just because people are different from you doesn't mean they aren't genuine. Not everyone will let you down. Don't run before you've given them a chance."

The shadows darkened and faded, and he angled his head. "Fair."

We were staring at each other, and we'd moved closer. Though we weren't touching, it felt like we were, like every nerve in my body was alert and tuned in.

A buzzing phone startled us apart. Not mine for once.

His focus lingered on me before he pulled out his phone.

"Soph?" he said. "Whoa, slow down. Breathe. What's wrong? Start over."

He took a single step back, remaining close.

His brow wrinkled. "I don't know. They might've meant it. Or . . . Yeah, I guess. I really don't know."

He looked helpless, sounded lost and slightly broken over the fact that he didn't know what to say to whatever it was his sister had told him.

I didn't know what was going on, but I could tell Gabe wasn't equipped to handle it.

I held out my hand. He blinked at me, so I raised my eyebrows and wiggled my fingers. When he lowered the phone to my waiting hand, I felt oddly gratified.

I raised the phone to my ear. "Hi, Soph, this is Gabe's friend. My name's Evie."

He twitched but didn't move to reclaim his phone.

"You answered the other day," she said, sniffling.

"That's right. Gabe and I are working together this week."

"I'm glad he made a friend. He's terrible at that."

I smothered a laugh. "I'm glad too. Sounds like you're having trouble with something. Can I help? Sometimes you need another girl to listen."

"I got invited to a party."

"Is that bad?"

"I don't know. What if they didn't mean it?" My heart clenched at her small voice.

Ah. She meant, what if they invited her so they could mock her, or it was a setup or a trick. Gabe had said she wasn't the best at social cues and that the last time people had been nice to her, the situation hadn't ended well.

"No wonder Gabe couldn't help. Does he even know what a party is?"

She laughed quietly, and he quirked an eyebrow at me. I returned the gesture.

"Did they tell you to bring alcohol or dress in costume or bring your flute to play?"

"No. Why, should I do those?" she asked.

"Definitely not. If they had, it might have been a trick. The fact that they didn't is a good sign. Is the party in a safe location?"

"Someone's house."

"Can you find anyone who wasn't in the group that invited you who might be going too?"

"Maybe a girl in my math class . . ."

"Good. Try to find the person who's hosting on social media, see if there are pictures from past parties so you know what to expect. Be careful not to accidentally like something."

Her laugh was stronger this time.

"When is the party? Will Gabe be back?"

"No, it's this weekend."

"Hmm, okay. Can one of your other siblings take you? Help you check it out before you go inside?"

"Yeah, maybe."

"Here's what you're going to do. Wear something casual,

jeans and a cute shirt. Don't arrive at the time they gave you—wait half an hour, then watch people go in before you do, make sure you recognize them. Don't drink anything you haven't opened yourself, and don't leave your drink anywhere. Make sure a family member can come get you, and text them if you feel uncomfortable. Once you're inside, find one person who's standing alone and say hi, then ask them what they like, what shows they're watching, what their favorite hobby is, get them talking and listen."

"Wow. Wait, I'm writing this down."

I smiled.

"I probably shouldn't sing, right?"

"You go to a music school, don't you?"

"Yeah."

"Don't start the singing, and if spontaneous singing occurs, it's probably safer not to join in. Or if you do, watch the leaders and stop as soon as they do."

"I can do that. You're good at this."

Good at knowing how to fit in, how to be exactly what people expected? Yeah, Gabe had made that point abundantly clear. "When I get home, I could come over and we could hang out and I can give you more tips."

"That sounds fun. How did Gabe make a friend as nice as you?"

"I'm very persistent," I said, and Gabe rolled his eyes at my repeating the phrase. "I'm giving the phone back to your brother. Can't wait to meet you."

My fingers brushed Gabe's as I handed him the phone.

Whatever Sophia said softened Gabe's face. He maintained eye contact with me as he listened.

"I'm glad she could help. . . . Yeah, she's all right. . . . Fine, yes, I do like her, she's my friend. . . . Yes, I'll make sure she comes over. . . . I'm not answering that."

I cocked my head, and he smirked.

"Gotta go. Yeah, yeah, love you too." He lowered the phone.

"What didn't you want to answer, *Gabriel*?" I asked.

An eyebrow rose. "Wouldn't you like to know."

Desperately, especially since they'd been talking about me.

His face sobered. "Thank you. For doing that. Even if I wish you'd told her to stay home."

"She needed help that you were clearly incapable of giving. And that help isn't telling her to avoid all social situations forever." I nudged his arm. "She seems cool. I'm going to bug you until you introduce us for real."

"I don't doubt that. If I tried to avoid you, you'd hunt me down."

"I would," I said. Then added, "Thank *you*. For trusting me with her."

His head bobbed. Like he recognized that I understood the weight of that trust and he appreciated it.

I narrowed my eyes playfully. "See, what did I tell you? Sometimes letting people help works out."

"Or you're just unusually good at connecting with people, and most are still the worst."

I rolled my eyes.

"Seriously, though. I appreciate it." His forehead wrinkled.

"It's weird not to be at school with her. I don't know her life like I used to. I can't help worrying, but I don't know how to help. I want to take her back to when she was little and happy and ran around singing without a care."

This time, I took his hand. "She's lucky to have you. I wish my brother cared a fraction of how much you do."

"If your brother doesn't see how amazing you are, that's his fault. Your friends and family are lucky to have you."

"That includes you now. Friend."

"Lucky me, then." His deep voice and burning gaze implied *friend* might not have been the word he was thinking of.

Something warm and electric stretched taut between us.

Could we ever work? We were teamed up here for the project with no choice. He was a loner, uninterested in the social stuff that I loved. He wasn't going to attend baseball games or prom or senior-year parties with me.

But we could visit museums and take a class together at the library and—

Was I being naive? Thinking he'd want to keep hanging out, after barely tolerating my attempts at friendship? Thinking a week in Venice might make me the exception to his anti-people policies?

It was safer not to let myself consider a future, but I was imagining one anyway.

Chapter Twenty-Seven

We'd been roaming slowly, and when we came to a bridge, a man popped up in front of us. His black-and-white-striped shirt, black pants, and boater hat with a red ribbon fit the image in my head of a classic Venetian gondolier. He pointed to a small boat and asked if we wanted a ride.

Riding in a gondola felt like something that had to be done here. It also felt like something romantic to do with a date.

The idea that maybe I wanted this to be one terrified me.

Gabe was watching me with his usual steady expression, the one where his eyebrows had lifted enough to say he wasn't annoyed or mad or uncomfortable. They were . . . expectant. Waiting. For me to decide.

"We should, right?" I hoped my voice didn't reveal that my heart was thumping. "We can't visit Venice without riding in a gondola. And you love canals. I'd hate to deny you the opportunity to get up close."

His lips twitched. "No jumping in, though. I promise."

The man helped us into the boat, which was shiny and

black. It sat right above the water and had one low seat. The gondolier stood behind us as we settled into it, and it forced Gabe and me to nestle close, like in the elevator.

The sky was fire and magenta, the water liquid silver. On one side of the canal, the buildings were illuminated and the stone glowed. The smooth water was so close I could reach out and touch it. We passed under low bridges that forced the gondolier to duck and made the air cooler. Many other boats were out too. Some gondoliers were singing, but mostly it was quiet, peaceful. The man's paddle made the slightest ripples as he dipped it in and out, and we rocked occasionally when larger boats passed and their wake disturbed the water.

Gabe and I were silent as the boat wound through side canals. The sky darkened, and the church dome and tower were outlined against the rose-and-blue sky.

I shivered.

"Cold?" Gabe shifted. Our elbows brushed. He twisted to partially face me. Studied my face. Lifted his arm in invitation.

Suddenly I wasn't cold at all. That liquid silver was in my veins, oozing through me with steady warmth.

I swallowed hard, nodded, not at the question of whether I was cold but at the invitation. I shifted toward him as his arm settled around me and pulled me against him. Heat seeped into my side, so the half pressed to him was no longer chilled. His hand came to rest on my upper arm. I held my breath for several seconds as the boat glided on. Gabe was relaxed. I tried to exhale the tension from my shoulders and sink deeper into the seat—and him. His thumb made lazy circles against my arm, like he didn't realize he was doing it.

The glittering reflections and glowing sunset had moved inside me. The gentle rocking of the boat kept me nestled against Gabe.

"It's magic," I murmured.

"Everyday magic." His voice was soft. Reverent.

My breath caught. Was he thinking of the Elven Realms? It was one of my absolute favorite quotes. Or was it a coincidence that he'd used the same phrase as Bastian?

"Don't grow so eager for elven magic that you lose sight of the everyday magic."

"Everyday magic?" Ana asked.

"The way a plant drinks sunlight and converts it into a flower. The way wood and strings make vibrations in the air that touch your deepest emotions. The way the scent of familiar perfume transports you through time to the last hug you received from your mother. Simple things that most people fail to appreciate. Everyday magic."

"What . . . what do you mean?" I asked Gabe.

He shifted slightly. "You know, not like real magic. But still amazing."

I swallowed hard. That didn't tell me much.

"I don't know," I said. "This feels beyond everyday. More."

Gabe hummed softly. "Maybe so."

We were facing forward, watching the water slip by and the buildings drift past. Longing hit me to face him, to press my lips to his. To have his arms come around me fully and tug me closer, for his thumb to trace those soft circles on my face.

My heart beat out a rhythm as it attempted to escape my chest. Did I turn? Did I remain motionless? Would he want that?

"You're awfully quiet," he said.

"I thought you liked silence."

"Coming from you, it feels sad."

His words were warm honey in my veins.

"And maybe," he said, "I don't hate talking when it's with you."

Before I could process the meaning of that, he shifted me toward him.

"What are you thinking?" he asked. "For real. Not like the game you play, about which superhero is best."

"Superman, obviously."

His arm tightened, a teasing warning.

I lifted my eyes to his. They were dark pools, his brow the softest I'd ever seen it. His throat bobbed with a swallow.

"I'm thinking . . ."

The problem was, I wasn't. Zero coherent thoughts resided in my brain. Words had thrown themselves overboard and dog-paddled away.

Our heads angled so slowly, inching closer. My lips parted.

Gabe's hand pressed against my shoulder, drawing me toward him, and mine reached out to lay flat against his chest. His heart thudded under my palm.

A wisp of his breath teased my lips.

The boat rocked, and my head knocked Gabe's. Pain shot through my forehead.

We jumped apart, rubbing our heads. He huffed what might have been a laugh.

We settled into our seats, arms touching, but nothing else.

My pulse raced, and my forehead throbbed. I was disappointed, but I was afraid to find out whether he felt the same or was relieved that the canal had conspired against us.

After we docked, Gabe offered a hand to help me climb onto the dock. He didn't release it as we moved away. In fact, he readjusted to slide his fingers through mine. I glanced at him. He was studying the area, concentration written on his face. When he moved, it was deliberately, along the waterfront, down a quiet street, then another. I didn't ask. Just clutched his hand and stayed beside him, not wanting this evening to end.

He let out a soft hum of approval. Ahead was a dark area, with golden lights pooling in the water. I let him take me onto the bridge, stone with an ornate railing.

He stopped in the middle and tugged me to face him.

I stared up. He stood so close, I had to crane my neck to meet his gaze.

"Gabe?"

"Evangeline." His voice was barely more than a vibration.

My stomach was plunging into the depths below as my heart soared.

"I believe we were in the middle of something."

He stepped closer so our thighs brushed. One hand cupped my face. His head dipped. Paused. My arms slid around him, my palms spreading across his spine.

Our lips met, and those twinkling lights exploded behind my closed eyes. It was comfort and thrill, warmth and sparkles.

His kiss was deliberate, with the same easy confidence he exhibited in everything. Not in a rush, but not lost. Intentional, to enjoy the moment and be fully present.

I didn't know how many ages passed while we kissed, but when we broke apart, I was breathless. I'd been breathing him in for so long that my lungs had forgotten real oxygen and needed time to adjust.

He cleared his throat. "You were right." His voice was hoarse. "Beyond everyday magic."

"Way beyond," I managed.

He kissed me again, briefly, then took my hand. We kept moving, unhurried.

Soon I stopped, forcing him to halt with me. "Sorry. I have to talk about that."

"Surprised you waited this long." His mouth tucked in.

I shoved him lightly. "So you want to talk too?"

"I just knew you would." He blocked my view of anything else, and his hands cupped my face. "You want to know what this means, and what happens next, and if you were good at it, because you like to succeed."

"Wait, was I not good?" I hadn't kissed a ton of guys, but so far, I'd had no complaints.

His eyes smiled. "It was the best kiss I've ever had."

"Please tell me it wasn't the only one. Wait, no, don't tell me." I didn't want to picture him kissing anyone else.

He trailed a finger down my face. "I like you far more than I thought was possible."

"That's a big change from not liking me at all."

"Sometimes I surprise myself. You surprised me too."

I reached up tentatively and rested my palm against his cheek. His head tilted toward it, and I shivered.

"So . . . where do we go from here?" I asked. "I like you too. I know we're very different, and our lives are very different, and I understand if—"

"Shh." He placed a single finger on my lips. "I could say the same to you. Why don't we sleep on it."

"You think I don't know what I want?"

"What do you want, Evangeline?"

"To spend time with you. All the time. Constantly. To hear your thoughts and your jokes and"—I smoothed my fingertips across his eyebrows—"see you frown and smile, even if the smile needs some practice. You could wake up tomorrow and decide I'm too much, I talk too much and I care too much about what people think. Or that I'm not enough, that you want someone more independent or who can help you—"

"Hey. You don't have to help me with anything. That's not how it works. I don't like you because of what you can do for me."

My heart was doing a good job attempting to escape my chest.

He took my hand, and we resumed walking.

"So we both sleep on it," I said, "and if I want to kiss you again tomorrow . . ."

His lips quirked. "I'll consider it."

We paused around the corner from the hotel. Gabe backed me against the stone wall, bent his head, and kissed me again. Like the first one, it was both leisurely and intentional.

I clenched his shirt in my hands. "We haven't slept on it," I murmured.

"It's not tomorrow yet, Whitmore."

I tugged his shirt to bring his lips to mine again.

We entered the lobby to find half of our class hanging out. Were we being open about this? Should I reach for his hand? Show him I wasn't embarrassed to be seen with him?

Before I could decide, he gave me a tiny smile and a salute and went upstairs. I was kind of relieved. I didn't know if I wanted to share him yet. Not because I was afraid to admit I liked him, but because talking about the magic might make it vanish.

Chapter Twenty-Eight

Natasha was in the room when I arrived. Most of my brain remained outside, reliving those kisses. Lost in the beauty of a Venice night and the way my entire body tingled at the memory of Gabe.

"You are alive," Natasha said.

I blinked and tried to focus on her. "Of course I am."

"I didn't see you all day."

Guilt wormed through me. "We had lots to do."

Like flirting and holding hands and kissing and romantic gondola rides. I didn't want to tell her about it, though. It was too new, too uncertain.

"How was your day?" I asked.

Her face went pink.

"Natasha Gutierrez, what does that look mean?" I sat on my bed and faced her.

"Nothing. I had to sit next to Alex at dinner. I was saving you a seat, but you never came, and he took it."

I raised an eyebrow. "Doesn't sound like you hated it."

"Whatever. Are you wearing the new dress tonight? We're running out of time to find your mystery guy."

Angelo. I'd forgotten about him completely for the last several hours. I had three nights to decide if I wanted to meet without masks, except now I wasn't sure how I felt about that. Should I say something to him about Gabe and end whatever undefined thing lay between us? But then, Gabe and I hadn't defined things either. He'd left our situation vague, made no promises. I didn't know if he wanted a relationship or just kissing or just kissing in Venice.

Why hadn't I pressed him? Too late now.

I took my new dress from the wardrobe. It had totally been worth risking using my emergency card. The outfit was a replica of Ana's gown from *Bay of Phantoms*, when she made her return to Venezari society after escaping the elven realms. The deep blue fabric shimmered. I would have tweaked a few elements if I'd designed it, but it was gorgeous. And perfect for a ball.

After I did my darker makeup and put my hair up, I twirled for Natasha.

"You look fantastic," she said. "It almost makes me want to go with you."

"Did you want to come? I'm sorry I didn't ask this week."

She waved a hand. "No, it's fine. It's your thing."

"Yeah, but that doesn't mean we couldn't have enjoyed it together."

I thought of the past couple of days with Gabe, him being

patient while I sketched, or me waiting for him at the museums, us just being with each other. The simple pleasure of someone else's presence. I never realized before that I often did that for other people but never asked anyone to do it for me.

"Too much excitement for me," Natasha said. "I like sleep. Text me if you have problems in the lobby."

"I will."

It would be harder to sneak out while wearing the dress. I saw why Ana wore trousers. I couldn't imagine fighting dark elven creatures in a skirt this voluminous.

I wished I could show it off to Gabe. What would he think about the club and the cosplay and my art?

There was still a chance he was Angelo. Did I want to risk asking early?

It wasn't that I feared Gabe's opinion. He would likely approve—of the sneaking out, and of the fact that I'd been taking a risk for something I loved. But if Angelo wasn't Gabe, would it affect our new relationship, if a couple of kisses could be called that? Would I secretly be curious about a relationship with Angelo, or would I choose Gabe anyway? And if Angelo was Gabe, what did it say that we'd spent all week together and hadn't figured it out? That we didn't know each other as well as we thought? That we didn't trust each other enough?

I had no good answers, so I would do what I'd been doing all week—wait and see what happened. Enjoy the evening with Angelo, hear what Gabe decided tomorrow after sleeping on the kiss, and save my decision for the last night.

My skirt swished as I crossed the lobby, which was thankfully empty. I couldn't have run from classmates while wearing this.

"Wow," said Angelo when I joined him in our usual meeting spot. "You look amazing."

His voice sounded lower and rougher than usual.

"Thanks." I smoothed the skirts. "New jacket?"

"You weren't the only one who went shopping."

"I like it."

Over his usual black pants, he wore a midnight-blue elven-style tunic made of a fabric that shimmered slightly in the faint light and nearly matched my dress. The crisp lines made his shoulders look broad, and the tails added elegance.

We went by land so I didn't risk tripping on my dress while climbing into a boat and falling into a canal. The sheer amount of fabric, once wet, would quickly drag me to the depths.

The skirts swished as we walked through the silent streets. We didn't speak, and I didn't know if it was a comfortable silence or a loaded one. I likewise couldn't tell if the fact that we were walking farther apart than usual was deliberate—on my part or his—or necessary because of the size of my dress. Or maybe I was imagining it.

This outfit was more conspicuous than my others, and the few people we passed stared. Normally I wouldn't mind being admired, but tonight the attention made me self-conscious.

Images flitted through my mind of what awaited, dancing in the ballroom or the magical forest. But I was also remembering the day with Gabe, the fun we'd had exploring, the peace and quiet, being together without talking, the fact that he was finally opening up and how much I liked it. The way he felt comfortable, like sinking into a book, when the story absorbed you, the real world faded, and your troubles dimmed.

My gaze slid sideways, assessing Angelo's height and the way he carried himself, comparing him to Gabe. The mask made it hard, since Gabe's eyebrows did so much of his talking.

Angelo was extra quiet tonight, and I started to ask if he was okay, but I didn't know where the conversation might lead or how prepared I was for the directions it might go.

When we arrived, we found that others had dressed for the occasion too, in gowns, nice jackets, or formal elven tunics. A buzz of excitement filled the air, and I was glad we were here at the right time to attend one of these.

We followed the crowd upstairs. The ballroom had been transformed. Hanging lanterns gave the space a golden glow, somewhere between the magical elven ball and an elegant Venezari one.

A man in a shiny silver tunic stood at the front of the room and said, "We'll begin with dance lessons."

Angelo extended his hand, head cocked, eyes shadowed beneath his black mask.

I gulped, stepped closer, and took his gloved hand. He clasped mine gently and rested the other on my back, warm and solid, keeping a respectable distance between us. The dim lighting and masks gave me the courage to meet his gaze. His eyes were definitely brown. Familiar? I wasn't sure.

Could he tell how fast my heart was beating?

The teacher guided us through basic steps. Angelo was smooth and elegant, his posture straight, his moves confident, like he'd done this many times. If that wasn't hot, I didn't know what was.

Could Gabe dance? He moved with the same easy confidence as Angelo, but I couldn't picture him on a dance floor. Unless public libraries offered ballroom lessons.

Instrumental music, sometimes airy and sometimes elegant, played over speakers and perfectly captured the feel of both a historical time period and a magical realm.

My skirts swished around Angelo's legs as we moved, and the idea crossed my mind that I wanted to remove his gloves and feel his hands on mine, before I wondered if it was betraying Gabe to consider a more intimate touch with Angelo.

I kept starting to speak and then chickening out. It wasn't like me, not having words. Angelo didn't speak either. He spun me like an expert and pulled me back in close.

We switched partners when others drew near, but we always ended up together again before long, magnets drawn to each other. I was aware of his presence despite the crowd, the way Ana always knew where Bastian was and when he was watching her.

We took a short break for tiny sandwiches and sparkling wine or punch, like in the book.

More people arrived as the night went on, until the room was full. Who would have thought that a modest-sized city had so many Elven Realms fans?

"Do you think everyone knew about the ball?" I asked.

"Lots of visitors do seem to know what's happening before we do."

"If I attended for a single night, I would choose a ball. It's amazing to imagine where everyone might have come from."

"Makes you feel less alone, doesn't it?" His voice was deep.

"Yes. Exactly."

That was how I felt here at the club, but also with him. Like I was part of something bigger, like Ana and her crew. That because others loved what I loved, I wasn't alone.

The music shifted to a slower song, and Angelo's arms tightened around me. I let my head rest on his shoulder, which pressed my mask awkwardly into my cheekbone. He drew our clasped hands up and held them against his chest. We drifted for a few steps before I remembered Gabe and startled, putting more distance between us.

If Angelo thought my reaction was weird, he didn't say anything.

Bottled-up questions pressed against my ribs. I tried to ignore them, live in the moment, and not think about the next day or the next week.

When the music ended and everyone slowly exited, we were among the last to leave. It was nearly closing time, and no one lingered. The market and the other rooms had been closed tonight, all attention on the ball.

When the guard opened the door for us to leave and we stepped into the night, I was exhausted but exhilarated. My feet were tired from dancing, but I was wide awake.

I seized Angelo's hand. "Let's stay out longer. Not go back yet."

His masked face tilted down toward me. After a moment, he said, "Okay."

We had two more nights, including a possible reveal on the final one, but somehow tonight felt like the end. Like nothing could top it. Returning to the hotel and taking off my mask and this gown would mean something was over, the spell broken, the magical realm cut off forever.

We moved slower than ever as we roamed the city.

"What did you like best this week?" I asked. "I liked LARP-ing, but if you repeat that, I'll deny everything."

He laughed. "The whole atmosphere. Getting to . . . see everything."

What had he been about to say instead?

"It was nice having company." His voice was softer.

"It was. Thanks for being my partner in crime."

"Anytime."

"It was nice to talk to people about things that no one in my real life would care about," I said.

"Would they listen, though, if you wanted to talk?"

I hummed. "Most of them? Probably not."

"You need new friends, then."

A tiny pain stabbed my chest. "It's not their fault. I don't tell people how much I like the books."

"But you've been so passionate about them. The art."

I shrugged. "Most of my friends wouldn't understand."

"I'm sorry."

"What about you?"

"I . . . don't talk about it much. But I could. With some people. If I wanted to."

Who did he mean? If this was Gabe, did he mean his sister? Or . . . me? Maybe he thought he could trust me? I was being ridiculous. This could've been Bryce and he meant Dai or his mom. Or a guy from another school who I didn't know.

We found a small bridge and sat on the top step.

"I'm glad we ran into each other that first night," I said.

"Curtains will always make me think of you."

I laughed softly. "And cats, you."

Lights danced on the water. Tiredness was creeping in, in the form of contentment. I wanted to cling to the last traces of magic before they vanished forever. No matter who he was and what we decided, I wasn't sure if I could fully recapture in real life the joy this week had given me.

I shifted to face him, and our knees pressed against each other's. The silence was heavy with things unsaid. Faint light gleamed on his mask, but his eyes were more shaded than usual. I lifted my hand, traced the edge of his mask. He sat very still.

I swallowed hard and dropped my hand into my lap. His head lowered to watch its progress. He tensed, as if debating reaching out to take it.

The urge seized me to take off my mask now, to forget our

earlier agreement. Break this barrier, see who he was and what the future might hold. But was I ready to know for sure and shut other possible doors?

"Angelo." My voice was half sigh, half hope.

My chest heaved with the effort to keep my breathing steady. His shoulders had stiffened. Was he having the same mental debate?

When neither of us spoke, I finally settled on, "Thanks. For everything this week. I've had a great time with you."

"I have too." His careful, soft tone matched mine. "Are you still considering . . . do you want to . . . ?" He reached for my face but stopped.

He didn't need to finish. "Do you?"

"It's your choice. We can remove our masks now. We can wait until the last night as planned. Or we can leave this here. Be grateful we made a friend and leave it at that."

"I'm still considering," I said, and he nodded. "Thank you for letting me be myself this week."

"Always be yourself, Fantasma." He helped me to my feet and drew me into a hug. My hands clasped around his waist. We stood for a few heartbeats, and we both pulled away at the same time.

"Should we get back?" I asked.

"Yeah."

We didn't immediately move.

He took my hand with his gloved one, squeezed once, and started walking.

Despite our clasped hands and our arms brushing, it felt like a canal was forming between us, a broad one with no bridge or boat or way across. He was Bastian preparing to return to the elven realms and seal the breach for good. If I didn't have the courage tonight, would I find it in two days?

Our walk was silent. Angelo waited while I took out my key at the hotel's side door.

"You go on," he said. "I'm going to walk more."

I nodded.

"Tomorrow?" he asked, and my chest expanded.

"Tomorrow," I said.

I slipped inside, circled the breakfast tables. Stepped into the lobby.

And found Natasha and Mr. Owens waiting.

Chapter Twenty-Nine

I froze. Debated making a run for the door and pretending I hadn't seen them, though they were the only people in the lobby and therefore impossible to miss.

Mr. Owens stopped pacing and faced me. "Evie? Is that you?"

I gulped. Terrible, ill-advised responses raced through my mind.

Who's Evie? I have no idea what you're talking about. Who are you?

Guilt was written all over Natasha's face, like the time she'd eaten my stash of Sour Patch Kids, the closest to lawbreaking she'd ever come.

I might have fooled my classmates as I hurried through the breakfast room, but in this brightly lit space, with my best friend right there? Yeah. Mr. Owens wasn't going to buy phrases in bad Italian and me making a run for it.

I slowly reached up and untied my mask, clutching it so the

edges pressed deep into my fingers. The rush of air on my bare skin, normally a relief each night, felt like I was naked, exposed in front of him with no defenses.

"Would you care to explain where you've been and why you're arriving at"—he checked his watch—"five a.m.?"

No, actually I would prefer to dive out the window into the canal and swim away, thanks for asking.

"I'm guessing that's not an option?" I asked.

Wait. Had I said the first part out loud?

I was tired, and I'd been spending too much time with Gabe this week, and apparently those two factors obliterated the filter between my brain and my mouth.

"Sorry," I said. "I'm sorry."

Mr. Owens was staring at me like he didn't recognize me. Given the outfit, that was fair. Also given the attitude. I hated the confusion on his face, so similar to the expression my mom wore when she talked to my brother. I had never, ever wanted that look pointed at me. My stomach was tying itself in knots.

"I, uh, heard about a ball tonight," I said. "I sneaked out. I know I shouldn't have. I know I broke the rules."

"Were you alone?"

Saying yes might make this worse since going out by myself was more foolish. But I refused to get Angelo in trouble, and admitting I'd been out with a guy I didn't technically know might be a more terrible answer. Where was Angelo, anyway? He'd said he was going to walk, which meant I had to get Mr. Owens out of the lobby before he returned.

"Yes," I said.

Mr. Owens's face screamed disappointment. The knots in my stomach tightened.

"Do you know how dangerous that is? In a foreign city?"

"I do. I'm sorry."

Mr. Owens looked at a loss for how to proceed.

Him and me both.

"I need to call your mother. That's why I was looking for you. She was trying to reach you, and when she couldn't, she called Natasha, then me."

"Is everything okay?" New panic flared inside me.

"She said it wasn't an emergency."

I exhaled. That was a relief, but then why had she called at five in the morning?

"I knew where Evie was, though, so she wasn't unsafe," Natasha said. "Like I told you."

"A buddy system only works if you can get in touch with the person, Ms. Gutierrez. I watched you call Evie several times with no response."

I hadn't checked my phone in hours. Oh no.

My teacher's face flickered as he seemed to have a mental debate. Surely I wasn't the first rule-breaking student he'd had to deal with on a trip. Just the most unexpected one.

What was a person supposed to do in a situation like this? This was exactly why I followed the rules. To avoid this dizzying, nauseating, might-puke-in-the-lobby feeling, and the heavy weight of disappointed expectations crushing my lungs.

"You've never done anything like this before," Mr. Owens said.

Other than the previous five nights . . . I continued to clutch my mask, trying to look repentant and keep the puking at bay.

"We only have two more days. How's your project coming?"

"Please don't punish Gabriel," I said in a rush. "I don't want his grade to suffer because of me. I want to do my part of the project, however you'll let me."

Grades. Would Mr. Owens lower my art grade for this? Would the infraction go on my perfect record and ruin my shot at the citizenship award?

"Since you're eighteen, it's technically legal for you to do as you please. But you did agree to the trip rules. We need to call your mom and let her know you're okay."

Or I could hide behind that curtain again and go with my plan from the first night, to stay there forever.

Glancing at the door, hoping Angelo was safe and wouldn't get in trouble, I slowly dug out my phone. Sure enough, I had tons of messages and missed calls.

Better get this over with so I could get Mr. Owens out of the lobby and clear a path for Angelo. Saving him was the best I could do. It was too late for me.

I hit Call and held my breath.

"Evie, are you all right?" my mom answered. "I've been calling you."

"I'm fine. What's going on? Why'd you call so early?"

"Would you care to explain the charge on your emergency credit card that showed up as Fantastical Stitches?"

I smoothed a hand over my gown, the reason for that charge. So much for my hoping she wouldn't see it until I was home.

And, seriously? That question couldn't have waited until a normal hour?

Who was I kidding. It was my mom. Of course it couldn't.

"I, um, bought a dress. For a ball."

"A ball? Is that where you were? Mr. Owens said you weren't at the hotel?"

"Yeah. I went out. A special-occasion thing. Natasha knew where I was, and I had my safety whistle."

"But you weren't answering your phone. Were you out all night?" She sounded more baffled than concerned. The credit card use was more alarming to her than my sneaking out.

"Kind of?" I squeaked.

"I'm glad you're okay." I heard the unspoken *but* before her tone shifted. "I know I teach you to be independent, but there's safety to consider. I never expected something like this from you."

From the kid who worked so hard to never cause trouble.

"I won't deny I'm disappointed," she went on. "In the poor decision-making, and in making your teacher worry."

Why was the lobby so hot? My head felt disconnected from my body, my limbs shaky. "I know. I'm really sorry. So . . . what now?"

"I won't demand that you come home," my mom finally said, and I tried to exhale quietly. "That's too much work for your teacher, and the trip is almost over. But I expect you to behave, to do exactly as he says and whatever he thinks is fair. No more using the emergency card for frivolous purchases. Once you get home, we'll discuss this. May I speak with him?"

I handed the phone to Mr. Owens, who walked to the other side of the room.

Natasha was watching me with such pity that I felt like a natural disaster. I played with the laces on my dress, fighting the urge to pace, pass out, or run away.

Mr. Owens returned and handed me my phone. "We agree you can remain with the group. But I expect perfect behavior for the next two days."

"Yes, sir. Thank you."

"You've been up all night. Do you need to stay here for the day? I'll have to leave Ms. Reyes with you."

Because I couldn't be trusted anymore. It was a dagger in the heart. "No, sir. I'll rest for a bit and be down in time to meet the group."

We had an all-day tour of the city of Vicenza scheduled. I almost wanted to stay behind. I was exhausted. But if I went, I could behave and prove he could trust me. Plus, if I missed the tour, people would wonder why.

Mr. Owens nodded, reluctant, and gave me one final distressed look that made me want to melt into a puddle and ooze away toward the nearest canal.

He escorted Natasha and me upstairs and watched us enter our room.

Getting caught had been a possibility all week, but I'd had so many successful nights that I'd begun forgetting about the prospect, convinced I'd be okay and no one would know. It figured that my mom's obsession with checking credit card statements had been my downfall.

"I'm so sorry," Natasha said as soon as she closed the door. "I tried to convince your mom you were sleeping and it was too early for a phone call, but she insisted on talking to you. Then I used our cover story, that you'd taken sleeping meds and I couldn't wake you, but she didn't buy it. Once your mom called Mr. Owens, he came to the room and then I really couldn't do anything."

"I don't blame you." I dropped my mask on the nightstand. "I should have checked my phone. I didn't mean to stay out so long. It was my fault."

"You look like you might pass out. Do you want to sleep? I'll leave so you can rest, then bring you breakfast and wake you up in time for the tour."

"You're the best." I didn't deserve her kindness after I'd made her lie for me and gotten her in trouble too.

Natasha offered a sympathetic smile and left.

I stripped off my dress and hung it in the wardrobe, then flopped onto my bed. I wasn't sure if I'd be able to sleep. Yes, I'd been up all night. But the panic, the worry, the dread of punishment and disappointment were a big ball inside me and my mind was racing. Recalling Mr. Owens's face. Imagining the exact expression that my mom would have been wearing.

Had I blown my years of being precisely the daughter she wanted and needed? Had I destroyed the trust of my favorite teacher? And would my choices hurt my best friend?

I couldn't stop my body from trembling, and the simplest actions were challenging like my muscles had decided to stop working. I took a hot shower, washed off my makeup, and stared at my face. I looked pale, tired, weak.

I climbed into bed and fought the urge to scream into my pillow, trying to focus on breathing slowly, wishing for the oblivion of sleep.

I must have slept a little, because the next thing I knew, Natasha was saying my name.

I rolled over, exhausted, heavy. My worries flooded back immediately.

I checked the clock. Just enough time to get ready. Natasha knew me well.

"I'm sorry," I said.

"Why?"

"Mr. Owens is mad at you too."

"I knew the risks when I agreed to help. How was the ball?"

"Good and weird and I don't know. Angelo and I almost took our masks off, but I chickened out."

"Does this mean Operation: Mystery Man is over? We had it down to two people."

"We did? Wait, the mission had a name?"

"Yeah, I guess I didn't get to tell you yesterday. About the candidates. How did you not know about the name?"

"I don't know if I want to know who they are." I stumbled to the bathroom, leaving the door open as I washed my face and opened my makeup bag. "Ugh. Getting in trouble is terrible for your complexion."

"Are you going to tell the others?" Natasha asked.

She meant Bryce and Dai, about Mr. Owens discovering

me, but I pictured Gabe. He wouldn't care about the sneaking out. He'd probably tell me where I'd gone wrong in getting caught.

Except . . .

"You said there are two candidates left. Who are they?" My voice sounded resigned.

Before Natasha answered, I knew. Because it was the two people who would make my life most complicated.

"Bryce and Gabriel. Which, I know, is weird. I don't see either of them doing the stuff you've described."

"Most people would say that about me." I added more concealer, which was not enough to help the bags under my eyes.

"I guess so," she said.

"Please don't mention this, okay? I don't want anyone to know."

"Of course I won't."

What would have happened last night if I'd removed my mask with either Bryce or Gabe, and we'd talked for real?

Most likely I would have gotten Angelo in trouble too.

We made it downstairs just in time, and I shoved toast into my mouth as we entered the lobby. Everyone was there but Gabe. What did that mean? That he'd been out all night and was tired? That he'd been caught after Mr. Owens busted me? Or that he didn't care about Vicenza and had decided to call in sick?

"Morning," Bryce said. "What are you thinking?"

I blinked at him. I had nothing.

"Hey, are you okay?" His fingers brushed my arm.

I had nothing to that either. He didn't look exhausted like he'd stumbled in at five a.m. Or later, since by the time Mr. Owens escorted me upstairs, Angelo still hadn't arrived.

"Just tired," I said.

He was nice enough that he didn't even give me a strike for not answering the original question.

Gabe strolled down the stairs, and his gaze found mine. His brow wrinkled like he sensed something was wrong.

My attention jumped between them. Bryce, who was always moving, always helping, friendly with everyone, who had been my friend for years. Gabe, who was the opposite, deliberate and contemplative and reserved. Who I had kissed. My face warmed.

"Glad you finally rejoined us, Mr. Martinez. Is everyone ready?"

Mr. Owens wasn't looking at me. On purpose? How disappointed was he?

We trooped out, and I let Bryce get ahead and fell into step with Gabe.

"Hey," he said.

"Hi. You were late."

"You weren't in the lobby early like usual, so I went to my room to stall and give you time to arrive."

"Oh. Thank you."

"What's wrong?" he asked.

"What do you mean?"

"You look awful."

"Thanks. Way to make a girl feel special."

"You okay?"

"I don't know."

"Is this about last night?"

My heart stuttered before I realized he didn't mean the ball and the club but the kiss. "That part of yesterday was perfect. Other than the mild concussion."

We smiled at each other, and I ducked my head.

His smile said he might not regret it, might want to do it again. I longed to ask what he'd decided after sleeping on it, but surrounded by classmates wasn't the place for that conversation.

For now, I settled for saying, "I talked to my mom this morning. She's not happy with me about some stuff."

He studied me. "Do you want to talk about it?"

"Thanks, but maybe later."

He nodded. "Need advice on dealing with disappointed parents?"

"What have you got?"

"Don't say more than you have to. Let her do the talking, get it out of her system. When you do talk, keep it simple. Agree with everything she says."

I made a noise.

"What?"

"I can't see you agreeing with people."

He raised an eyebrow. "When your mom says you shouldn't have tried to hit a guy, what's getting you out of that conversation faster—*I know and I'm sorry*, or *He was asking for it*? Even if the second is one hundred percent true, the goal is to end the lecture as soon as possible."

"I thought the goal was to make her trust you again."

"One conversation won't do that, no matter what you say. The goal the first day is not to make it worse."

"Ohhh, you know from experience, don't you?" I poked his arm. "You totally said the guy was asking for it."

"I didn't say I was telling you what I did, just what you should do. I'm aware that I'm not the best example."

I laughed.

He looked pleased with himself, and I realized that my nausea had subsided.

His face grew serious. "It will suck at first, but she'll remember that she trusts you. Helps if you're extra good for a while."

"Is that what you did?"

"Does that sound like something I would do?"

"Not really."

He grinned.

"Sounds like I'm learning from your mistakes."

His lips tilted up. "At least someone is."

I laughed again. He was right—it was going to be awful. But it was the first time I'd done anything bad, so maybe I'd get through it. And maybe Mom would un-ground me in time for me to go to college in the fall. Or maybe not, and then my problem of not knowing what to do would be solved because I could stay locked in my room.

"Thank you."

Gabe bobbed his head.

I shoved his arm. "You're not bad at the advice thing."

"You haven't tried my advice yet. Save that thought until after you see if it works."

"If it goes badly, can I blame you?"

He shrugged. "Sure."

"I'm kidding. I'm the one who messed up."

"By messing up, I assume you mean getting caught?"

I shoved him again, and he laughed.

"Now I'm dying of curiosity, Whitmore."

"I might want to tell you. Just . . . later."

"Fair enough."

Maybe I did want to tell him everything, about the club and my art and Fantasma. I could trust him. He wouldn't judge or laugh. But if I did, we would need privacy, because if he was Angelo, it might turn into an awkward talk about the secrets we'd been keeping. And if he wasn't, I'd have to choose.

I would put off the decision until the end of the day.

I was becoming a master procrastinator. Mom would not approve.

Gabe's pinkie and ring finger linked around mine briefly, then let go. His mouth tucked into a tiny smile. Mine did too.

Gabe and I reached the boat and were jostled apart as everyone loaded.

Neither he nor Bryce were in trouble today, so hopefully Angelo had avoided Mr. Owens.

My blood pressure spiked. Angelo.

There was no way I'd be able to go to the club again and meet him for real, and he would never know why.

Chapter Thirty

When we switched from the vaporetto to the train at the outskirts of Venice, I wasn't able to make my way back to Gabe. Natasha dragged me with her to meet Alex, and we sat with him and Dai in four seats that faced each other. After how much Natasha had helped me this week, I owed it to her to meet the guy she hate-liked.

My eyelids were drooping, and I had trouble concentrating, and I wanted to sleep, but I forced myself to chat for the ride to Vicenza, which took about an hour. I also had to force myself to stop craning my head to see where Gabe had ended up.

Occasional glances out the window revealed that after crossing the bridge and passing through an urban area on the mainland of Venice, most of the trip went through green countryside, fields dotted with trees and old farmhouses.

After we reached the station and exited, Mr. Owens led us through a park, then up a street of shops and restaurants. Though the stone buildings weren't too different from those in

Venice, it was strange to be in a city with wide streets and cars after a week of canals, alleys, and boats.

As our group moved along, taking up a whole block as we spread out, I watched for Mr. Owens so I could avoid him. I should have wanted him to see me, to prove I was following the rules and staying with the group, but I was afraid to know if he looked at me differently now.

I tried to maintain my usual happy face and friendly questions so no one suspected anything was wrong or learned I'd gotten caught sneaking out. Not only would it affect my reputation, but then Angelo would figure out who I was.

Gabe didn't walk by my side, but he moved past me a few times and brushed my hand before shuffling away. When it happened for the third time, sending shivers up my arm, I hurried to keep up with him.

I raised my eyebrows. Mine weren't as expressive as his, but they held a clear question. "Ashamed to be seen with me, Gabriel?" I emphasized his full name.

"Figured you didn't want people gossiping about you, Whitmore."

"Maybe I don't care. Although," I said, "this is more fun." I held him back with me as the group filed around a corner and slid a hand up his arm.

His eyes glinted. He lowered his head, hesitated with his mouth an inch from mine, and lifted his eyebrows in question. I replied by pressing my lips to his. The kiss was short and intense, then he smiled and moved on, forcing me to hurry not to get left behind.

Warm bubbles fizzed inside me as I watched the back of his head.

I guessed that confirmed we both wanted the kissing to continue.

Our first stop was a Gothic cathedral, and a tour guide met us outside. The architecture portion of the trip was the reason we'd come to Vicenza, to see buildings throughout the city designed by a famous architect, including part of this church. Most of the architecture students, Dai included, moved closer to the guide to listen. I didn't object to learning, but I was happier to be in a beautiful old Italian city, flirting with a cute guy, than learning about old buildings.

Which, sure, maybe that made me shallow, but whatever.

Gabe hadn't bothered with the audio device, but he was studying our surroundings with interest.

"I thought you liked learning," I said.

"I'd rather do it on my own, learn what I want to."

"But guides are so knowledgeable."

"So is Google."

I rolled my eyes. "Not the same."

He smirked and drifted away as the guide led us through the interior, showing us chapels and monuments and art. When he mentioned the crypts, Gabe's eyes found mine from across the group. One eyebrow quirked, and I smiled.

I joined Dai, who was studying the arches overhead, and when I passed Gabe, I reached out to stroke his hand with my pinkie and didn't look back.

Our group moved on to a basilica with classic windows

designed by the famous architect. The church was connected to a large plaza, with a red brick bell tower standing in contrast to the white facade of the church.

As I circled the pillars guarding an outdoor walkway, a hand grasped my arm. Gabe steered me into a dark corner and kissed me deeply but quickly, leaving me out of breath.

"You're right," he murmured. "This is fun."

His hand trailed across my lower back as he ducked away, right before a few classmates arrived and I forced a normal greeting to hide my racing heart.

My insides were dancing at the thrill of the game.

I was trying not to let my imagination run wild, wondering whether Gabe would officially want to date, whether he would hang out with me and my friends at school, whether he'd go to events like prom. I knew if I wanted to keep spending time with him—and I did—that it might look different from dating a usual boyfriend. I also knew there was a chance Gabe would want to leave this in Italy. Partners for a week, no complications.

For today, until we had a chance to talk, I would let him be a nice distraction from the trouble I was in and the abrupt ending to my visits to the club.

And I would enjoy the fact that he was a great kisser.

Bryce did the hard work for me at lunch—convincing Gabe to sit with us. Under the table, his foot brushed my ankle, his calf pressed mine, and his hand occasionally rested on my thigh. I returned the favor by linking my foot around his, resting my knee against his leg, and letting our elbows touch.

It was the thrill of finding the club, the happiness of exploring Venice, the adrenaline of sneaking out, laced with the simple comfort I always experienced in Gabe's presence.

Our tour concluded at the Olympic Theater, an impressive brick building that had a gorgeous interior of white stone, columns, statues, and seats facing a stage.

"Can we go up there and sing?" Dai asked.

I had to bite my lip to keep from laughing.

"At least he asked first," Gabe murmured.

I told Natasha that Gabe and I wanted to use the return trip to discuss our project—which we did need to do, to add anything from today that wasn't related to sneaking kisses and touching each other when no one was watching. We sat next to each other and managed to focus for a few minutes before his leg pressed against mine and my shoulder leaned into his, and passing a laptop back and forth became more an excuse to brush fingers than to work.

"I'm assuming that sleeping on it worked for you?" I asked.

"I want to kiss you more, if that's what you mean."

I shivered. "Pretty much."

But how long did he want to keep kissing me? I shifted toward him.

"I think . . . I might want to tell you what happened last night. And some other stuff. But"—I peered backward between the seats to see who was sitting near us—"not here. Tonight?"

"Of course. There's something I want to tell you too."

My insides jumped. Would his willingly talking to me ever stop making me happy? What did he want to discuss? The club, if he was Angelo? Or our future?

It was evening when we returned to Venice, and I ended up next to Bryce, Dai, and Natasha as we walked toward the hotel.

"What are you thinking?" I asked Bryce.

"How sad it is that so many modern storytellers rely on anti-heroes and have moved away from classic heroes like underdogs and noble protectors who fight against darkness."

"That was deep, bro," said Dai.

Wait, what? Bryce's words sounded familiar.

Angelo had said something nearly identical, when we'd discussed tropes we liked. Underdogs. The fight to protect the light.

I slowed and stared at Bryce. His dark hair and brown eyes. His height.

Something clenched in my chest.

And my stomach plunged.

Apparently, I'd been hoping Angelo was Gabe. We would talk later, and I would tell him about the club, and he would say he was Angelo and that he was so glad I was Fantasma because he wouldn't have wanted her to be anyone else.

This wasn't how it was supposed to go.

And now, faced with the possibility of Angelo being someone else, I knew with certainty—Gabe was the one I wanted. I could give up Angelo if it meant keeping Gabe.

But I had to know for sure.

Bryce stopped too when he realized I was studying him. "What is it?"

Did I dare risk asking? Had he said that to drop a hint? Maybe he suspected I was Fantasma and was digging for clues?

"Are you . . . Angelo?" My muscles tensed as if bracing for his answer.

Bryce blinked. "Who's Angelo?"

My breath froze in my lungs. Natasha's eyes were wide.

"What are you talking about?" Bryce's brow creased in confusion.

"Ha. Nothing. Never mind. A guy I met this week." I was talking too fast. My whole body felt flushed.

"Angelo," he said. "That name sounds familiar. Is it from those Elven Realms books? Like Matt and Sanjay were asking about? That girl they saw wasn't you, was it?"

My laugh was high-pitched. "Do you think I would do something like that? It doesn't matter. Angelo is no one important."

Why did my heart feel like it was trying to escape? Where was all the air?

I spotted movement. Gabe was hesitating at the corner a few yards from where we'd stopped. How long had he been there?

His gaze locked with mine. A range of emotions flickered across his face. Shock. Confusion. Hurt. Then his eyes shuttered, and his face went very blank.

Had he heard all of that?

Time stopped.

He was Angelo.

Of course he was.

I should have seen it days ago. Who else accepted me,

encouraged me? Who else allowed me to relax and open up and be myself and challenged me and made me laugh?

It couldn't possibly have been anyone else.

And he'd heard me say I thought *he* was Bryce. Then dismiss everything we had shared together.

No. No, no, no.

I was such an idiot.

Gabe broke eye contact and ducked around the corner.

I raced after him.

"Where are you going?" Dai called.

I didn't stop. But when I rounded the corner, there was no sign of Gabe. I speed-walked to the next corner, looked up and down the street, didn't see him anywhere.

This was what he did—went off alone. How he preferred to be. But it hadn't hurt this badly before, like he'd ripped out my heart and taken it with him.

Curse my stupid mouth. One hasty guess, one careless remark, wanting to sound cool and casual, acting impatiently instead of waiting to talk to Gabe, and I'd messed up the best thing that had happened to me.

It hadn't been the masks that had given me freedom—it had been Gabe. Not only at night but also every day this week.

He had every right to be hurt or disappointed that I hadn't known.

Wait.

Had he known I was Fantasma? Or had he learned the truth just now, when I said his nighttime name? From his face,

I thought he'd been as surprised as I was. Like he was having the same realization at the same time. Did he think that I had known all along that he was Angelo?

Surely he hadn't spent days pretending he didn't know all those secrets about me. Right?

The idea of him knowing more than I did unbalanced me. But I couldn't be sure. I needed to talk to him, to find out.

What exactly had I said? That Angelo wasn't important. Then I'd mocked the thing we'd shared together.

Gabe didn't trust people, assumed the worst about them. I knew exactly how he'd interpret my words—they would have confirmed his initial fears about me, made him think I was like the people who had been horrible to his sister, or his supposed friends who'd forgotten him. He'd think I hadn't taken our nights together seriously, or that I'd been toying with him all week. That what we had didn't matter.

A whirlpool in my stomach threatened to make me sick.

I had to talk to him. Easier said than done since he had vanished into the maze that was Venice, and good luck finding him. He was an expert at being alone. Which should have told me something. I should have questioned whether this was worth it, whether I wanted to pursue someone who might not want to be pursued, who had made it clear that talking ranked up there with root canals on his scale of fun.

But I wasn't letting him go. He was worth the effort. I just had to figure out how to find him.

Clearly, though, my current strategy wasn't working.

My breathing was heavy as I made my way back to the hotel.

My friends were waiting in the lobby. Thankfully, Mr. Owens was not.

"What was that about?" Dai asked.

I looked at him. Natasha. Bryce. Three of my closest friends. Suddenly, after driving Gabe away because of my desire to seem perfect, the last four years of lying to them felt not only absurd but shameful.

A boulder settled in my stomach. I was letting everyone down today.

No one was in the breakfast area, so I waved them to follow me and take seats.

I debated asking if they could keep a secret, but keeping secrets was what got me into this mess—in trouble with my mom and Mr. Owens and alienating the guy I liked.

My fingers laced together, tight, twisting, and I braced myself. "So . . . I lied to you. That girl Sanjay and Matt saw sneaking out? That was me. And this morning Mr. Owens kind of caught me staying out all night."

Natasha looked sad, while Bryce and Dai were staring at me like I had morphed into a twisted dark elven creature.

"That doesn't sound like you," Dai said.

"They said the person was wearing a costume, right?" Bryce asked. "What were you doing?"

I tried not to squirm. To speak confidently and own what I liked, the way Gabe would tell me to. "There's a secret fan club in the city, an Elven Realms one. I love the books and I wanted to find the club."

"Did you?" Dai asked.

"Yeah. It was amazing. I've been sneaking out every night."

He blinked at me. "That's why you've been less like you this week."

That, and kissing Gabe.

Dai pouted. "I want to go. You should have invited me."

"Then she would have been caught much sooner," Natasha said.

"Sucks that Mr. O caught you," Dai said. "How much trouble are you in?"

"To be determined. He talked to my mom."

"Ouch."

That heavy, ill feeling of disappointing people washed over me full force. "Yeah. They didn't send me home early, so that's good. And I never get in trouble. But sneaking out at night in a strange city wasn't the smartest move. I know that."

Dai waved a hand. "Eh, Venice is fairly safe. The best part about new places is finding the hidden things, the secrets, the stuff not everyone else sees."

"I doubt my mom and Mr. Owens share that philosophy when it involves me breaking the rules," I said dryly.

"Why didn't you say anything?" Bryce finally spoke.

"I guess I was embarrassed. Fantasy books and cosplay and fan clubs don't really go with the image, you know?"

Bryce rolled his eyes. "Dude, Tanaka plays with pigeons. Your hobby is way better than that. Besides, I said I liked the books." Hurt seeped into his expression. "You didn't trust us?"

It was another knife in my already stabbed chest. "I don't

talk about it often. It was something I shared with my dad, and it was easier to keep it private."

Dai's face softened.

"You talked about the books with people at the club, right?" Bryce asked. "But not with us, your friends?"

"I'm sorry." My voice was small.

"Is that what that Angelo thing was about?"

"What made you think of that antihero topic?" I asked instead of answering.

Bryce lifted a shoulder. "Matt mentioned the books, and it made me remember reading them."

Ugh. I had blown things up with Gabe because of that.

"Can we go with you to the club tonight?" Dai asked.

I blinked at him. "Did you miss the part where I got caught? I can't go back. Mr. Owens will probably be guarding the exit."

"Hmm." Dai had a calculating light in his eyes that meant trouble.

Natasha's mouth was set in a grim line, and Bryce's face held betrayal.

On top of that, in the time we'd been here, Gabe hadn't come through the lobby, and I didn't know how to find him.

Chapter Thirty-One

After telling Natasha I'd join her soon, I lingered at the front desk while my friends went upstairs. I'd realized I didn't have Gabe's number.

I smiled at the clerk. "Hi. I need to reach one of my classmates. He left his phone and I want to return it, but I don't know what room he's in."

"I can't give out that information."

"That's okay. Can you call him? Gabriel Martinez?"

I leaned against the counter as he dialed. 406. Bingo.

"No answer," he said.

"Okay. Thanks for trying."

Before he could offer to hold the nonexistent phone, I hurried to the fourth floor and knocked on the door of room 406.

Then I waited. And waited.

It made sense that Gabe wasn't there or he would have answered his room phone. Then again, maybe he wouldn't have. Sophia seemed to be the only one he tolerated talking to on the phone. I knocked again. Still no answer.

"If you're in there, I'm sorry," I called. "I know what you heard, but that wasn't what I meant. Can we talk so I can explain? Please?"

I waited a few minutes. Then tried again and called in a fake voice, "Housekeeping."

Brilliant. I should have figured out the Italian word. Unsurprisingly, that strategy failed too.

"What are you doing?"

A woman with an Italian accent, wearing the uniform of actual housekeeping, watched me warily from the end of the hall.

"You are disturbing the guests," she said.

"Sorry."

I'd have to try again later. I trudged downstairs. I didn't know if I was mad at Gabe or hurt or both. My insides were jumbled up. I just knew I had to see him and figure this out.

Obviously he didn't share that desire.

My phone rang as I was returning to my room. My mom. The hall was empty, so I leaned against the wall and answered, both too numb and too nervous to talk to her.

"Am I interrupting any work?" Mom asked.

"No, I'm done for the night."

Because I couldn't find my partner, and I couldn't go to the club. At least I could finally sleep. Ha. Like that was going to happen after the past few hours. And after this inevitably doomed conversation. I doubted I could rely on the sweet oblivion of sleep to escape my mess.

"Good," Mom said. "I wanted to talk."

This time I managed to keep it to myself that I would rather jump into a canal than have this discussion. "Okay."

"Help me understand why you'd do something so dangerous and reckless."

I remembered Gabe's advice about how to respond when you were in trouble. "I'm sorry. I know."

She waited. Apparently, his advice wouldn't work with her. Unfortunately, I might not have the chance to tell him about it.

I thought of his other advice, the part I'd used when talking to my friends earlier—that I should be myself, be honest. Opening up to my friends had made me feel terrible and guilty, but it had been nice to get everything out in the open and stop hiding.

Maybe I needed to do that with my mom too.

"I wanted to see a fan club," I said. "Not a party club. A place for people who like the Elven Realms books, with costumes and games and stuff."

"The Elven Realms?"

"You know, the fantasy series that Dad and I read together? I love them."

She was silent a moment. We rarely talked about Dad, always focused on the next task, the next event, the next project. Looking forward, not back.

"Why didn't you ever mention it?" she asked.

I shrugged even though she couldn't see me. "I didn't want to hurt you. You know, with the reminder of him. Plus, I wanted to keep it just for me. Reading the books, doing art, wearing costumes. I feel like I always have to be the best at everything.

I wanted something that was fun. I really am sorry for breaking the rules."

After a pause, Mom's voice sounded curious when she asked, "Did I make you believe you couldn't have fun?"

"Sometimes." All the time.

"I'm sorry you felt like you had to hide this." She sighed. "You took on a lot after your father died. I relied on you too much. I should have seen that you were missing so many aspects of your childhood. I'm sorry for that."

Before this trip, I had never thought I needed an apology or that she'd done anything wrong. Now, I wasn't so sure. But I also didn't feel ready to express that sentiment, so I didn't know what to say.

"We'll talk more when you get home, okay?" she asked.

"Okay. Oh, Mom? One more thing." Might as well go all the way. "All those college acceptances? I have no idea what I want to study."

"What do you mean?"

"Exactly what I said. I don't know what to major in or what I want to do with my life. Like, no clue whatsoever."

"Sweetie, you're eighteen. That's normal."

"Really?"

"Of course. You think I had everything figured out before I started college? Do you know how many times I failed or changed paths?"

"Really?" Apparently that was the only word I could manage.

"I'm happy to help you discuss options. You'll find the path for you, when the time is right."

Wow. Why had I been keeping this a secret for so long? If she was going to be this understanding, I should have brought it up sooner. "Thanks, Mom. Love you."

I was dreading an interrogation about my interests and possible punishment, but at least, like Gabe had advised, I hadn't made the situation worse. And telling the truth had me feel lighter. The secrets had been a heavier burden than I'd thought.

Natasha was waiting for me when I entered our room.

"Everything okay?" she asked.

I dropped onto my bed. "I told my mom the truth."

"How'd she take it?"

"Who knows? She can't fathom my sneaking out, but I think it will be okay, eventually. Can I confess to you something I told her?"

"Of course."

"I do fan art. For the Elven Realms. I met people at the club who know my work from online."

"Okay. Wow. I knew you liked to draw, but what's fan art?"

"Drawings or paintings of things from the books. How I imagine them. I post on a fan forum. I'm kind of well known."

"Cool. You've always been good at art. Why didn't your mom know?"

"So she didn't get all *her* about it."

"Good point. I mean, you could have told me." Natasha's face and tone were mild, but her words felt like a condemnation.

I gulped and ducked my head. "I know. I should have trusted you. Like I should have trusted Dai and Bryce in the first place with the fact that I like the books. When I started high school,

I was so afraid that I wouldn't be popular, that I wouldn't fit in or would disappoint my mom. I wanted to manage my image, I guess. Then the longer I went without telling you, the easier it was to keep it that way, especially since it meant also talking about my dad, and I told myself it wasn't a big deal."

Her face softened. "I'm sorry if I did anything to make you think you couldn't tell me. I should have asked you more questions."

"It's not your fault," I said with conviction. "If I had told you, maybe we would have talked more."

She scrambled over to my bed and wrapped her arms around me. "So. Now can I ask what's up with Gabriel?"

Though she shifted away from me, I didn't meet her eyes. "What do you mean?"

"Please. I heard you asking about him. I saw you with him today. You chased him through the city."

I covered my face. "I like him."

"Wait. Your nighttime guy. It's him, right?"

"Yes, but don't say anything. He obviously doesn't want anyone to know."

She nodded, her face assessing. "Whoa, so you fell for him during the day and also at night?"

"More during the day, I think? But it helps knowing that the person I talked to every night is also him."

"Why didn't you say anything? That's why you ditched us all week, isn't it? To be with Gabriel."

"Sorry about that." I had too much to apologize for lately.

"He doesn't seem like your type, but if you like him, that's what matters."

"I think he's the type I didn't know I wanted but that I need. The rumors are wrong. He didn't get arrested, he didn't go to juvie, he didn't terrorize hamsters. He's pretty great. He's nice. Well, he's sarcastic and doesn't like people. But he's funny and he makes me relax and he likes art."

"As long as he treats you well and makes you happy."

"He might, if I could find him. Guessing that Bryce was Angelo and mocking cosplay drove him off."

Natasha's face lit up. "Have you checked his room?"

She was ready to launch Mission: Find Gabriel. I wasn't sure if I wanted to stop her or hug her again. "No answer, even when I pretended to be housekeeping. I stood outside for ten minutes knocking until a maid told me to leave."

"I admire the persistence. Where else could he be?"

"He has no problem skipping required things, so the only guarantee is the airport the day after tomorrow." I didn't want to wait that long. Plus, no matter that movies kept selling airports as romantic places for deep confessions of love, trying to talk about feelings with Gabe in a public place wouldn't end well. "We have to finish our project tomorrow, but I can see him doing it himself."

"What about the club?"

"We had planned to meet again tonight. Well, my nighttime alias had planned to meet his. But there's no way I can go again."

Besides, Gabe didn't know I'd been caught, so he would assume I'd be going tonight. Which meant he might not, to continue avoiding me.

"We could make it happen," Natasha said.

I shook my head. "Too risky. What if Mr. Owens checks in? Or is watching the lobby?"

"If you're sure," Natasha said.

"I'm sure."

It was the right decision, but that didn't lessen the sadness pressing against my rib cage. If Gabe did go, I'd miss my best chance to talk to him. And if I wasn't there, I'd confirm the assumptions he had surely made about me, that I didn't care about Angelo, that my image was more important than he was.

I wasn't ready for my time at the club to be over. What was I missing tonight? The thought of the magic continuing without me should have been comforting—I knew I didn't have forever, and I did like the idea of other fans carrying on after I left. That didn't ease the disappointment that I was so close but couldn't be there.

But I'd already failed my teacher and my mom, and I did not want to experience that again. Not to mention the more severe consequences if I were caught a second time. I couldn't risk making things worse.

Everything I'd done at the club was playing through my mind. I saw it with new eyes now, imagining Gabe behind that mask. The games, the dancing, the talks. Exploring the city at night. If I'd been brave enough the night before to take off my mask, would he have done the same? We would have had a good laugh and kissed and avoided the awkwardness and misunderstanding and me trying to find him.

I sighed.

"Do you . . . would you want to show me your art?" Natasha's voice was oddly vulnerable.

A warm-blanket feeling wrapped around me, easing the sadness. "I'd like that."

I pulled out my phone and sketchbook, and for the next hour, I geeked out with my best friend, telling her what she was seeing and letting her flip through something so personal that I felt like I'd opened a new part of my heart to her.

She didn't seem bored, or criticize me, or tell me I should pursue art. She asked questions and complimented my work.

When I put the sketchbook away, she asked, "Will you loan me the books when we get home?"

"You tried them once. You didn't like them."

"I want to try again, for you. Plus, then I can show up Alex and prove fiction is okay."

I laughed. "So you plan to keep talking to him? I thought he was horrible."

"He's only partly horrible. The books?"

"Deal. Now tell me more about Alex."

Things with Gabe may have been a mess, as uncertain as the rest of my future, but for now I would choose to focus on one amazing thing in my life—my best friend.

Chapter Thirty-Two

Mr. Owens approached me at breakfast the next morning. Although I'd slept surprisingly well—and longer than I had any night this week—I wasn't sure I was ready for this conversation. He hadn't checked on me last night, making me glad I hadn't betrayed his trust by sneaking out again. Although I had spent a good amount of time wondering what I was missing at the club and whether Gabe had gone.

"Good morning, Evie. Where's your partner?" Did he sound more formal than usual or was I imagining it?

"He'll be down soon so we can finish our report."

Gabe was dodging me, and I was still covering for him. Maybe he was right, and I was too nice.

"Good, good." Mr. Owens started to move away.

"Mr. Owens?"

He paused.

"I'm sorry I disappointed you. This has been an amazing trip. I'm grateful I had the chance to come."

His face softened. "I'm glad."

"When we get home, I have some art I'd like to show you. If that's okay. Something I've been doing for fun."

"I always enjoy seeing what my students are working on. I'll look forward to it."

I had no idea if he knew what the Elven Realms was, but he would appreciate my work. After he'd been so supportive for years, I wanted him to know how he'd helped me.

He left me to my meal, and by the time I finished eating, Gabe still hadn't appeared.

Embers of anger stirred inside me. We needed to finish our project. It was important to my grade, even if I had been lax in thinking about it this week. Was he going to avoid me all day? Do it himself? Or assume I would? Or turn in a separate project, because he was upset?

I could focus on the project and forget about him. Except his knowing I truly cared was important, more important than my grade, and I couldn't stand the thought of him thinking badly of me or feeling hurt because of my careless words.

We should have been out somewhere fun in the city today, writing our report and sneaking kisses. Where was he? Had he climbed out a window, using a bedsheet as a rope, and lowered himself into the canal and swum away? Or hired a getaway gondola?

My classmates were either heading out or sitting around the lobby with laptops and their partners. Dai, Bryce, and Natasha stayed in the breakfast room to write. Or, to watch Natasha write. She sent me a pitying look and nudged an empty chair toward me.

I sat, alternating between flipping through the drawings I'd done for our project and watching the stairs for Gabe. After an hour that lasted a lifetime, I knew I had to do something drastic.

"I need a plan," I announced.

Natasha perked up from her laptop. "Good thing I excel at those."

"What kind of plan?" Bryce asked.

He'd been distant this morning, though Dai had already forgiven me.

"I need to find Gabe," I said. "Then I need to get him somewhere alone so we can talk."

"Why is he avoiding you?" Dai asked.

Gabe's secrets weren't mine to tell, but I could give my friends something. "I did something dumb yesterday."

"Been there," Dai said. "You need a grand gesture."

Yes. Perfect. Something to prove to Gabe that I wasn't embarrassed of him or myself or my interests. I needed him to know that I wasn't mocking him or toying with him and that none of this week had been a game. He wasn't temporary. And I wasn't giving up.

But he was private. He wouldn't want a public gesture, for everyone to see. And there was the minor problem of not knowing where he was.

"Grand gestures depend on being able to find the person." I motioned to the Gabe-less lobby.

"I sense a group project coming on," Natasha said.

Dai rubbed his hands.

Bryce studied me. I swallowed hard and met his familiar gaze. His eyes softened.

"Whatever you need," he said, and I gave him a small smile.

Natasha grinned. "Excellent."

They had a project to complete as well, and I hated to distract them. But how could I refuse what I'd dreamed about, having a crew like Ana's for an important mission? The remains of guilt over keeping secrets from them faded into warm gratitude.

Natasha whipped out her phone. "What do we need to do?"

"Step one, find him."

"Leave that to me."

Her detective skills hadn't given me tons of confidence that she would succeed where I'd failed, but I supposed part of working with a team was trusting them.

I sorted through ideas of what Gabe would like, what would show him that I was the person he'd gotten to know all week, not the one he feared, not the one who'd said those careless things. Gestures that would mean something to him.

"I need a place to meet him," I said. "Somewhere quiet."

I did a search on my phone. Hmm. The city had several libraries, but one was a museum, and some were attached to universities, so I couldn't tell if any of them would work. Art museum? Too public. Café? Too boring.

Then I remembered the evening we'd talked about scenes we hoped to see if the books were made into a TV show. Angelo had mentioned the fight in the garden.

A quick search revealed a few gardens throughout the city, including one near Saint Mark's that looked appropriate.

"Here." I sent my friends a location pin.

"So we find him and get him there and you're waiting," Natasha said. "What else?"

The idea further solidified in my head. "I need to get something from my room. Time to do a drawing. And cream-filled croissants."

Dai raised his hand. "Ooh, I'll handle those."

"We both will," Bryce said.

I laughed. "Please don't eat them all before we find him."

Dai shrugged. "No promises."

Bryce elbowed him. "Don't worry. I'll keep Tanaka from feeding them to the pigeons."

Natasha was watching me. "Alex can help me find Gabriel, if you want to draw."

"Thank you. I'll get my stuff and go ahead and wait in the garden. I can find a bench and draw."

I went to the room and grabbed a jacket, my sketchbook and colored pencils, and the other item I needed.

Problem: it wouldn't fit in the purse I'd been using.

Oh well. I switched back to my bag with the incriminating Tigers patch. At this point, I didn't care if anyone recognized it.

Dai and Bryce were gone when I went downstairs.

"Alex is on his way," Natasha said. "We'll find Gabe."

I hugged her. "I owe you."

"No, you don't," she said firmly. "This is what friends do."

Heat pricked my eyes, and I shook my head to make the feeling pass.

I was glad the place was near Saint Mark's Square and therefore easy to find without Gabe navigating. I crossed the whole square to reach the Grand Canal. A row of gondolas covered in bright blue cloths were lined up amid wooden poles, the turquoise lagoon stretching behind them. Water lapped the stone bank. Not too far down, I found the park.

I passed through an ornate metal gate, and a gravel path crunched under my feet. Bushes and trees reached taller than my head, making the city vanish except for the bell tower sticking up in the near distance. I'd entered another world. Vivid green surrounded me on every side. Trellises covering part of the walkway formed a tunnel of green, and purple irises and white hydrangeas added color. A freestanding brick water fountain with a white lion's head and ivy wrapped around it added an ancient feel. This was perfect.

I bypassed the benches on the main paths and found one tucked into a hidden corner near the lion fountain, then took out my sketchbook. The scene I wanted was clear in my mind, and the garden faded as the drawing sucked me in.

I was so lost in the scene taking shape on the page that I jumped when people stopped in front of me. It was Dai and Bryce, who handed over a paper bag.

I peeked inside and inhaled the sweet smell of baked goods.

"They're delicious," Dai said, "but I left some for you."

"Thank you," I said. "For everything."

"I'm still mad you didn't take me to the club." Dai narrowed his eyes playfully. "But I hope everything works out."

Bryce's smile was genuine. "Good luck."

I set the croissants next to me and quickly finished the drawing.

As I was packing my pencils, Natasha texted.

He's on his way.

My heart leaped. Was he coming for real? What had she told him? Had she had to convince him? And was there a possibility he'd told her he was coming while he actually planned to run away and keep avoiding me?

What did you say? I asked.

You'll see.

Once again, she was not as reassuring as I would have liked.

I fought the urge to pace and watch the gate. Twisted my hands in my lap. Picked up the bag of pastries, then set it down.

Footsteps crunched on the gravel.

And Gabe stood in front of me.

Chapter Thirty-Three

My heart skipped a few beats before lodging in my throat. Why did he have to look so good? He had a backpack slung over one denim-jacket-clad shoulder. His posture and expression indicated caution, a careful blankness that didn't reveal his thoughts about being here.

I wanted to jump up and throw my arms around him, but that might scare him off.

"You came." I tried to match his casual vibe. "How did Natasha find you?"

"She didn't. I found her while I was looking for you."

My breath hitched, and I tried not to let hope burst too brightly inside me. "You were looking for me?"

"May I?" He gestured to the bench, and I hurried to move my backpack and the bag of croissants to make room.

He sat, not touching me, but not at the complete opposite end, which I hoped was a good sign. He studied the garden, taking it in in his deliberate way. The corners of his eyes softened.

"Nice place. Lacking in dark elves to fight."

Light kindled inside me. He remembered mentioning the scene, and he knew I'd been paying attention. "Best I could do on short notice."

We were silent.

"I'm sorry for what I said," I blurted out as he said, "I'm sorry I ran away."

"You are?" I asked.

He shifted, angling himself toward me. Our gazes locked and held. Maybe he planned to speak, but I couldn't wait.

"I know what you heard and how it sounded," I said. "I promise I didn't know you were Angelo. Not until yesterday when I was dumb enough to think it was Bryce. As soon as I said it, I realized I was wrong. Did you know I was Fantasma?"

I held my breath, hoping he said no, because if he had known, my opinion of him was going to take a hit.

"No. I suspected for a couple days, but I didn't know for sure until I heard you with Bryce."

I exhaled slowly. "You know how on the train I said I wanted to talk? I was planning to tell you about the club. About these books I love and how I've been sneaking out to a fan club, and that I met this guy I liked, but he didn't compare to the guy I fell for without masks, during the day. And I was hoping you were going to tell me you were Angelo."

His eyebrows inched up in the middle. "Last night you weren't sure you wanted to meet."

I gripped the edge of the bench. "It wasn't that I didn't trust you, you or Angelo, but I didn't want to risk messing up what we had in either relationship, so I pulled away. But then today

I knew I wanted to keep kissing you as Gabe, and I didn't want secrets between us."

"I let you pull away. As Angelo, I did too. I suspected Fantasma might be you, but if I'd been wrong, I wasn't sure if I wanted to know who she was because I was happy with Evie." His eyes had gone molten brown, warming my insides.

I laughed softly. "We made a mess, didn't we? Did you go last night?"

He shook his head. "I wasn't quite ready to talk. Wait—you didn't go?"

"So . . . you know how I was in trouble yesterday? Mr. Owens caught me when I got back from the ball."

"What?" Gabe's voice came out loud for him. "Sorry. I'm sorry I didn't know. I would have taken the blame."

"I know you would have, but I was mostly concerned with making sure he didn't catch Angelo too. I really am sorry for yesterday. I know what it must have sounded like. Bryce said something that reminded me of Angelo, and the words slipped out, and then I panicked. It was the old me, hiding myself."

His brows lifted. "There's a new you?"

"I'm working on it. Thanks to you. I told my friends and my mom about the books and my art. I was honest about the job and college stuff too."

The warmth in his eyes sent tingling to my core.

I started to reach for his hand but stopped. "I didn't mean that Angelo wasn't important, that *you* weren't important. I'm done hiding what I like and what I want. I knew immediately what you must've thought, but then I couldn't find you."

He sniffed. "I did exactly what you accused me of, assuming the worst, not trusting you. I had time to think last night, and I realized that I do know you, and no matter what it sounded like, I knew you weren't really like that. When I first heard you, I thought you wanted it to be Bryce and would be disappointed it was me."

"The opposite, actually," I said, and his lips twitched upward. I fixed him with a serious look. "If we're going to make this work, you have to talk to me. Or if you need space, tell me."

"I promise. I shouldn't have run off."

"Were you in your room last night?" I asked.

"Yeah, why?"

"Did you not hear me knocking?"

"I didn't hear anything."

"I stood out there forever."

"Which room?" he asked.

"Room 406."

"I'm in 409."

I groaned. "Then someone else heard a very nice apology. Also, can I have your number? The reason I went to your room is that I couldn't call you."

His eyes crinkled. "Only if you promise not to actually call me."

"You're ridiculous."

"You like it."

I did. "Oh. I have an apology for you."

"Didn't we just do that?"

I handed him the croissants. "Will you share a croissant with me?"

"I love sharing. I'd enjoy it very much, Evangeline."

When we finished, I gave him the drawing. It showed the two of us standing on a bridge over a canal, wearing regular clothes but each of us holding our nighttime masks.

After he finished studying it, his gaze lifted to mine and lingered, intense and steady. "I love it."

I extended a hand. "Hi, I'm Evie, and I love the Elven Realms, and I do fan art and cosplay and occasionally LARP."

His hand closed around mine, warm and gentle. "I'm Gabe, and I also love the Elven Realms, and I fell for someone who is from another world but who feels more like home than any place possibly could."

My insides went gooier than the croissant cream at his quoting Bastian. "And you dance. Wait, you were really good. How did you learn?"

"Sophia's quinceañera."

"Aw, that's so sweet."

"Stop it." His lips twitched.

A thought occurred to me. "You impersonated a cat."

"You pretended to be a ghost. We both did things we aren't proud of, Whitmore."

I laughed.

He picked up his backpack. "I have something for you."

"You do?"

"I knew I needed to apologize, and I went out this morning

to get it, but when I came back to the hotel, you were gone. Thankfully Gutierrez told me where to find you."

That's what Natasha had meant. She hadn't needed to do anything, because Gabe had found her first. I took the bag he handed me. Inside, I found the copy of *Mask of Souls* I'd admired at the first bookstore we visited, in Italian, with a gorgeous cover. I turned the book over to admire the scene that filled the dust jacket. Opened it and ran my fingers over the familiar but not-familiar words.

"I love it. Thank you. But I'll need someone who can read Italian to help me."

"I think that can be arranged."

Our gazes locked.

"I have one more thing for you too," I said. "At first I felt more like myself at night, wearing that mask with Angelo. But I realized that spending the days with you, with no masks of any kind, was better. On that note . . ."

I took out the other item I'd brought, my silver mask. In the epilogue of *Bay of Phantoms*, Bastian gave Ana his magical mask because he was choosing to stay in the human realm with her and wouldn't need it anymore.

Based on Gabe's expression, he understood the symbolism, but I quoted the scene anyway.

"For ages, I watched you from afar, this mask my only connection to you. Now I have no more need of it, for I have something infinitely better. No masks between us, no barriers, just you and I together, and I will face what comes with you by my side."

Gabe cradled the mask in his lap as gently as the hand that

rose to cup my face. We leaned toward each other at the same time, and our lips met. This kiss started soft but quickly deepened, and I clung to his shoulders. His hand slid behind my head like he never wanted to let go.

After we broke apart and I caught my breath, I asked, "Could you ever bring yourself to keep spending time with a friendly, popular girl who talks too much?"

"If you can bring yourself to keep trying with an antisocial guy who dislikes most people and prefers museums and libraries to parties." The hand on the back of my head shifted to rest against my neck, steady against my racing pulse.

"I can, if you'll take me to those museums and libraries with you."

"Deal. And . . . I suppose I could live through prom. If you're with me. I'm still holding out hope for the murder barn, though."

"Maybe I'll book one just for you." I paused. "No, I already made one grand gesture today. I'm not sure I can go that big."

His thumb caressed my jaw.

I poked his arm. "Will I have to work as hard to get you to use *boyfriend* as I did *friend*?"

A slight smirk played on his lips. "Depends what you have in mind to convince me."

I moved closer and kissed him again, my hands holding his face in place.

"Nope, not enough," he said.

"You're so demanding," I murmured against his lips, and did it once more.

He hummed. "Getting there. So. Club tonight?"

"I don't want to risk it. We can spend the evening together as us, somewhere safer. Besides, I gave up my mask."

One corner of his mouth lifted. "You want it back, though, don't you?"

"I mean, it was a lot of work, and I really like it . . . But it made for such a nice gesture."

He laughed. "It really did."

He lifted the mask to my face and put it on me, his fingers gentle as they tied the ribbons, brushing my jaw. He traced the outline of it.

"Beautiful," he said.

We sat like that for I didn't know how long, until the breeze and nearby footsteps and a chirping bird reminded me of where we were.

"We need to finish our project," I said half-heartedly, though I didn't move.

"I brought my laptop. We have time. As long as we can take breaks for this."

He kissed me once more, angling his head to reach my mouth beneath the mask.

"I think that can be arranged," I repeated his words. "You feel like that for me too, you know. More like home than anywhere I've been."

The warmth in his eyes melted me. "Beyond everyday magic," he said.

I couldn't have agreed more.

Evie's Guide to the Elven Realms

THE BOOKS

The Elven Realms: A world of twenty-plus fantasy books, comprising multiple interconnected shorter series, set in a universe where parallel realms exist: human, regular elven, and corrupted dark elven. Breaches between the realms sometimes allow the three worlds to bleed into each other. The overarching series is set across many countries and time periods and is full of politics, scheming, romance, and action.

Mask of Souls: A trilogy set in the fictional city of Venezari, which resembles historical Venice. The subseries centers on a crew of young people who learn of an impending invasion by dark elves and must protect their city.

Mask of Souls: Book 1, in which the crew learns of a looming dark elf invasion and must pull off two big heists to learn more about the dark elves and how to strengthen the magic separating the realms in order to protect their home.

Bridge of Echoes: Book 2. After a betrayal leads to the crew accidentally opening a breach between realms and getting sucked into the elven realm, the characters are trapped and must find their way home, trying to recruit human and elven help along the way.

Bay of Phantoms: Book 3, in which the crew has returned to the human realm but the dark elves are invading, and they must use the allies they've gathered and the magic they've learned to protect a city that's now fully aware of the other realms.

THE CHARACTERS

Andriana "Ana" de Rossi: Clever and feisty, a member of the Venezarian nobility and the latest in her family to lead the Sentinelle. She is fascinated by magic and loves the game of playing two roles, one with the nobles and one with her secret crew. She always has a plan.

Luca: A member of the city guard originally from the poor part of Venezari. He daily risks his job to help Ana after she rescued him from a dark creature and he learned of the elven world. He can be counted on to make a joke at the wrong time and to carry lots of weapons.

Clio: Ana's best friend, a merchant from the nearby country of Halla who sells legal goods and not-so-legal ones. She can find anything for a price, as long as you don't ask where she got it. She loves to bargain and sees everything as a deal to be made.

Izak: A sailor from the country of Krijeka who, after deserting his crew in Venezari for mysterious reasons, can never go home again. He now works as a gondolier and helps Ana patrol. He's quiet, steady, and observant, unless crossed, and then he can quickly turn deadly.

Pietro: The youngest son of a noble family that's friends with Ana's, he's a priest in training with a thirst for knowledge and a penchant for picking locks and sneaking into places he shouldn't go because he doesn't believe in secrets. He's not afraid to question the powerful church.

Bastian: Captain of the elven guard, he has kept an eye on the human realm for years. Ana can see him through her magical mask. He's a powerful fighter and magician who can craft new magical items on the fly during battle, and his motives are at first unknown.

THE WORLD

Sentinelle: An ancient secret society charged with keeping the elven realms a secret from humans by bolstering the magic that keeps the realms separate and covering up intentional or accidental elven incursions.

Venezari: A human city of canals and guilds, with nobility, a duke, and an influential church. In the time of the trilogy, it's the center of a powerful, sea-based republic.

Moravion: A beautiful and magical elven city that exists parallel to Venezari and can be glimpsed in Venezari when the magic separating the realms is weak.

Ellurai: The elves' name for themselves. They can pull magic from the air and infuse it into inanimate objects to give them special properties. They are great artists and powerful warriors.

Calurai: Also known as the dark elves, they pull magic and infuse it into living beings, which creates deadly, corrupted creatures. They live in the third, shadow, realm.

Acknowledgments

I remain in awe every time I reach this point of writing a book. I'm so incredibly grateful that I get to publish these stories and that they're reaching readers who are willing to go on adventures with me and my characters.

Thank you to my husband, Russ, for being my biggest fan and supporting this wild dream. Thanks for letting me drag you all over Venice taking notes and pictures on my first official book research trip, keeping me well supplied with pizza, pasta, and gelato. There's no one I would rather adventure with.

Like Evie's dad did for her, my parents instilled in me a love of reading and books. Thank you, Mom and Dad, for encouraging my imagination, providing lots of reading material, and forgiving me all the times I was lost in a book when I should have been doing something else.

Thanks to my editor, Wendy Loggia, for consistently helping make my books better and for championing my stories. It's been so much fun traveling around the world with you through fiction!

To the rest of the Delacorte Press/Delacorte Romance team: Ali Romig, Colleen Fellingham, Heather Hughes, Sarah Lawrenson, and so many more. Thank you for all you do to make the book magic happen. And thank you to Ray Shappell and Libby VanderPloeg for another perfect cover and for somehow always capturing exactly what the book needs.

As always, thanks to my intrepid agent, Eva Scalzo, for your hard work, support, and encouragement. I'm grateful to have you by my side on this journey.

Josiah, thank you for letting me borrow your conspiracy theories.

Amanda Stevens and Jason Joyner, I can't thank you enough for reading, critiquing, and being cheerleaders for my books. Critique partners who can truly be called friends are a gift.

To my friends in the Fellowship and KidLitNet: books brought us together, and I'm grateful for your friendship and support.

Books are not only transportive magic but also gateways to meeting people who experience that magic with you. Thank you, reader, for picking up this book! Every reader who posts, shares, likes, comments, sends a note, or buys or checks out a book truly helps sustain authors, and I'm grateful for each one of you.

And finally, thank you, Jesus, for loving me, saving me, calling me to tell stories, and writing the greatest story of all.

Love is on the horizon. . . .

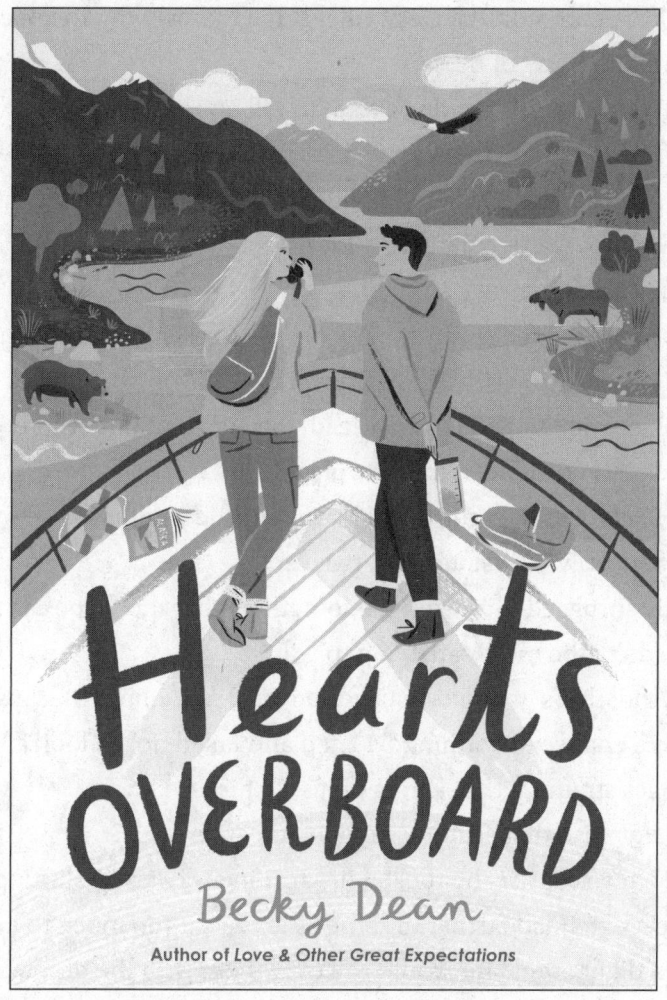

Hearts
OVERBOARD
Becky Dean

Author of *Love & Other Great Expectations*

Turn the page for a preview of another Becky Dean romance!

"You get the aisle one." I pointed. "This one's mine."

"Is that another airplane rule? Planning to submit a complaint?"

"It's a common courtesy rule. I don't know why I expected you to know any of those."

"Are you sure? You don't want to tell on me like you did with the fireworks? Or the Christmas when I opened the presents early. Or the picnic where I accidentally knocked over the drink table. Wow, there really are a lot of examples of times you got me in trouble."

I refused to feel guilty for any of those. He could have burned the house down with those fireworks. "Maybe you should reconsider the life choices that lead you to situations where you could get in trouble in the first place."

He nudged the armrest. "I'll arm wrestle you for it."

"Seriously? What are you, twelve?"

He shrugged. "It seems like something that should be earned. Wouldn't it be more satisfying to win it?"

"And that's why you suggested arm wrestling? Because I stand a chance of winning?" I tried and failed not to look at the muscles straining the sleeves of his T-shirt.

"Not with that attitude, you don't."

To my surprise, he tucked his arm in awkwardly, shifting so his feet extended farther into the aisle. Was it too much to hope that a flight attendant would roll over them with the drink cart?

"How do you think you did on finals?" he asked.

The annoying thing was, for all that Tanner acted like a dumb jock, he competed with me for near-top grades. Despite having no ability whatsoever to pay attention in class, to take actual notes, or to do homework more than a day—or a class period—before it was due.

"Great," I said. "What about you?"

"Also great. Better than great."

"I guess we'll see."

Final grades would be uploaded to the online portal later this week, and I was glad they would arrive on a port day since we wouldn't have internet when the ship was at sea.

He shifted. "Sorry about, you know."

His voice was serious now, and a rare solemn expression flickered across his face.

Did he mean Friday? My public humiliation? The new nickname? My neck grew hot, and I couldn't decide if I wanted to snap at him or pretend I had no idea what he was talking about.

"You're better off, anyway," he went on. "Caleb is boring."

"Doesn't that mean we're perfect for each other?"

He shifted again. "You're not boring."

"That's not what you said on Friday."

"What?"

I snorted. "Like you don't know."

He frowned and opened his mouth. Then his face morphed— he crossed his eyes and stuck out his tongue.

Seriously?

Oh. A baby in front of us was staring at him over the top of the seat.

Fine. It was better if Tanner and I ignored each other. I smiled at the baby, who barely noticed me, sucked in by Tanner's goofy faces. A tiny hand came through the seats, and he let the kid grab his finger.

It was not cute. At all. Nope. And I definitely wasn't watching.

The seat in front of me reclined violently, trapping me in a tight prison.

"Will you stop?" came a woman's voice from directly behind me, sharp and loud. I jumped.

I couldn't make out a guy's mumbled reply.

"This was supposed to be a fun vacation," the woman went on, and like, come on, lady, the whole plane doesn't need to hear your business. "You didn't want to see the beach, the Dodgers game was too crowded, the Walk of Fame was dumb. Why did you even want to come?"

"But . . . I had a great time, babe. Because I was with you."

Hearing a couple fighting was near the top of my *things I don't want to do* list. I tried to reach down, hoping to find earbuds, but I couldn't get to my backpack on the floor with the seat in front of me reclined so far.

"You know what? I can't." Her voice rang out. "They say traveling together is a good test, and we failed. It's over."

Heat spread up my neck as my stomach sank. Every second of last Friday washed over me. The eyes on me. The whispers. The need to escape. This guy had fewer options than I'd had, unless he could get a flight attendant to bring him a parachute.

Silence surrounded us, heavy with awkwardness. The hush of people who very much wanted not to have witnessed such a private moment.

"But," the guy said, "I love you. I don't understand."

I hoped I hadn't sounded so desperate in the parking lot. My heart twisted for him.

"That's the problem. You don't." Her voice lacked sympathy. "This week, we were on totally different pages."

Of course they were seated two feet from me and not thirty rows away. Because that was my life lately.

"But—"

An elbow bumped mine, and the man's reply was smothered as Tanner settled his noise-canceling headphones over my ears. They were playing a loud rock song, but he tapped his phone and handed it over, loaded to his Spotify account, which included a wider variety than I would have expected.

The music completely drowned out the couple.

My heart stuttered. I tried to peer at him without moving my head.

But Tanner returned to playing with the baby in front of him and didn't acknowledge me once.

Hearts Overboard excerpt text copyright © 2024 by Becky Dean.
Cover art copyright © 2024 by Libby VanderPloeg.
Published by Delacorte Press, an imprint of Random House Children's Books,
a division of Penguin Random House LLC, New York.

Delacorte Romance

IT'S A LOVE STORY.